Spirit Talker

Helen McIntyre

Contents

Chapter 1

H aving an inability to remember anything before the age of eight can admittedly be a bit of a bummer, but it's one hell of an ice breaker. You know that question you're always asked in awkward social situations? That whole 'state one interesting fact about yourself' spiel when, in reality, you're about as fascinating as a damp sock? It's perfect for that.

When expanding on it to the point where I'm telling complete strangers how this memory loss was the result of a car crash that brutally killed both my parents and older sister, things can become a little uncomfortable.

As I found out at a job interview at Build-A-Bear when I was sixteen, oversharing isn't always the best way to deal with a nerve-racking situation. Got me the job, mind you. Probably out of complete sympathy, but hey, a job's a job. I generally just leave it at the 'I can't remember anything before the age of eight' stage, and then bullshit about falling out of a tree or something.

The plan from here on out is to not even go that far. It's not important. As great of an ice breaker as it is, I always end up becoming the sad little orphan with a weird history, who people are scared of upsetting. It's easier just to hide it, not that Annabel would agree.

"So when someone asks what our parents do for a living, you're going to say what? When people ask about growing up, childhood memories?" she demands.

She's sitting at the end of my new bed with her legs crossed, and her lip is twitching slightly. Her pale blue eyes are narrow, which is arguably a nice break from their usual activity of rolling around her eye sockets in disapproval.

"No one actually cares enough about that crap to ask it, Annie. I'll say they're bankers, or some shit. No one cares about bankers."

Annabel huffs. "So when a semester ends and everyone goes home, but you stay here, what are you going to say?"

I roll my eyes. She's being paranoid. It doesn't have to be a big deal, and I'm hardly traumatised from the whole dead parent thing. Thanks to my good friend, amnesia, my family is just a picture, and my past life is just a pretty bland, sad story.

"No idea. Doesn't matter." I shrug. "Sheesh, you think too much. I only moved in five minutes ago, least give me a chance to breathe. It's fine, I'll figure it out. There is this magical thing--not sure you've heard of it, so buckle up and prepare to be blown away--this magical thing called lying--"

"Oh, piss off. You shouldn't meet a load of new people, then immediately start lying right off the bat."

I sit up in my bed, which is surprisingly comfortable, and laugh. "Most people don't bring their sister along to university, but I can't exactly be honest about that."

"That's different," Annabel mutters.

I raise my eyebrows. That shut her up. She lifts her hand to her face and rests her head on her palm. She's making faces and muttering under her breath, which is always a clear sign that she's bitching about me to herself. She doesn't exactly have the option to complain about me to anyone else, I guess. Sucks for her.

"It's just easier," I pipe up, interrupting Annabel's conversation with herself. "And hey, I can't live in the past forever. I need to get over the whole dead parents thing."

"That's a healthy approach," she mocks in response.

I vaguely gesture into the air. "We all have our flaws. I'm studying for a degree in Civil Engineering here, not psychology. You expect too much of me."

Annabel mutters something under her breath, and I respond by blowing her a kiss. She shoots me a scowl, then vanishes. She's so easy to wind up today, it's great.

I take my sister's strop as an opportunity to soak in my new university bedroom. It's pretty nice, and bigger than any of the rooms I temporarily lived in growing up. Due to my lack of living relatives, I was able to get the highest student loan possible, alongside a grant for foster kids who haven't been slaughtered by the education system by the time uni comes around. Swings and roundabouts, and all that.

It means I've been able to afford one of the nicer student halls, all with a complimentary mood lamp. I'd be lying if I said that wasn't the deal breaker for this place. My walls are bare and everything is uncomfortably tidy for my liking, but I've already established a small pile of needless junk on my desk in the corner of the room, so I'm getting there.

"Your flatmate is hot, go find out if he's single."

The sound of Annabel's voice makes me jump. She wasn't gone long. Shame. I say this to her, which gets me the biggest glare yet. She's back on my bed, sitting in the same cross-legged position as before.

"Sorry to break it to you, but I don't think you're his type." I laugh.

"Shut up, I'm just curious." She pouts, twirling her black hair around her finger. "Having a crush on someone when you're dead sucks balls, Felix. Remember James? We were practically Romeo and Juliet, if you forget about the whole him not knowing I existed thing."

"Should've thought about that before you died then."

Annabel scowls. With a wave of her hand, she lifts a pair of boxers from the pile of underwear in the corner of the room, and lobs them directly towards my face. I smack them away before they reach me, and they fall onto the floor beside my bed. It adds character to the room, so I leave them lying limply on the carpet. To that, Annabel gives me the finger.

Despite the fact I've now surpassed her in age--she was sixteen when she died, and hasn't aged a day since--it's usually jarring not to think of her as eons older than me. It's times like this I begin noticing myself overtaking her though, and I don't like it. I really don't like it. Spirits don't age, mentally or physically, and so eventually I'll be a miserable old man while she'll be stuck as a naïve teenage girl.

"Right," I announce, snapping myself out of my daydream. "While you ponder over what could've been, I'm going to put my food away before everyone else takes the good cupboards. Go make a jigsaw or something."

Annabel rolls her eyes at me before disappearing, and I jump off my bed to grab the bags of food I bought from the supermarket down the road. I picked up mainly freezer food, you know, the stuff with zero nutritional value you can shove in the oven and be done with. The last time I attempted cooking anything creative, I half melted a baking tray, so I try to keep it as simple as possible.

There's only one other person in the communal area as I barge open the door, and he's sitting on one of the stools beside the long island with his arms crossed as if he's the kitchen's bouncer or something. He's a tall, lanky kid whose hair looks greasy, but he might have just gone overboard on the hair wax.

We greet each other, and normally I'd spark up some conversation, but this one bag is so goddamn heavy that I might collapse at any moment if I don't set it down. I drop my stuff onto the off-white countertop, and start searching for empty spaces to put everything away.

I'm so preoccupied with my food that it takes me a while to notice the room slowly starting to fill up with the rest of my flatmates. It's excruciatingly awkward because no one is saying much, and I'm too busy trying to shove a kilo of jacket potatoes into a cupboard to come to their rescue. I rarely find situations awkward, so this kind of thing doesn't faze me. Occasionally bumping into dead people with missing limbs and flesh dripping down their face does that to a guy.

All the small talk has been addressed, and so everyone's now just standing around avoiding eye contact with one another. We know each others' names, ages, hometowns, degree courses, and all that boring stuff, not that I remember any of this information considering I have the memory of a deformed goldfish.

Annabel is standing against the wall beside me, giggling at my poor attempts to store food. It's times like this I wish I could address her in public, but one of my earliest memories is realising how bad

of an idea that is. In response to the one family photo that was constantly shoved in my face after the accident, I'd spend hours telling
the doctors that Annabel was alive and point to wherever it was she
was standing at the time. Unsurprisingly, they'd glance at each other
with a look that suggested they were seriously considering getting
an exorcist on speed dial. I eventually just started agreeing with
whatever they told me was right.

Annabel starts laughing at me--needlessly loudly, I might add--as
I try to balance five jars or pasta sauce on top of each other. One
of my three female flatmates, the prettiest, clears her throat and
finally speaks.

"Uh, so... What's the most interesting fact about you all?"

Great. I couldn't make this shit up.

"I'm bilingual. I guess that's interesting, right?" one of the other
girls, the one with bleached blonde hair, pipes up.

"I can speak four languages," the tall, lanky boy cuts in.

"Oh, cool." The girl blushes.

Right, well if I ever need someone to ruin the mood, I know who to
call. It's silent again for another minute or so. I'm too busy trying to
strategically balance a bunch of bananas on top of my pasta sauce
castle to contribute anything. I'll get these stupid potatoes into a
cupboard somehow; I can't let them win.

"Um, well, I'm the only boy in a family of five sisters," a boy with
a shaved head finally says to break the silence. He looks at the guy
beside him, indicating his turn.

"I can eat a whole onion in thirty seconds." There's an enormous
grin on the guy's face as he talks, and I get the impression he doesn't
quite understand the concept of oversharing.

As he speaks, Annabel nudges my arm and nods at him en-thusiastically. This must be her Romeo. His hair is an unnatural blonde colour, and he's dressed like he researched what a university student looks like so he could resemble one. He's wearing a Yankees snapback with a Chicago Bulls jersey, and I get the feeling he's a fan of neither, nor is he American. I raise my eyebrows at Annabel. Really?

"Uh, okay, cool," the olive-skinned girl who asked the initial question begins. "I didn't give you guys mine, so... Well, mine is more of a story than a fact. Until I was about six, I used to think fish were called puppies, and so when I was younger I always begged my parents for a puppy. One day my dad bought this gigantic fish tank for the living room because of something to do with feng shui, I don't even know, and I was absolutely ecstatic, and... and I've just realised how shit that sounds now."

Hey, that one was actually kind of funny. The girl's cheeks have turned a flushed pink, and I'm so amused by her story that it takes a while for me to realise that I'm next in line. Everyone's eyes shift to me, and I have no choice but to to dismiss the potatoes that were keeping me safe up until now. As if it's some knee jerk response, my instinct is to spill the memory loss story, but I keep my mouth clamped shut. I dart my eyes towards Annabel, but she just shrugs at me.

"I..." I begin, stammering slightly. If I'd had any sense I would've planned this out while the others were barfing out their fun facts, but common sense is something I severely lack. I glance at my potatoes, and mutter the first thing that pops into my head. "I eat potatoes."

What is wrong with me?

"What? As in exclusively? Just potatoes?" Tall and lanky asks me as if I'm dumb.

"Oh, like, you're vegetarian?" the blonde girl questions.

I respond with a shrug, and everyone nods, with a few people saying cool. Most just gaze at me like I've strangled a kitten, which is fair enough. I might as well have told them I speak to dead people. I'm not a vegetarian. Never have been. Couldn't even attempt to guess why I didn't deny that.

We quickly move on and turn to the last girl. She's separated herself from the rest of us, opting to sit on one of the lumpy sofas beside the window, as opposed to near the kitchen island in the middle of the room. She has dark skin, and her hair has been weaved into countless intricate braids that highlight her striking features. She's staring outside the window with a small smile on her lips, but looks up as she's asked for her fact.

"Oh, groovy, is it my turn?" she questions softly. She clicks her tongue as she sits up a little on the sofa. "Sorry, I was watching the ducks. I communicate with spirits."

What the--I lose my grip on the potatoes I've just spent ten minutes trying to shove into my cupboard, and they crash to the floor with a heavy thud.

Chapter 2

"What would she gain from it, y'know? Makes her seem different and unique or whatever, sure, but it's such a random thing to make up. I don't know, Felix, this definitely needs further investigation," Annabel rambles as she paces back and forth in my room.

"All right, Poirot, calm down."

"She didn't make a big deal out of it either. All of the phonies we've met before have been so dramatic and in your face, but she said it like it was the most normal thing ever."

"Uh-huh."

Annabel stops pacing and faces me with her hands on her hips. She raises her eyebrows. "Are you even listening to me?"

"I just think it's horse crap. She had no idea you were there earlier," I reason.

"Just because she didn't make a song and dance about it, doesn't mean she couldn't see me." She rolls her eyes. "And ugh, at least make the effort to learn her name. It's Ava. Ava, Katie, Carmen, Jamie, Tom, and Mason."

"Yeah, yeah. Did she look at you at any point?"

"Well, no, but--"

"There we go then. If she could interact with you then she would've acknowledged you, she couldn't not," I argue. "Whatever, I'm just pissed that half my potatoes are bruised, and don't even get me started on the fact I'm going to have to eat all my bacon on the sly."

Ava's announcement caught me off guard at first, I'll give her that, but it's nothing worth dwelling on. It made the kitchen awkwardness peak because the sentence, I communicate with spirits, is a bit of a conversation killer. It's not like speaking to dead people is exciting, anyway; they generally whine at you until you sort their shit out for them, and that's that. Bit annoying, if anything.

One of the boys, Tom I think, is organising a flat party here tonight, so I'm hoping throwing some alcohol into the mix will have us all acting like best friends in no time. Annabel is still blathering on when I hear a quiet knock on my bedroom door. I tell her to hush, then swing it open to see a pair of dark brown, almost black, eyes gazing into my own.

"Whoa, hey," Ava says as if she didn't expect anyone to open the door she just knocked. "Tom said pre-drinks start in an hour, and the cleaners come every other Friday."

Bit weird. I thank Ava and go to close my door, but she stops me.

"You're the one with the funny name, aren't you?"

"Uh, probably. It's Felix."

"Groovy, like the cat?"

I nod slowly. Ava shoots me one more toothy smile before stepping away and moving on to the next door. Okay then.

Annabel has disappeared by the time I turn back around, and so I take it as my chance to pull open the drawer I've already christened as my alcohol stash. It only has a bottle of bourbon and a few beers in it at the moment, but it'll soon bloom. Before I can take that thought any further, one of the beers flings out of the drawer and lands with a thump onto my bed.

"You can't get drunk on your first night here, that's not fair!"

I spin around to see that Annabel has returned with her infamous scowl. While never knowing my mother can often suck, it's not all bad when her replacement stalks me every second of my life. I miss the days--well, day--when she had no idea who I was. She was a lot less annoying back then.

We didn't recognise each other after the accident, but I quickly figured it out from the family photo that was shoved in my face daily, as the doctors and psychiatrists attempted to spark my memory. It was just the one. My parents must have hated photos or something.

"Felix!" Annabel whines.

I grab a different bottle from the drawer, crack it open with my teeth, and flash Annabel the most sarcastic grin I can muster up.

"I'm going to be bored all night, please?" she pleads. "And stop trying to wind me up!"

"I'm your brother, annoying you defines my existence." I wink at her, but she just pouts even more. "C'mon Annie, it's freshers' week, I'm not spending it sober. I'm not going crazy every night or anything, but at least let me have some fun."

She mumbles something under her breath and, knowing she can't argue back, disappears in a strop. Alcohol tampers with my ability to interact with anything non-living, by which I mean it removes all traces of the ability. I can't see them and I can't hear them. I sure have no complaints, but it leaves Annabel with no one to talk to.

Once I'm done with the beer, I open my drawer to bring out the bottle of bourbon. I don't know what I'm expecting when I wander into the kitchen, but it isn't the uncomfortable social mess that I stumble upon.

Everyone is in there, but Tom and Mason are the only ones talking. If it wasn't for the music blasting from someone's portable speaker, it would pretty much be silent. The rest of my flatmates are quietly sipping their drinks and avoiding eye contact with one another. Tough crowd. I set my bottle of bourbon onto the kitchen island, pour the brown liquid into the bottle's cap, and take a shot. Anything to spice up this night.

Two hours, five games of Irish Snap, and who knows how many drinks later, everyone's shells have practically exploded open. Around fifteen other people have arrived by now, and there's a large group in the midst of an intense debate over the legalisation of cannabis. A bit predictable, but hey, whatever keeps conversation flowing.

I'm a little concerned about Jamie, the lanky kid, as he's slumped on one of the sofas looking like he may possibly die some time soon. Ava and Carmen are chatting beside the kitchen island, while Tom and I sit with our backs against the large window that looks down on the canal running alongside our building. And I feel fantastic.

"You fancying any of the girls?" Tom asks me, making me open my eyes I didn't realise had closed.

"Huh?"

"Carmen's the fittest," he elaborates. "Not spoken to her or any-thing, but I'm gonna go for it. Not like that's important, right?" Tom winks.

"How d'you know you'll like her if you've never spoken?"

Tom laughs, but I'm missing the joke. "You're funny, I like you," he says.

He's still laughing as he stands up and leaves the kitchen to presumably go to the bathroom. I still don't get it. I mull it over in my head as Carmen jumps off her stool and heads over to me. Oh shit, did she hear all of that? I'm still thinking over what Tom said when she sits down into the space he left behind.

"Hey," she begins. "I've not really spoken to you properly yet, so figured I'd come over."

What did Tom mean, goddamnit? I suck at riddles, man. I've been trying to learn the she sells sea shells one since I was a foetus, but can't even get past the first--Wait, no, is that a tongue twister? Are they the same as riddles? Hang on, what was I trying to figure out? Oh, the Tom thing. Yeah, I mean, if he's not spoken to Carmen, how can he know--

"Oh, wait, he just wants a one-night stand!"

"Pardon?"

It suddenly occurs to me that I said that out loud. I stammer as my muddied mind tries to conjure up an explanation. "Nothing, I just--It was something Jamie said."

Considering the guy's currently half conscious and in no state to be argued with, I figure that was the least harmful thing to say. If anything, Carmen looks even more confused. Her eyebrows are furrowed, and her plump lips are parted to leave her mouth slightly agape.

"Sorry," I try again. "I say things."

I don't know why I end it there, but I do.

"Um, okay."

"Sorry, again. If it's any reassurance, I've no idea what the hell I'm on about either. I liked your story, by the way, with the goldfish and the puppies and the feng shui," I say in a poor attempt to change the subject.

"Thanks," she replies. She leans in and takes a sip from the plastic cup in her hand, but locks her eyes on me the whole time. "Now c'mon, what's your secret."

"Huh?"

"The vegetarianism thing is cool--I sure couldn't do it, but you're definitely hiding something. You were going to say something else, but you didn't."

She's good, I'll give her that. There's a glimmer in her yellow-brown eyes as she watches me expectedly, and she smells like vodka. I tell her she's wrong, and she tells me she's right, so I tell her she's wrong again. I'm studying her lips and they're a little chapped, but I kind of want to kiss them and I'm not sure why. All too soon, Carmen turns away as her laugh circles the air around us. She has a small bump on the bridge of her nose.

"I'll get it out of you one day, you hear me?" she says as she takes another sip of her drink. She faces me again. "Can't be any stranger than Ava's fact."

"Oh, you'd be surprised." I mutter, half to myself.

"Ha! So there is something!"

Damnit. Oh, she's really good. Either that, or I'm an idiot. Probably the latter. I shrug as indifferently as possible, to which she raises her eyebrows. She's notably tanned, but other than her angular eyes, her features look European.

We're both silent as we scan each other's faces, and we remain like that for a while, neither one of us daring to leave the eyes of the other. It's Carmen who caves first, as she turns away with another airy laugh. Finally, I focus my attention back to what's ahead of me, and staring straight back at me from the far corner of the room is a tall figure with irises blacker than anything I've ever seen.

The cup in my hand falls to the floor. I'm distracted as Carmen stands up and says something about kitchen roll, but my eyes soon flicker back to the corner of the room. It's still there. It's staring at me. Every inch of my body has suddenly turned numb. You can't see them when you're drunk, you can't see them, you can't see them.

I feel sick. I feel really sick.

I'm imagining this, I have to be. There's a cartoonish frown on its grey face, and its hollow gaze is filling me with an immense feeling of emptiness. Its arms hang limply at its side, and if I didn't feel like I was in the midst of choking, I'd find its gangly limbs and knobbly knees almost comedic. I want to turn away, but I can't. I'm fixated on it. I'm cold. Why is it so cold? The sound of the party has become a monotonous buzzing sound underneath my heavy breathing. Why is it staring at me?

"Felix? Hey, are you all right?"

I need to get out of here.

Looking anywhere but the corner of the room, I jump up from the floor and charge towards the doorway. Everything is spinning. I barge into someone as I leave. They say something but I don't hear them, and my vision is beginning to blur.

"Felix!" a voice calls after me. I ignore it.

Once I've left the room I quicken my pace, look back up, and it's there. Slightly hidden under the shadows, it lurks at the back of the hallway, its blank stare boring into me. This isn't real, you're making it up, this isn't real. Slowly, as if inspecting me, its head starts to turn sideways.

Nope.

I turn on my heel and head straight for my flat's exit. I stumble slightly, and I'm not sure if it's due to the dizziness or the drunkenness. The creature is already standing at the end of the next hallway. I avert my gaze to anything other than it, and charge down the stairs.

I don't stop until I reach the ground floor, by which point the urge to throw up has overcome everything else. My vision is so blurred that I can barely see, and my skin is crawling. I shove open the front door to inhale the fresh autumn air, and it's more intoxicating than any drug could ever be. Within seconds, my vision is switched off like a light, I stumble to the ground, and suddenly there's nothing.

For a moment, I consider the possibility of being dead.

"Whoa, are you okay?"

The voice is smooth and melodic, and if this is how angels sound then I can't complain. A hand brushes my cheek, and it's ice cold against my burning skin. This death thing is nice, I'm down for this. As I flicker my eyelids open, I'm momentarily disappointed to realise that based on the fact I'm sitting on the damp concrete outside my university accommodation, my back against the the brick wall, I'm alive and kicking.

Directly in front of me, her legs crossed in the same way Annabel crosses hers, is Ava. She's waving her slender hand in front of my face. I try to speak but my voice is lost.

"Here," she says, handing me the cup in her hand.

As I drink from it, I'm surprised to find that the clear liquid inside is nothing but water. I glug it down my throat as if my sanity depends on it. It's drizzling and the air is a lot snappier than I remember it being earlier, but it relieves me. I'm sweating out the entire Lake District. I thank Ava before handing back the near-empty cup of water.

"I can't hear them when I drink."

I narrow my eyes at her, confused. She lifts her head up to the dark sky, and I mirror her to see the moon barely peeking through the dark clouds. I lower my head as Ava lowers hers, and she chuckles at the bewildered expression still planted on my face.

"The spirits. I can't drink, otherwise I won't hear them."

Maybe Annabel was right about her. I mean, that can't be a co-incidence. I have the sudden urge to tell her everything, to know if she understands what I am, to ask her if she saw the creature that drove me insane moments ago. But I don't. I'm honestly doubting that thing was even real now. It wasn't like anything else I've ever seen.

"What do they look like?" I ask quietly, grasping onto the hope that I'll hear something that makes sense.

"Oh, whoa, no, I can't see them. No one can see them."

Well, this is awkward.

"Are you feeling better?" she questions, and I'm grateful for the change of subject.

"Yeah, thanks, I--I guess I drank too much or something, I don't know. Just wasn't feeling great," I say as I scratch the back of my head. "What happened? I don't really remember, I mean, did I pass out?"

Ava nods. "You looked like shit."

I laugh. "Cheers."

She parts her lips to speak, only to hesitate, but eventually says what's on her mind. "Sorry to sound rude but I can't read your aura, and it's been bothering me all day." She pauses. "Can I try something? Would you mind?"

For reasons beyond me, I say yes. I blame it on the small amount of alcohol I'm yet to sweat out. Ava reaches out and cups her hands around mine, which look shockingly dull and white compared to hers. I've never seen anyone focus on anything as intently as she's focusing on me right now. She frowns.

"Maybe it's the alcohol," she mutters. "Whoa, okay, clear your mind. Focus on your breathing and nothing else, and don't let your thoughts wander. Close your eyes, that always helps."

I obey Ava like a well-functioned robot, mainly because I'm pretty tired by this point and can't refuse a bit of shut-eye. I empty my mind as best I can, and concentrating on my breathing is helping me calm it. This is nice. I could get used to this. I'm so engrossed in the experience that I barely notice the falling sensation, or the high-pitched buzzing that's becoming increasingly louder.

There's a face, a woman's face. She's screaming something but I can't hear her because the humming in my ear is too loud. Her brown hair is tangled and sprawled over her face, and there's blood streaming from her nose. There are tears flooding her eyes. She keeps screaming. She keeps screaming, but I keep not hearing her. Her eyes are the wildest I've ever seen.

The humming sound comes to a sudden stop, and what follows hits me like a freight train. There's screaming and crying and a deep rumbling shaking the earth I stand on, but I can't see anything but the face in front of me.

"Don't look at them! Listen to me, don't look at them, okay? Pretend they're not there! Don't look at them, please, don't look at them!"

And then everything is black again. I dart my eyes open and yank my hands away from Ava's without a second thought. My head feels light again, my vision blurred.

"What's wrong? Did something happen?" she enquires.

"I just--I just feel sick again, sorry, I--uh..."

Ava says something else but I don't hear it. That face, those eyes. I know them. I know that face. It's not one I recognise from memory, but it's one I know. From the one photograph that's ingrained into my memory, I know that face as my mother's.

Chapter 3

If I didn't know any better, I'd honestly think I spent last night ingesting acid, not alcohol. My throat is killing me. I'm graced by the presence of Annabel at the end of my bed, who doesn't look the slightest bit like she wants to brutally murder me. I'm about to roll my eyes at her and tell her to relax when the events of last night flood my mind. Seeing my mother's face, hearing her voice, Ava, that--that thing. I jump up in my bed, and all at once I'm fully awake.

"Did you see that thing last night?" is the first thought I manage to transfer into words. "And Mum, she--I, what was that thing?"

Annabel narrows her eyes at me. "What the hell are you on about? You went haywire last night, y'know?"

In an attempt to straighten out my thoughts, I get out of bed and sit down onto the chair beside my desk. Everything still makes no sense. I spin around so I'm facing Annabel, whose big eyes and white face look the most perplexed I've ever seen them.

"Sorry," I finally say. "I--When I was at the party, when I was talking to Carmen, there was this thing in the corner of the room and--I--I don't even know, it was freaky as shit, Annabel. Its eyes were black and it was following me. Didn't you see it?"

She slowly shakes her head. "I'm beginning to wonder if you actually just had a psychotic episode here, Felix."

I'm barely making any sense, am I? I shake my head. If Annabel didn't see that thing, then it can't have been real. If it had any relation to the spirit world, she would've been aware of it, and it sure as hell wasn't related to the living one. Maybe I just drunk something bad, or someone thought it would be funny to spike my drink. But then what about my mum?

"Were you there when Ava was doing her mystic mumbo-jumbo with me?" I ask, to which Annabel nods. "Okay, so this'll sound crazy but I saw something. It was like a dream, except I was fully awake, and--"

"So like a vision? Oh, awesome, maybe you're getting superpowers."

"Stop making it sound all fun and exciting, it was creepy as shit," I mutter. "Whatever it was, I saw our mum. I heard--"

"You saw Mum?" Annabel's eyes are huge, practically the size of her head.

Her memory of life before the accident is just as bad as mine, so it doesn't surprise me that this amazes her. It was a bit odd for Annabel to have forgotten everything; while the majority of spirits aren't aware they're dead at first, they rarely forget who they are.

I nod. "Yeah, I heard her speak, she was... Shit, what was she saying?" I struggle to bring the memory to the surface. "She was telling me not to look at something."

"How sure are you that you weren't hallucinating?"

"Honestly, not very."

Annabel goes to say something else, but is interrupted by a swooshing sound. It isn't until Tom is standing in front of me with an enormous smirk slapped on his unshaven face that I realise the sound was my door opening. A knock would've, y'know, been nice. He has a red apple in his hand, and he's wearing nothing but a pair of white briefs. Annabel is gawking at him, while I'm trying not to throw up.

"Hey mate! Heard you freaked out last night," he says. He bites into the apple, and it's really damn loud. "A few of us are heading over to campus to check out the freshers' fair in half an hour or so, if you fancy it."

"Dress code isn't strict, I take it," I attempt to joke, motioning to his underwear.

He doesn't get it.

It's an unusually warm September morning, and the university has an alluring charm I couldn't see in the February rain when I visited on an open day. A few of my flatmates have sunglasses perched on their noses, and Ava has even brought along what she referred to as a parasol, but I think it's just a fancy umbrella. She's walking ahead of us, almost skipping slightly, and it's clear no one knows what to really make of her.

The heart of the uni is The Cavern, which was originally a medieval manor house, but it's been distorted by years of extensions and modernisation. It's now filled with restaurants, cafés, lecture theatres, a student pub, the students' union, some shops, and the like. Behind the building is an open field where the fair is being held, and it sure isn't hard to miss.

I don't think I've ever seen so many stalls in my entire life, or so many fanatical young adults in bright green t-shirts with the phrase here to help planted onto them. I can just make out the large lake populated by ducks and manmade fountains at the bottom of the field, but I can't focus on it for long because we've barely stepped onto the grass when a green t-shirt warrior approaches us.

He's speaking way too fast and way too enthusiastically about the university's fabric society. I wish I was kidding. The guy finishes his speech by pointing us in the direction of his stall.

"Groovy, yeah, that's so cool, we'll totally join. Thank you so much," Ava says in a voice that could melt a frozen heart.

The guy nods at us with an accomplished expression on his tanned face, and begins his search for more victims. Ava faces us, her smile oozing with innocence.

"I'd rather saw my head off."

To that, she spins back around and continues leading us into the fair. Jamie, who blatantly has the hangover from hell but won't admit it, has been whining throughout the whole walk. He's dragging himself along beside me, regurgitating complaints like a mentally deficient parrot.

"I don't see why it was imperative we visit this today. If any of you had bothered conducting any research beforehand, you'd already be aware of all of the events and societies available. It's just an inconvenience."

"Headaches getting worse, is it, Jay?" I ask before he can continue his complaining.

"It's Jamie," he barks in response. "And I'm fine, shut up."

Bit harsh. It doesn't help that he speaks like an eighteenth century nobleman. I've no idea why he came along; he could've just stayed in the flat with Katie and Mason. Jamie mutters something under his breath and storms ahead to catch up with Tom and Ava, leaving

Carmen and me to follow behind. She rolls her eyes as if to say ignore him, as Ava stops in front of a stall a few yards away.

Once we reach her, I acknowledge the society she's stopped at, and I'm half tempted to gouge my eyeballs out of my skull. The A4 banner sellotaped onto their table reads Paranormal Society.

It's kind of funny, really, how the moment I decide to pretend this stuff doesn't exist, it starts following me everywhere I go.

Ava is quietly reading through their information booklets, while Tom tells the society members a story about his grandmother, who apparently haunts his downstairs bathroom. Ava eventually scribbles her name down onto the sign up sheet, and just when I think I've escaped, Tom makes a joke about how hilarious it would be for us all to join the society and go on flat ghost hunts. He promptly signs us all up.

"Leave me out, mate, I'm good," I interject as he's writing down our names.

He ignores me.

By the time we've investigated the rest of the fair, I'm so hungry I'd be willing to snack on the grass we're standing on. I've collected a pencil case worth of stationary, alongside at least five shot glasses, and even some complimentary mayonnaise. I don't like mayo, but it was free, so it would've been crazy of me not to pick some up.

My indecisiveness forced me to sign up for a load of societies I know I'll never attend, but I figure it's best to keep my options open. Tom and I both signed up to the boxing society because I've done that since I was a kid. The only other one I'm likely to attend is the percussion society, and that's purely for free use of a drum kit.

Carmen suggests we get some food from the burger van at the bottom of the field, and there are no protests on my behalf. We head in the direction of the lake, and join the growing queue. I'm about to order a cheeseburger when Carmen starts discussing vegetarian sausages, and I sort of just stand there nodding my head, not quite sure why she's saying all this to me. Then it occurs to me that I'm an idiot, and recall what I said when we all first met. Crap. I must've been staring at the menu for ages because Tom, who's next in line, starts bugging me to hurry up.

"I'll have..." I try, but my voice trails off.

Should I just own up? I glance at Carmen, whose honey eyes watch me expectantly, and instead of doing the sensible thing and admitting I'm not actually a vegetarian, I go right ahead an order a vegetarian hot dog.

God, I hate myself.

I continue to order some large fries and a side of onion rings to make up for my loss, and a bottle of water to be, y'know, healthy.

"Hungry?" Carmen laughs as she and I find a place to sit beside the lake.

I glance down at the food in my hands as we sit onto the dry grass. It's not that much, is it? Compared to her small portion of chips, sure, but hell, I'm a growing boy. I take a bite out of my hot dog, and it tastes a lot less like cardboard than expected. I'm actually impressed.

Annabel has appeared by this point, and she sits opposite us eyeing up my onion rings. Being unable to remember anything other than her afterlife, food is one thing she can't get her head around. She doesn't quite grasp the need for it, but thinks it always smells good.

"You feeling all right today?" Carmen asks me, drawing my attention away from my sister. She waves Tom over to the space we've found. "Ava said you passed out last night, after you did a runner."

"Oh, yeah, nah I'm good," I reply absentmindedly, dissecting my hot dog. "Sorry about that, by the way."

"I've been eliminating options," she continues.

"Huh?"

"Of what your secret is." She points a chip at my face as she begins stating her theories. "I hear you talking to yourself a lot in your room, so you might have smuggled a pet in without telling us. You have suspiciously big eyes and long eyelashes for a guy, so maybe you're actually a woman. Also, you're the only one yet to talk about your parents, so they're probably part of MI5 or something," she concludes, finally popping the chip into her mouth. "Am I warm?"

I raise my eyebrows at her, and it's enough for her to take my answer as a resounding no, despite the fact she's close on some level. As far as I'm aware, I'm not a woman, but the story of my parents is a weird one, and she just doesn't realise I'm not talking to myself.

"Not even lukewarm?" she asks, and I shake my head. "Damn it."

Tom, Jamie, and Ava sit down opposite us, and I smirk at Tom as he shivers when he sits beside Annabel. She edges away slightly. Jamie, who hasn't bought anything for himself, frowns at my food with such disgust that you'd swear I was eating an infant child.

"Not hungry?" I ask, nodding at him. "You can have some of my chips, if you want."

"I'd rather eat something more... nutritionally valuable," he mutters in response. He mumbles a lot, doesn't he? "You've no idea under what conditions that food has been prepared. I certainly didn't notice any hygiene certificates."

"Your loss." I shrug, shoving a chip into my mouth.

Within ten minutes, every last crumb in the cardboard box has made its way into my stomach. I could probably eat more. Ava has been glancing at each one of us frequently throughout our meal, but she's barely said a word. I think everyone else has noticed because Jamie keeps scowling at her, Tom's watching her, and Carmen has asked her if she's okay three times.

Annabel hasn't said a word to me, and I'm wondering if it's because she's worried Ava will hear her. I'm still undecided on that front. What she said about losing her abilities when drunk was a strange coincidence, if it was one, but it just seems so unlikely. I've never met anyone else like me. Eventually, she speaks up.

"One of you has a spirit attachment, but I can't figure out which one."

Annabel and I glance at each other.

"What does that mean?" Carmen responds.

"There's a spirit following you."

"No way... Is it going to kill us?" Tom gasps, wide-eyed. "Oh my god, I had a shiver earlier, did it walk through me?"

I fail not to laugh. Besides Ava, no one else appears to find it as hilarious as I do, and it results in some confused glances in my direction. Way to be subtle, Felix. I look down in an attempt to shift away the attention. She must be referring to Annabel, she has to be. Holy shit, maybe she can do what she says she can after all. Annabel quickly disappears after shooting me one more shocked look.

Everyone's giving each other the is this girl crazy? look, and it's a sharp reminder of why I've never told a living soul about what I can do. Tom continues asking questions, and as each one is answered by Ava, Jamie becomes more and more restless. He begins sighing at her and rolling his eyes, and I'm half-tempted to punch his smug face. Tom is in the middle of another story about his toilet haunting grandmother when Jamie finally says whatever it is that's making him so agitated.

"You know, Thomas, psychics feed on your desires and use manipulation to convince you of their abilities," he announces.

He stands up and turns to face Ava, while lifting his hand over his eyes to block out the sun.

"Simple physics invalidates every single thing you've said. Kinetic energy is responsible for the movement of objects, not dead people, and the suggestion of there being a place for spirits to gather and spend eternity in bliss is absolutely preposterous. There is no brain activity after death, and the soul is a fictitious concept conjured up thousands of years ago to comfort people about the prospect of death."

"Oh, whoa, no... Sorry, you don't understand," Ava responds. "They manipulate energy, you see, that's how they have the ability to move things. The soul is a separate entity all together. It doesn't matter what the body is doing because the spirit is released the moment you die. It's like, whoa, they don't all just magically appear in this eternal place. Some are stuck here to complete unfinished business, or to redeem their living selves, or carry out a duty. Only then can they leave and--"

"Oh, come on. You may be able to convince these... people," Jamie interrupts, motioning at us still sitting on the grass. I'd love to hear what he was going to say before he settled on people. "But I've got far too much of a scientific nature to fall victim to this type of manipulation."

He doesn't stop there. He continues his elaborate speech, discrediting every single thing Ava has said about spirits. I'm not even kidding anymore, I actually want to hit him. I clench my jaw in a bid to calm myself, but it's bloody difficult.

Annabel, no doubt sensing the drama, has returned by this point. She's sitting nestled up to me, watching Jamie with narrowed eyes. If it was appropriate to do so, I'd push him into the lake. He's standing on the edge, so all it would take is a tiny nudge. He's still ranting. Every word he speaks makes me more and more agitated. Not believing in this stuff is fine, but there's no need to single Ava out and be an arsehole over it.

"I apologise if I've offended you," Jamie continues, briefly redeeming himself, "but I'd recommend perhaps seeing a psychiatrist. It may be an issue, something from childhood perhaps. It's common for children to conjure up these stories in their heads to deal with some kind of trauma or difficulty."

I'm done with this jerk. My jaw is locked, my fists are clenched. An overwhelming anger is building up inside of me, and I'm worried I might genuinely jump up and shove this idiot into the lake behind him. I'm clenching my jaw, and I don't know if it's a bad hangover symptom, but my skin doesn't feel like my own, and my body feels light.

"Has anyone in your family passed away? Perhaps it's your way of coping."

That's it, I'm done.

"Oh, shut up, Jay."

The sentence has barely left my lips when, out of nowhere, Jamie stumbles backwards. As if someone physically pushed him, he stumbles backwards and doesn't stop falling until his back has disturbed the still water of the lake. Whatever the case, he sure as hell didn't just fall.

He re-emerges with his soaked hair sitting like a dead animal on his head, and a face redder than a fire engine. Tom bursts out laughing, Carmen lifts her hand to her mouth and gasps, and Ava watches with a smirk while I whip my head to Annabel with a crazed look on my face.

"Annie!" I whisper a hiss. "Appreciate the thought, but Jesus, I didn't want you to throw him into the lake!"

Annabel gapes at me, her face somehow looking paler than usual. She glances at Jamie flapping about in the water, then returns her gaze to my face.

"Felix, that wasn't me."

Chapter 4

I would be lying if I said I had high expectations of what my degree course would be like, but I didn't think it would be this bad. I've just finished my first week of lectures and seminars, and I'm bored half to death. I was hoping the stereotype of civil engineering students learning about nothing but bridges would be diminished when I arrived at uni, but apparently not.

We've been reassured by countless lecturers in tweed suits that we will explore other things, but I can't say I'm holding out much hope. I'm not even sure why I chose this degree. I thought it'd be useful, but I'm wondering if choosing something more creative would've been better for my sanity. A degree in drumming or something, that would be cool. I hope that's a thing.

I'm pondering over my poor life decisions as I stroll in the general direction of my flat when a car horn almost makes me wet myself. A bright red Mini Cooper pulls up beside me, and I stop in my tracks. The passenger seat window is cranked down, and peering over it with a pair of round sunglasses on is Carmen. In the driver's seat sits Ava, who gives me a soft smile.

"Get in loser, we're going shopping," Carmen says with a wicked grin on her face. Ava laughs, and I've got no idea what's going on. Carmen lifts her sunglasses to the top of her head. "No seriously, we could really do with a bit of help. Ava's picking some stuff up from home, and we need a bit of muscle."

I shrug. Why not? I'm just flattered to have been referred to as muscle, really. Carmen hops out of the car and jumps back in, this time sitting in the back to allow me to squeeze myself into the passenger seat. I knew Ava lived quite locally, but I didn't realise she had her own car, let alone one this nice. Both the outside and inside of it is spotless, and as it's the classic model, it sure can't have been cheap. As we make our way out of the city and towards the suburbs, the girls start talking about Jamie's dip in the lake last week.

"Ava reckons he pissed off some dead guys, so they pushed him," Carmen says from the backseat. "What do you think. Ghost or no ghost?"

I shrug. I do a lot of shrugging, don't I?

"Do you believe?" Ava interjects. We stop at a red light, and her eyes bore into me.

I have to stop myself from shrugging for the umpteenth time. "In ghosts?" I ask, to which she nods. "I dunno."

Carmen announces that she does, but Ava says nothing. Her dark eyes continue to gaze into mine, and I get the feeling she knows I'm hiding something. Ever since she failed to read my aura, she's been spending a lot of time watching me. Then again, she stares at everyone. The traffic light turns green, she mutters a groovy, and accelerates forward.

It takes just over half an hour to reach Ava's house, and I initially think she's having us on. After driving through a narrow country lane for a few minutes, an old English country house begins to slowly emerge through the trees. Its beige bricks have yet to be exposed to the strangling grasp of the modern world, and being three storeys tall with too many windows to count, it's enormous. Foliage crawls up the house's walls, and from afar the vines resemble serpents clinging to the bricks for dear life. Ava pulls up outside the porch as if we've arrived at her house, and it takes me a moment to realise that we have.

"You live here?" I ask, dumbfounded.

"It's like, whoa, yeah, big, I know. People always say so."

I can't stop gawking. Carmen's mouth is agape, and as we glance at each other, I know she's wondering why Ava willingly lives in our small flat when she has Buckingham Palace barely half an hour away. That's sure as hell what I'm thinking right now, anyway.

Ava hums to herself as she leads us inside the building, and once I catch a glimpse of the main hallway, I actually think I might develop heart palpitations. In the centre of it is a grand staircase leading the way to the upper floors in a dizzying spiral, its wooden steps perfectly polished. Portraits of people wearing old-fashioned clothing and long beards frame the walls, and exotic plants and flowers cover any remaining floor space. For the second time, Carmen and I turn to each other in amazement.

We follow Ava up the staircase, and as I scan the cream walls, I can't help feeling like the people frozen within the portraits are staring at me. The next hallway, while not as grand as the downstairs one, is still impressive. The walls are almost bare, but the exotic plants remain to fill the long space.

Ava leads us through a door, and we find ourselves standing in her bedroom. I'd be fairly confident on betting that her four-poster bed is bigger than my entire bedroom at the flat, and all of her furniture, from her wardrobe to the chest at the bottom of her bed, looks like it's come straight from and eighteenth century lord's house.

Ava pulls her braids up into a ponytail before heading over to the wardrobe and opening its doors. She motions us over as she begins shuffling through racks of clothes. Carmen questions her over her parents as we're sorting through them, and due to my growing belief of Ava's abilities, I'm half expecting her parents to have also kicked the bucket. I quickly find out that's one way we're not similar; her folks run their own business in the city, and work most of the day. Based on this mansion of a building, it must be a pretty successful one.

Once a sizeable pile of dresses has been accumulated, Ava turns to me. "There are a few books I need from the library, would you mind finding them for me?" she asks, to which I nod. "Groovy, thanks! They're pretty heavy, so I don't think I could carry them. Here," she says a she delves into her skirt pocket. She hands me a piece of lined paper. "These are the titles I need. It's the room next door to this one, to the left."

Ava thanks me again as she grabs some of the clothes on the floor, while Carmen picks up what remains. We leave the room, and the girls turn right to head outside to the car, while I turn left into the library.

I didn't expect this room to be small, but there's a library, and then there's this. By this point, you'd think I'd have grown accustomed to every single item in this place looking like it cost no less than a grand, but evidently not. There's not a single wall visible; each one is framed by bookshelves, and in the middle of the room stands an intimidatingly large globe. Circling it are several leather chairs, all adorned with enormous cushions. There are small tables dotted around the room, and placed upon each one is a pile of books.

I glance down at the list in my hand. This might take me longer than I thought.

"Holy mother of Baby Jesus." Annabel.

I turn to see her standing beside me, and slapped onto her face is the stupidest grin I've ever seen. She promptly begins exploring the room, accompanying an impressed gasp with every object she looks at. Annabel has read more books than I could even try to count, and has always insisted that she'd have studied English Literature at university, so this is heaven for her--no pun intended.

I laugh. "Cool, right?"

She turns back to me. "Can we live here, please? Marry Ava, whatever it takes, I don't care."

I don't respond to Annabel, and instead watch her with raised eyebrows as she bounces around the room like a deranged puppy. As I begin my potentially lifetime long search for Ava's books, I start to pick up on a pattern. Every single one is spirit-related. I don't bother opening any of their pages at first, but curiosity eventually gets the better of me. They're written in old English, and some of them seem to even be written in a Celtic language. It's difficult to make sense of much, but I can gauge vague ideas.

"Hey, Annie," I call, gesturing my sister over. She looks up from the globe in the centre of the room, then manifests herself beside me. "According to this, you can make yourself visible to anyone, not just me."

"Does it say how?" she asks as she stands on her tiptoes. I lower the book for her.

"Nah, it claims to be unknown, and extremely rare. Says that most spirits fall into that state of being accidentally, which I guess explains why random people experience ghost sightings occasionally," I reply. "I'm calling bullshit."

"Y'know, for someone who can see dead people, you're quite the sceptic."

"What can I say? I'm very self-critical." I wink at her. "Nah, I don't know, it all just sounds like a load of made up shit to me, like stories parents would tell their kids to scare them or--"

"I told you you talk to yourself a lot."

I jump at the sound of a voice coming from the doorway, and slam the book shut. Standing there with a lopsided grin on her face is Carmen, who probably thinks I'm a goddamn psychopath. I stammer and feel my cheeks rapidly burning, but she just laughs and wanders towards me. When she notices the book in my hands, she reads the title and smiles.

"Ava's into some weird shit, fair play," she mutters. She takes the book and begins scanning the pages. "It's so interesting, though, don't you think? I've always been fascinated by the concept of there being something after all this, something bigger than us."

I don't really know what to say, so I just say, "yeah, dead things are crazy, right?"

Why do I always make myself sound like such a halfwit around this girl?

She doesn't seem to hear me, to my relief, and continues speaking. "The suggestion that we're born, we live, we die, and that's it has always terrified me. I want to feel like things matter, y'know? I was only six when I realised I was going to die. I remember lying in bed one night and, I don't know, it just occurred to me. It was all I could think about for years, and everything I did felt so irrelevant because I thought it would all come to an end eventually anyway."

As if she'd forgotten I was in the room, Carmen looks up at me and shakes her head, as if snapping herself out of her thoughts. She apologises--for what, I'm not sure--and begins reading a passage from the book aloud. It takes me longer than it should to realise that she's reading a non-English section. I watch her in both confusion and awe.

"Welsh," she explains. "My grandfather's from there, and my mum grew up there. Fun fact: she's also Malaysian, and my dad's half Spanish."

"Wow, that's different," I reply, finally able to conjure up coherent sentences. "Makes my family history of Sheffield sound a bit shit, really. Saying that, my grandmother was from Stoke-on-Trent. Exciting stuff, I know."

Carmen's airy laugh fills the room, and she proceeds to read the rest of the page she's on. Annabel is peering over her shoulder to read the contents of the black book, but moves back when Carmen shivers. I say my family derive from Sheffield, but they could have originally been Norwegian pig farmers for all I know.

My mother had no siblings, which meant no cousins or aunties and uncles for me, and only her mother was still alive when the accident happened. She kicked the bucket after a few years, and was too old to be able to care for me up until then anyway. No one could be traced on my father's side, and my grandmother had never met any of his family, so that was pretty much a brick wall.

"My folks are already demanding to come and visit me," Carmen announces as she closes the book and places it onto the pile I've accumulated. "They divorced after having a handful of affairs each, and they're in this constant battle of beating one another to the mark. Being the first to visit me at uni is one of those marks, but I'd rather not see either of them for as long as possible, to be perfectly honest."

Geez, that was candid. I always feel like I should resent people for saying things like that about their parents because I can't even remember mine, but I don't. I figure just because someone has something you don't, it doesn't make their version of it better. It hardly sounds like that in Carmen's case, anyway. I expect to see a glint of sadness in her eyes as she finishes speaking, but there's nothing. She talks about it as you would about the weather.

"Your folks still together?" she continues, and I immediately wish there was a sadness to distract her from asking me that.

I hesitate, but eventually nod my head. I figure it's not really a lie. Wherever they are, I've always assumed they're together. I'm just taking her question in its most literal sense.

"Lucky," she says as she traces her fingers along the spine of a book. "Apparently, fifty percent of marriages end in divorce nowadays. My plan is to live alone on a farm, maybe raise a few alpacas or goats, not sure yet."

"That's very specific."

She shrugs her shoulders. "I like alpacas and goats."

Carmen stays in the library with me for a while, aiding me in my search for the books on Ava's list. Annabel gives us a hand too, but I have to stop her when Carmen spots a book being slightly nudged out by an invisible force. I shoo her away when Carmen isn't looking, to which Annabel protests but eventually obeys. She's never been the best at subtlety. Carmen makes a ghost joke, but doesn't seem to think much of it. By the time Ava enters the room, we're in search of the last book.

"Groovy, thanks!" she exclaims in an overly joyous voice. "I just, whoa, totally forgot about all these. Which ones do you have left?"

She wanders over, her bare feet tapping against the wooden floor, and takes a peek at the list on one of the tables. She nods to herself, then promptly heads towards the back of the room. Within seconds, the final book is in her hands. This one is notably smaller than the rest, and doesn't appear to be so old.

"This one's basically a watered down version of the ins and outs of the reflective world--the spirit world. I thought that maybe some of you guys would be interested in it. The language is a lot simpler, and it assumes the reader knows, like whoa, nothing at all."

"So like ghosts for dummies?" Carmen replies, to which Ava smiles, then nods. "Yeah, I'll definitely take a look at this. Thanks."

As Carmen takes the book from Ava, I have to bite my tongue to stop myself from protesting. I really want to take a look at that thing. Regardless of whether or not Ava has genuine supernatural abilities, my curiosity can't resist it. As we begin loading the books, alongside the rest of Ava's stuff into the car, I consider my options.

I could steal the thing from Carmen when she's not looking, or I could even get Annabel to do it for me, though that would be risky. I could simply ask to have a look at the thing, but I don't want to seem too interested in it all. My head is beginning to hurt, so I figure that's enough thinking for one day. As we're throwing the last pile of stuff into Ava's car, I realise that my head really is aching. A lot.

"You all right?" Carmen asks, to which I wave my hand at to signal a yes.

She doesn't look convinced. We pile into the car, and as I shut the passenger seat door I realise my fingertips feel numb. My skin feels irritated, and my hands are clammy. I'm seriously beginning to wonder if there's something wrong with me. Carmen and Ava are discussing something, but I'm not listening. I can't seem to turn my focus away from the aching in my head or the strange feeling in my gut, or at least I think I can't until I glance back towards Ava's house as we're driving away.

Peering outside the window of the library we were in moments ago is a slender figure with a large frown, and deep black eyes. Its head turns as the car does, and as suddenly as it appeared, it's gone. That explains that, then.

Chapter 5

Everywhere I turn, I'm terrified I'll see a pair of black eyes staring back at me. A few days have passed since I saw that thing in Ava's window, and I've not seen it since, but I'm constantly on edge. Part of me is still living in the hope that it's all a hallucination or some bizarre thing I've conjured up inside my own head, not that literal insanity is a great alternative to spirit-related stuff.

Annabel keeps going on at me to reveal all to Ava, but I just can't bring myself to do it. To get her alone is near enough impossible in itself, and I've only ever told one person about my abilities before. That resulted in the only foster parent I ever actually liked trying to literally section me, and then throw me out like a pair of old shoes.

Sometimes I wonder if I actually am insane, and that maybe every single thing I see is a figment of my imagination. What if I tell Ava everything, only for her to think I'm an absolute freak? What if she proves me wrong, and it turns out I am actually just crazy?

These questions are burning the circuits of my brain when I wander into the living area of my flat one Wednesday afternoon, and the first thing I spot is a small, brown book sitting on the kitchen island. I recognise it immediately. It's the book Ava handed Carmen the other day, the simplified one about spirits.

I drop the plate I brought in to clean up onto the countertop, right next to the two other plates I've yet to clean, and sit down beside the island. Everyone else has left the flat for a paranormal society meeting, which I gladly declined, so I've got at least an hour. Annabel's listening to some god-awful audiobook about a middle-aged divorcee who falls in love with a rich arsehole and adopts a puppy, or some garbage, so I'm even free of her for a while.

If she had it her way she'd probably stalk me every waking hour of the day, but I think she's gotten the message that being attached by the hip can be a bit much for me at times. She's pretty good at knowing when I want some privacy, and usually goes for a walk somewhere else for a few hours, or finds somewhere new to explore.

I flip open the book, and turn the slightly yellowed pages until I find the index. Hm. There are a lot more categories than I thought there'd be in a simplified version of something, half of which I've no idea what they actually mean. I figure the best place to start is the beginning.

I quickly pop back into my room to grab some writing materials. I'm soon hunched back over the book in the kitchen, with a pencil in my hand and a notebook by my side. I best write some notes for Annabel--I have a habit of processing information, only to verbally regurgitate that information in a way that makes no sense whatsoever to anyone but myself.

By the time I hear people returning to the flat, it feels as if I've been through the most intense academic session of my life. Ava is studying for a Law degree, so it should have occurred to me that her version of simplified reading will differ a lot from my version of it. I hastily slam the book shut, along with the small notepad.

Tom is the first to walk in, and judging by his wonky grin, he had a whale of a time at the society meeting. He immediately starts blathering on about how I missed out, how everyone there was weird as shit, and how much they all loved Ava. Jamie, who apparently attended for 'Scientific purposes' appears unimpressed, and follows Tom into the kitchen. The others must head straight to their bedrooms.

"They're real, man, I'm telling you now," Tom says to me as he opens the fridge and takes out a bowl of pasta that's been in there for at least a week. "The ghost people said it would make sense for my nan to haunt the bathroom because she had this thing for towels--used to collect them--and we had them all when she died. Kept them all in that bathroom."

"Ghost people?" I ask, struggling not to snigger.

"Yeah! The society members, and hell, even the president of it thought I was on to something. We're going on this trip to a haunted house before the semester ends, so I'll be able to flex my expertise then."

Tom continues rambling on about his paranormal experiences as he heats up his week-old pasta in the microwave, and I'd probably bet on it that he doesn't stop, even after he leaves the room. Jamie has been washing up some of his dishes the whole time, and when Tom disappears out of the door, he lets out a sigh.

"Enjoyed the meeting then?" I ask with a laugh.

"It's ridiculous, you're the only other one who doesn't fall for all of this preposterous storytelling," he replies, glancing at me from the sink. "I approached it with an open mind, and left finding the whole thing even more preposterous."

"Be careful," I joke. "You're near water. I wouldn't piss off anymore dead guys, if I were you."

He reddens slightly. "Shut up."

I roll my eyes as I pull my phone out of my pocket to scroll through aimlessly. I'm yet to figure out why Jamie is such an arsehole. He has a habit of redeeming himself briefly, only to ruin that within seconds.

"D'you know who keeps leaving their plates here without cleaning them? It's disgusting."

I look back up, immediately regretting it. Standing behind Jamie is an old woman with sagged skin and white hair. We've either acquired a new housemate, who happens to be an extremely mature student, or Jamie has made himself a new friend. I shoot my head back down as soon as possible, but it's too late. She saw me looking.

"Felix?" Jamie asks, but I don't remember the question.

"Hello? Can you help me?" The woman's voice, but I ignore it.

"Are they yours? Can you clean them if they are, please? It's not--"

"Hello? You looked at me, I--I saw you! Please, help. I know you can see--"

"--something crusty, it'll grow fungus and spread to everything else in the sink, it's hazardous and--"

"--need to talk to him, please! Answer me!"

I can't bear it anymore. I flick my head back up, and force all my attention onto Jamie, so much so that I barely notice the old woman standing over the kitchen island with her icy eyes boring into me. I glance at the plates Jamie won't shut up about. Turns out they are mine.

"Sorry," I finally say, still not letting my attention to waver from Jamie for one second. "I'll do it in a bit."

He resorts to the obligatory Jamie response by muttering under his breath, asks me to clean them again, and then swiftly leaves the room. I was hoping the old woman would follow him, but she doesn't. I groan and turn my attention to her.

"What is it?" I ask in a whisper. "It better not be about dentures because I swear to God, if one more dead old person whines at me to find something they've lost, I'm--"

"Shut it, boy, I'm not some incompetent pensioner," the woman snaps, lifting her chin. "No, I need Jamie to call me."

"Sorry to break it to you, but you're not going to be able to answer. You're..." I struggle to find a way to phrase it nicely, so I don't. "You've died, hence why only I can--"

She lifts her hand to silence me. "I can assure you I'm fully aware of that. I always answer my phone, so if I don't, he will know something is wrong. He called me this morning, so he won't for several days now. No one will find me, otherwise."

An image of this chubby old woman rotting in a floral armchair flashes through my mind, and I shudder slightly. At least she knows she's dead. It's always a lot easier when they know they've popped their clogs. It's way more common in the older generation because they're usually expecting it, as morbid as that may sound.

I click my tongue. "Well, I can try. You're his grandmother, I'm guessing? Won't Jamie's folks--your son, daughter, or whatever--check in on you? Don't take this the wrong way, but you've not got yourself the best kid there, if not."

The woman narrows her eyes and tuts me. "Don't be so rude, boy, did your parents raise you amongst a pack of wolves?"

Part of me is irritated by this woman's attitude, but another part of me is wildly entertained by it. She's what Jamie would be if he had any comebacks other than shut up.

"Yes, I'm his grandmother. His parents have passed on, so I've raised him since he was a teenager."

I cock my head slightly. "As in, they've died?"

The woman nods.

Shit.

I'm not too sure why because he acts like he has zero consideration for anyone else, but I feel bad for the guy. His folks died when he was a kid, and now the person who replaced them has left too. At least I can't remember the people I lost.

"I'll try," I eventually say. "I mean, I don't exactly rave about this whole speaking to dead people thing because I'm not sure if you've noticed, but I'm a bit of a rare case... but I'll try to put the idea of calling you into his head."

The woman thanks me before disappearing. Fantastic. Love it. As if I didn't have enough problems to deal with already. I throw this newfound mission into the tomorrow Felix's problem section of my brain, grab my notepad, and wander back into my bedroom.

Despite the gruelling process that was reading a chunk of Ava's book, it's opened my eyes to more than I thought existed. A lot of the stuff, particularly at the beginning, were things I'd already guessed for myself. Annabel pauses the book she's listening to as I enter the room, and asks me where I've been. After a brief explanation of Jamie's batty grandmother, I inform her of the notes I made from my reading. I plop myself onto my bed as Annabel joins me, and flip open the notepad to gloss over what I've written.

1. The world ghosties live in/their state of being/whatever is officially called the reflective world. Derives from the fact they're stuck in it due to unfinished business, the need to redeem themselves, blah blah blah.

2. Said ghosties have 2 states - open and closed. Open is where anyone can see them, closed is where nobody living can see them, but those with abilities can communicate

3. Ghosties have telekinetic powers where they can manipulate energy to move things, turn things on and off e.t.c. Powers are generally limited though e.g. can't just lob lamps at people's faces, unless they're a poltergeist. Additional abilities like telekinetic powers have occasionally been present in Spirit Talkers.

4. There are 2 types of ghosties - pure and dark. Pure are those who've died and are stuck in this world to complete a task, dark are the evil bastards. Dark spirits are generally murderers, rapists e.t.c. Poltergeist is a variation of a dark spirit. They become banished if they don't redeem themselves, and pure spirits can become banished due to failure to complete their task, killing a mortal.

5. Dark spirits can't communicate with each other, but can interact with pure spirits, while pure ones can communicate with everyone and their dog. Sucks for the evil guys

6. Originally 12 families with ghost-related abilities, but they've diminished and spread out over time, so few known families remain.

Annabel's whining at me to show her what I've written, and in fairness I did write it down for her to analyse, so I throw the paper down onto the bed for her to read. As she does so, my mind wavers back to Jamie and his grandmother. I wonder how long she's been dead, then realise how morbid I'm being and cut that thought short.

It's always amazed me how the deceased can trace someone connected to them so quickly, or at least those who understand they're dead, anyway. I figure it works the same way Annabel does with me. She describes it like a magnet; my presence and my energy is instantly distinguishable. It pulls her towards me, and so she can manifest to wherever I am within seconds. I briefly consider it having a relation to Ava and her auras, but I might just be getting carried away.

Whatever the case, I'm feeling worse and worse about leaving Jamie's grandmother rotting in her house as every second passes. I lift myself off my bed and head towards the doorway.

Annabel glances up from the paper. "Where are you going?"

"Just gonna check on Jamie, won't be long."

"Your third point, don't you think--"

"Hang on, I'll be back now."

I don't know if Annabel argues back because I'm swiftly out the door. Jamie's room is the furthest one away from my own, and so I slither quietly down the hallway. As I knock on his door, it occurs to me that I have no idea what the heck I'm going to say. I don't get the chance to contemplate it either because within seconds, Jamie's door is yanked open. His thick eyebrows are furrowed at the sight of me, and he's sporting that god-awful slicked back hairstyle.

"What d'you want?" he questions. "Have you cleaned your dishes?"

"Nah, in a bit," I say, waving my hand in the air. "I.. Uh..."

Jamie rolls his eyes and goes to shut his door, but I shove my foot in the doorway before he can close it completely. Screw subtlety.

"You should call your family."

There's a brief silence. "What?"

It's kind of difficult because considering my foot is the only thing keeping the door open, I'm having this conversation with a big plank of wood.

"I rang them this morning, it's fine," Jamie eventually continues.

"You should just check."

"Yes, sure, whatever." There's a muttering sound. "Could you move your foot, please?"

I don't think I'm going to get much further, so I pull my foot from Jamie's door. He mumbles a goodbye, mutters the word weirdo, and then he slams it shut. Oh well, I tried.

As I step back into my own room, it looks like a familiar face has followed me. Jamie's grandmother paces alongside my desk, and she's mumbling frantically while a look of immense fear floods her wrinkled face. Annabel watches her from the bed with wide eyes, and as I enter, they turn to me with a pleading look.

"Hey, you all right?" I ask quietly, not wanting anyone to hear me. "I spoke to Jamie for you, not sure I got anywhere though."

The woman turns to me and freezes. "You! I--You need to help me, someone is following me." She charges towards me and stands so close that if she were alive, I would feel her breath on my face. "I don't know who they are, or what they want, or--or why they're here, but I can feel them. I can--They're so dark. You have to help!"

I glance at Annabel, but she seems as dumbfounded by this as I am. Maybe this spirit isn't as put together as I thought she was. She's still rambling at this point, and I can barely understand a word she's saying, let alone make sense of any of it. I'm about to try and calm her down when, as if a light has been flicked off, she stops. Her mouth clamps shut, and she simply stares at me.

Her lips part, and she blinks slowly. "You're not safe here."

And with that, she's gone.

Chapter 6

An undying urge to hit something really, really hard has been gnawing at me lately. I'm practically jumping out of my seat with enthusiasm to meet up with Tom and head to the gym after this lab session. The boxing society are gathering there, and I missed last week's session because I had a nap that turned into a four hour sleep after my morning lecture. I can't say for sure why this urge to hit something has manifested itself, but I'm going to take a stab and guess it has something to do with the disturbing, confused state my life is currently in.

Jamie's grandmother hasn't paid me a visit since her meltdown the other day, and based on her famous last words, I may die at some point in the foreseeable future. On the cheery side of things, due to the fact my charade of being a vegetarian is still going strong, I've become an expert at cooking sausages when nobody's looking. I'm sure that'll come in handy at some point in the future. Might even be CV worthy.

We're meant to be designing three-dimensional underground transport structures based on equations given to us by our tutor, but I've got Ava's spirit book perched on my lap while I pretend to do work on the computer in front of me. Carmen's almost as useless as I am at leaving things around the flat, which I use to my advantage.

I've been trying to see if I can spot anything in the book about the creature I keep spotting, but haven't managed to find a single word on it. It's hardly helping with my concerns over possibility that I may legitimately be having psychotic episodes. I flick through more pages, only to be met with more and more disappointment as every page--

"Spirits appear as they did at their time of death once they have entered the Reflective World, but all physical appearance is discarded once they enter The Beginning," a deep voice booms above me, and I slam the book shut. The seminar tutor stands over me, his eyebrows raised. "As much as I love a good ghost story, I can't quite grasp what it has to do with underground means of transport."

I wonder if middle-aged men who make bad jokes are aware of how predictable their humour is. I say nothing in response, and instead just flash the scruffy haired man a sarcastic smile. I don't think he notices the sarcasm because he lifts his chin up in response, as if proud of himself for catching--and in his mind--scaring me.

Tom is already waiting for me outside the class when we finish, and he must've been waiting a while because he takes the piss out of the row I received ten minutes prior. He proceeds to ramble on about ghosts for the entire journey to the gym, and in a way, it's a good thing because it riles me up in preparation for hitting things.

I know I bring it on myself half the time, but a break from all of this dead people crap would be a godsend, even just for one day. Our flat is meeting up at one of the local pubs after this gym session, and I'm tempted to have a drink purely to do just that. I'm slightly concerned I'll develop an alcohol addiction if I continue with that attitude though, so I may pass.

The boxing session feels like it's over within seconds of arriving at the gym, and I spent the majority of it alone, hitting the biggest punching bag I could find. Other than some warm-up practices with Tom, I didn't particularly interact with anyone. I've never had much interest in actual fights. Considering my go-to instrument is a drum kit, I think I just like hitting things. I'm sure it's perfectly rational and healthy.

We all meet up outside The Cavern to walk to the pub Ava has recommended to us, and I'm surprised to see that Katie has actually showed up. She snagged herself a boyfriend a week into uni, and between us, I think we've seen her four times since. Unsurprisingly, he's here with her, in all his shaved head and steroid-induced glory. There's no sign of Mason, but that doesn't surprise me because he's made his own group of friends outside the flat.

We head off into the city, each one of us following Ava like a load of lost mongrels. We catch a bus just outside the university's south entrance, and it drops us off barely two minutes away from the pub. Jamie hasn't said a word during the journey, and there are plump bags under his eyes. His hair is unusually unkempt, and it's all suggesting that he did call his grandmother after all. I slow my pace as we approach the pub so that I trail along beside him at the back of the group.

"You all right?" I ask.

He just nods, shrugs, and follows everyone through the heavy wooden doors. Yep, he knows.

I could tell by the decaying stones this building is built from that this pub was an old one, but the interior stuns me. Thick wooden beams line the low ceiling, and more beams shoot from the floor to keep the roof sturdy. The chairs and sofas inside are covered in a deep red material, maybe velvet, and each seat is supported by a wooden frame decorated with intricate carvings.

The bar itself is enormous, and stretches far into the depths of the building. You'd probably catch the bubonic plague after forgetting to wash your hands at any of the pubs I ever stepped foot in back in Sheffield, but this place is spotless. I feel restless as we near the bar, so I figure I maybe do want a drink.

It's around six in the evening by now, and as it's a Friday, the pub is quickly filling up. Ava greets one of the old, bearded bartenders with bright eyes and an enthusiastic groovy, and they hug over the bar as if the man brought her up himself.

"So whoa, yeah, hey guys," she says, turning to us. "This is my dad."

Oh, turns out he did bring her up himself. Fancy that.

"Ah, you must be Ava's flatmates! Call me Mosi," the man says loudly, a South African accent shining through. He leans his elbows onto the bar. "First round's on the house, so make the most of it."

Always the observant type, at the notion of free alcohol, Annabel appears beside me with a hard glare in her eyes. She's such a mother, Jesus. I wink at her, and make an order for a bourbon and coke. I don't even really want a drink, I just want to annoy Annabel. I swear Mosi's dark eyes linger on me for a little longer than the others as he hands me my drink, but I might just be paranoid.

Drinks in hand, we find ourselves a booth nestled in one of the far corners of the pub. I squish myself in-between Carmen and Katie, who's already almost downed her first drink. Her boyfriend, who's sitting the other side of her, isn't far behind. The table is set against one of the large windows, which has an equally large windowsill, and so Annabel sits herself down onto that. She's still looking at me as if I sold her firstborn child to Satan.

There are four bartenders keeping the drinks flowing, three of which are alive. The not-so-alive one sits on a tall stool at the centre of the bar, with crossed arms and a proud smile. His hair is white and fluffy, and it sticks up on his head in a wispy tuft. He wears an old-fashioned suit--if I had to guess, I'd say nineteen-fifties--and has a pale complexion. I take my eyes off him before he can spot me looking, which would probably be rather unlikely considering how packed this place is, and take a sip of my drink.

"This place is beautiful," Carmen says once we've all settled into our seats. "Is this your family's pub?" she asks Ava.

"It's my dad's hobby," she replies. "My mum's family have owned it since the early nineteen-hundreds, but he, like, totally lives in it. It's technically my uncle's."

No wonder Ava is so minted. Her parents run their own company, while the rest of her family own a pub that's bursting at the seams with business. At least I know who to ask if I ever need to borrow a tenner. I take another sip of my drink, which so far doesn't seem to be helping with the restlessness that's niggling at me.

"This is the pub with access to the underground caves, isn't it?" Jamie asks, and it's the first thing I think he's said all evening.

Ava nods, while Tom stares in bewilderment. "Huh?"

Jamie grumbles something under his breath before elaborating. "They're artificial caves, believed to date back around a thousand years ago. The poor would occupy them during the medieval period, though more recently they were used as air raid shelters in the Second World War." Jamie waves his hand in the air as if the information he's stating is obvious. "You should really consider researching the city you're going to be living in for the upcoming three years."

With that, Jamie stands up and wanders back over to the bar. I hadn't even realised he'd finished his drink. At the realisation that Jamie is fetching himself another one, Katie leaps up, practically jumps over the table, and chases after him.

"Jamie's as cheerful as ever tonight, then. Bloody hell," Tom mutters. "Is that true? Are there really caves and shit here?"

"Yeah," Carmen replies. "Some of them are open to the public, like a tourist attraction. Didn't you notice the pamphlets about them from freshers' week? They were shoved through our door at least three times. Only fifteen quid for a family of four, apparently."

In Tom's defence, I was clueless about all this too. I always just ignore the pamphlets and vouchers rammed through our letterbox, and leave them scrunched on the floor until someone else bothers to move them. It sounds pretty cool, though.

The group continue to discuss the underground caves, while my attention briefly shifts back to the spirit behind the bar. He's watching the only barmaid pour a draft beer, and as she's about to let it run on for just a bit too long, it suddenly stops flowing. She's left with a perfect pint, and the old man beams at her. I like this guy.

"Does this place feel weird to you?" Annabel says from the end of the table, drawing my attention away from the bar.

I'm not sure how she's expecting me to answer in front of a table full of people, or what she means by weird exactly, so I just subtly shrug. She could be referring to the slight sense of restiveness I'm feeling, but I thought that was just me.

"Ask Ava if it's haunted or something, minus the old stiff behind the bar," Annabel continues to pry, but before I can respond, Katie reappears with a fresh drink in her hand.

"Guys, Jamie isn't boring, or an arsehole! We just did, like, three shots each at the bar." She fights her way back to her seat. Her boyfriend, who has been silently staring at his drink since she left, looks relieved to see his safety blanket return. "You lot totally lied about him, he's a blast."

I'm not sure if Katie realises that Jamie is right behind her, and has been since her initial announcement of him being a boring arsehole, but she doesn't appear to care either way. Oddly, Jamie doesn't seem fazed by the fact Katie basically just told him that we all hate him, and slumps himself back onto the end of the sofa.

"C'mon, Felix, ask her!" Annabel pleads again.

I shoot her a glare to see her with pouted lips and crossed legs. From what I've read of Ava's book, she can't literally hear every single thing a spirit says. The spirit has to make a connection to her somehow, and partly because I've told her not to, Annabel has yet to figure out how to do that. Nonetheless, when she's sitting on a windowsill inches away from Ava, while throwing my name out like it's going out of fashion, I can't help but feel a bit anxious.

Chapter 7

T he conversation has moved on to drinking games by now. Tom is explaining one he invented with one of his coursemates, which based on its inclusion of blindfolds and forced drinking, is probably illegal. By the time nine o'clock is rolling around, I'm only on my third drink, which is an orange juice and lemonade. The restlessness hasn't gone away, and I think the alcohol was only making things worse. On top of that, Katie hasn't stopped drinking since we got here, and if there's no one sober left to look after her, she might choke on her own sick at some point tonight.

We're at the bar after I promised to buy her a drink, purely so I can get her a water and tell her it's vodka. Her boyfriend has rendered himself useless by passing out an hour ago, so Ava and I have been trying to ensure she doesn't kill herself.

"You know what, Felix? It's mad. I can't remember you being this northern," Katie says through a laugh. "Like, you don't speak that northern, but you sound it. It's sexy. Sometimes I can't understand what you're saying, but it's hot--you're hot."

"Fantastic," I reply as I wave Mosi over.

This is the second time she's commented on my accent, and the fifth time she's called me hot. The first three times were when her boyfriend was conscious and sitting right next to her. Ava distracts Katie by starting a conversation about shopping, or clothes, or something similarly female-related, I imagine.

"Hey," I say as Mosi reaches us. His complexion is darker than Ava's, but their deep brown eyes are identical in colour. "Could we get some tap water for that one before she collapses and dies on your floor? Cheers."

Mosi winks at me as he turns to the sink behind the bar. I'm about to order another drink for Carmen because I remember hers almost being empty, but a high-pitched cackle stops me in my tracks. Katie's laughing hysterically. She's laughing so much that she backs up, and trips. Ava reaches out to grab her arm, but she's not fast enough.

Katie's falling, and her head is perfectly aligned to smack against the corner of a heavy, wooden stool. Panic floods me. The stool is too far for me to reach, but I shoot my hand out anyway, as if to push it away. And it moves. I don't have a goddamn clue how, but it flings out of the way, just in time for Katie's head to miss it as she falls.

Before I can even process it, Katie is lying on her back in hysterical fits of laughter while the stool now lies lifelessly on the floor, yards away from where it was moments ago. It must all have happened quickly because no one has moved much once it's over, but it feels like time has slowed down.

People rush to where Katie lies, while others watch the stray stool in bewilderment. I can't say I blame them; the thing did literally just fly across the room by itself. The feeling of restlessness is crawling through my skin now, and amongst the crowds and the humid air, I feel faint.

"Did you do that?" Annabel.

She gazes at me, her mouth hanging open. She starts rambling about the list I wrote after reading Ava's book for the first time, for some bizarre reason, but I cut her short and tell her to give me five. I don't know what the hell is going on. I just need some fresh air.

I stumble outside, and am surprised to find Jamie sitting on the steps leading up to the building. He flicks his eyes towards me the second I emerge, but they don't linger long. I think he wants me to ignore him. I do just that, primarily because I'll pass out if I stop paying attention to my aching head and clammy hands.

Simply leaving the cramped space of the pub has made me feel instantaneously better, though. As I'm about to step back into the place in an attempt to make sense of everything that just happened, Jamie stops me.

"Why did you tell me to call my family?"

"Huh? Oh, I--uh, I dunno," I answer pathetically.

"My grandmother has died."

The bluntness of his words leaves me tripping over mine. I stammer again. My mind frantically searches for the right thing to say, but I must take too long because it's Jamie who speaks next.

"It's just--I--She brought me up over the past few years, so it's.. it's weird, I mean... I don't know. My parents aren't around, so..." Jamie mutters, his voice turning quieter. The next sentence is a whisper, and I'm not sure I'm supposed to hear it. "I have no one left."

I'm not too sure why I say what I do next, but I figure it just wouldn't feel right lying at a time like this. If I can't be honest with him about seeing his grandmother, the least I can do is the second best thing.

"Mine aren't around either," I say quietly as I sit myself next to him on the concrete step. Why I continue, on the other hand, I assume is a burst of momentary stupidity on my behalf. "They died about ten years ago."

As the words leave my mouth, it feels like something has been crushing down on my chest since the moment I arrived in this city, and I never even noticed, like now that I've said that, I can breathe again. Jamie doesn't say anything in response, and I'm beginning to regret everything I've said when he eventually opens his mouth.

"Does it ever get easier?" His voice is barely audible.

Of all the questions he could've asked, he asks me one I can't answer. I've never wanted to remember my parents as much as I do right now. My mind flashes back to the party during freshers' week, when I had a vision of my mum, and I wish I knew something. Anything. I don't have the answer to Jamie's question, so I give him the one he wants to hear.

"Yes," I reply simply.

Jamie nods. We sit in silence for what feels like the rest of the night, but when I glance at my phone, I realise it's only been ten minutes. I can't stop going over what happened just now, and I don't think I've ever thought so hard about a bar stool in my entire life.

I didn't even physically touch the thing, so how it was pushed that hard by who knows what is beyond me. I know what Annabel's thinking; she's formulated this idea that it was all me, but surely I'd know if it was? I turn back to Jamie to catch him staring at me, but he quickly turns away.

"I don't mean to be an arsehole, I just don't know how to make friends," he mumbles as he stands up. He heads towards the pub's entrance, and just before wandering back inside, he turns back to me. "Thanks."

With that, he's gone. I don't find myself winning any alone time for very long though because minutes later, Carmen appears through the doorway. She's wearing a pair of tight jeans, and she's thrown on an oversized hoodie that's twice the size of her. Her dark hair dances wildly with the wind, and so she tucks half of it behind one of her ears.

As she spots me, a smile grows on her tanned face, and the innocence of that smile has a remarkable ability to make me forget anything ever happened. I'm standing now, with my back leaning against the jagged stones that form the medieval pub.

"So I think I've got it," Carmen says, standing beside me. I raise my eyebrows at her. "Your secret. You have a vendetta against stools."

I start laughing. "Oh, piss off."

Carmen elbows me, so I go to elbow her back, but she's too quick. She slaps my arm away before it can reach her side, and fist pumps the air in victory. I can tell she's drunk because she's hopping from one foot to the other, and slurring slightly.

"Only kidding, I doubt it's anything quite that interesting," she continues. "But! I have a real theory."

"C'mon then, I'll humour you."

"Close your eyes," she states.

"I dunno about that, mate. Not sure I trust you here."

Carmen doesn't say anything in return. She merely raises her eyebrows as a smirk reappears on her face. I challenge her by staring back into her eyes, but she doesn't waver, so I eventually give in. I shut my eyes, and briefly pray that she isn't about to dropkick me.

A few seconds pass, and I'm beginning to wonder if Carmen has run away to leave me standing here like an idiot with my eyes closed. I'm about to peek through them when a feeling of warmth hits me, just as a pair of lips clash against mine, and as if it's some primal instinct, I kiss Carmen back.

I raise my hand until it finds her face, and rest it gently on her cold cheek. She wraps her arms around my neck as I pull her closer, and I place my free hand on her waist underneath the baggy jumper she's wearing. As my fingers trace Carmen's hip bone, I have to stop my thoughts before they go in a direction I'd rather them not go when outside a medieval pub at nine o' clock on a Friday night.

I know there are more important things to deal with right now, but I can't say I give a shit. Besides, the longer we stay like this, the longer I can pretend everything's normal.

"Weyhey!" a familiar voice calls from the distance, and it's all over before I know it.

Carmen and I quickly part as if we just gave each other the most painful electric shock possible, and I look over her shoulder to see everyone leaving the pub. Tom leads them with a goofy look on his face, and I think it's a fair guess that it was him who called to us.

"Get a room, guys!" he continues. "In fact, we're all headed back now, so pick whose room you wanna get freaky in."

I don't say anything back; I just shoot him my middle finger. Tom laughs, as do the others, and continue on their way. Carmen and I follow behind, and as I feel my cheeks starting to burn and my mouth turning dry, I hurry my pace to catch up with them. Carmen is silent beside me, and I don't know what to say or do, or where to look, so resort to staring at her in a what the hell? kind of way. She stops me in my tracks as she fights off a smirk, stands on her tip-toes, and whispers into my ear.

"You're not gay then."

Chapter 8

Much to Tom's dismay, Carmen and I don't share a bed that night. Mosi invited us all to lunch at Ava's house before we left the pub, so I was told, so once we're all conscious and dressed, the plan is to head on over. Katie is still reeling after stool-gate, and Jamie's nabbed himself another horrendous hangover, so they've decided to pass. I, on the other hand, have been spending almost an hour glaring violently at a chewed pencil.

With a groan, I spin my chair to face Annabel, who's standing behind me with her hands on her hips.

"Mate, I have as much telekinetic ability as a toilet brush."

"Ugh, you're not even trying!" Annabel whines.

"I am!" I protest. "Can we just accept that stool-gate had nothing to do with me, nor did Jamie's dip in the pond."

Annabel crosses her arms with a roll of her eyes. A pained expression surfaces on her face, and it's one I recognise as her thinking face. She's lucky she's dead; it's not the most attractive thing ever. Her eyes roll around her sockets as she chases thoughts, while I stretch my legs so that they're resting on my bed.

We're due at Ava's in an hour or so, so we'll probably be leaving soon, and it'll be interesting to go back. Assuming her family is one of the twelve ghost-rearing ones mentioned in her book, I'm curious to meet her parents properly. I glance back to Annabel to see a mischievous look on her face, and I narrow my eyes.

"What is it?"

She responds by shaking her head, but her lips are tightly pressed together, and I can tell she wants to laugh. I ask her again, but she responds with a shrug. Jesus, she's annoying sometimes. A light giggle escapes her lips as she lifts one of my uni textbooks, and manoeuvres it to float around the space between us.

"What the heck are you doing?" I question her.

"Just playing," she mutters as her eyes follow the moving book. She turns her attention to me. "Did you hear Tom and Carmen this morning?

"What? No, I mean, what d'you mean?"

"Oh, I assumed you'd overheard them; they were pretty loud." Annabel shrugs, and the book she's floating around is starting to annoy me. "After seeing you eat each other's faces off--which was totally appropriate considering you'd just discussed dead parents with Jamie, by the way--but yeah, after seeing you, Tom must've felt threatened or something."

"Annie, what are you on about?"

She rolls her eyes. "They announced their love for each oth-er--Well, not literal love, but y'know what I mean. They fancy each other. Sucks for me because I was bidding on Tom to be my imagi-nary boyfriend."

I don't know why, but I stammer. What? Is she serious? I mean, I don't mind, I don't like Carmen or anything--I mean, she was the one who kissed me, and I just went along for the ride, that's all. I just... I don't know, I didn't expect that. Annabel's still holding the textbook above our heads, and it's becoming increasingly distracting.

"Oh, shit, sorry," Annabel says. "I didn't realise you actually liked her."

"What? Oh, no, it's--Yeah, nah, I don't, it's fine," I argue.

She raises her eyebrows and starts smirking again. If she wasn't dead and my sister, I swear to god I'd hit her. Why does she think this is so funny? I don't even have a thing for Carmen. Don't get me wrong, it would've been nice for her to say she had the hots for Tom before kissing me, but whatever, I don't care. I notice that my jaw is clenched, but can't remember doing it. Annabel is still smiling.

"Felix has a crush," she says in a sing-song voice. "Felix has a crush."

I'm not sure what I do next, exactly. I just know that I can't shout at her while everyone else is home, but I want to so goddamn badly because all I can feel is a sharp sense of frustration, and then I find myself sitting upright in my chair while my uni textbook slams into the wall with an ear-shattering bang. I stare, dumbfounded.

"Ha! I knew it! Get you riled up, and you're throwing things around like a teenage girl on her first period. No idea why we hadn't thought of that considering it's in every paranormal film, like, ever." Annabel's voice is filled with glee. "Don't get your knickers in a twist over the Tom and Carmen thing, by the way, I made it up."

After reaching the conclusion that I'm a hormonal mess with tele-pathically violent tendencies, I leave my bedroom to meet everyone in the kitchen. Carmen and Ava ask me if everything's all right because they heard a bang from my room, which I shrug off.

Carmen calls shotgun as we approach Ava's car, so Tom and I have no choice but to squeeze ourselves into the back of the small vehicle. As we leave the city and make our way into a maze of country lanes, I spend the journey reeling over the fact that I may, in fact, be a mutant. I'm still sceptical that the textbook was moved by me, but explanations are wearing thin. Annabel's theory makes sense, too.

Whenever something has seemingly moved by itself, I've been in a... shall we say, sensitive frame of mind. I've not always necessarily been angry--I wasn't angry during stool-gate--but I did panic, considering Katie was about to slam headfirst into a wooden chair. I kind of just want to pretend none of it is happening, to be honest.

Mosi is already at the door as we approach the house, and he waves to us with a massive grin on his face. The building is still as awe-inspiring as it was the first time I saw it. Tom, who's seeing it for the first time, is wearing the same facial expression Carmen and I wore during our first visit.

Mosi leads us into the living room, which I'd guess is the largest room in the house. It's furnished just as the rest of the house is; filled with archaic furniture, oak tables and chairs, two plush sofas that could seat at least a dozen people, and a grand fireplace at the end of the room. It's built from old stone, and the fire is roaring, its flames brushing the arch above it. The floor is wooden, the walls painted a neutral green colour, and the enormous television hanging above the fireplace juxtaposes the otherwise old-fashioned style of the living room.

We spread ourselves on the one sofa, while Mosi sits opposite us on the other. I sit next to Carmen, and as she glances at me with a smile, I turn my head away. Get yourself together, you piece of shit.

"Hello, dears!" a voice sings from the doorway, and I turn my head to see a tall, slender woman with beautifully dark skin gliding into the room. "My name's Nakato, but just call me Kato! I hope you all like lamb."

Carmen turns to me with furrowed eyebrows, as if she's trying to tell me something, as if we have a secret to share. I just stare back, bewildered at what it is I'm meant to be thinking. She gestures towards me, but I just keep gazing back at her.

"Felix is a vegetarian," Ava announces.

Oh shit, yeah, that. For Christ's sake, I really want lamb.

"Oh," Kato says as she bites her lips. "That's no worry, I'll make some stuffed mushrooms... Do you like mushrooms?"

"Yeah, cheers!" I reply with a nod.

I hate mushrooms.

I don't know why I keep lying about my culinary lifestyle, but apparently there's no stopping me. I can fling things across rooms, but can't be honest about my feelings towards fungi.

Ava's mum hums an unrecognisable tune as she sits herself next to Mosi, and she places her hand into his as he gives her a peck on the cheek. That's when the small talk begins. It's the usual stuff--our names, our ages, our degrees, our hometowns, etcetera. As the discussion moves on to the societies we're all members of though, the mention of the paranormal society gets Ava's parents' tails wagging.

Considering their potential knowledge of all things spirit-related, I listen intently, but in silence. I doubt I could get a word in with Tom here, anyway. He's rambling on about the haunted house the society are visiting soon, and Ava's parents look thrilled. They are one of the twelve families, on Kato's side apparently, and their family has lived in this house for generations.

Midway through Tom's classic haunted bathroom tale, Annabel appears beside the fireplace at the end of the room. She waves at me, as if I wouldn't have noticed her suddenly appearing directly opposite me, and gestures towards the doorway. I excuse myself, saying something about needing the toilet, and leave the room.

"Ask them about telekinesis!" Annabel demands, once I'm in the main hallway. "How it works and stuff, for you non-dead arseholes."

"Yeah 'cause that won't sound suspicious at all," I whisper.

"Oh, c'mon, it won't! Just steer the conversation in that direction, and ask when the time is right. You need to stop refusing help from people, y'know, we need to know more about what the heck is going--"

"It's you who has the spirit attachment, isn't it?"

My heart makes a leap for my throat, and I have to catch my breath. I turn back towards the living room to see Ava standing outside the door, her head tilted to the side.

"What? Uh, no, I mean, I don't think so," I say as genuinely as I can.

Ava nods slowly. Whether or not she believes my obliviousness to Annabel being attached to me by the hip, I don't know, but I've clearly not convinced her that this spirit attachment is all in her head. She doesn't pry further though. Instead, she just smiles, tells me she likes my hair today, and directs me to the bathroom. As I'm about to turn away though, I hesitate.

"Hey, Ava," I say. "I was reading the book you gave Carmen earlier, and I--I, uh, read this thing about moving stuff--I mean, people like you having telekinesis." I pause, and quickly try to conjure up something that won't sound weird. "Can you do that?"

Ava shakes her head. "Oh, whoa, no... My abilities aren't the strongest, truthfully, and that's pretty rare."

Of course it is.

"How does it work then? I mean, how do people do it?" I ask.

Ava says nothing for a while, and I'm beginning to wonder if she's forgotten what I just asked her. She grabs the hem of her dress and twirls it in-between her fingers, then nods slowly.

"Energy manipulation. It's the same way spirits do it, according to the literature. It's, like, all about channelling energy and controlling it, like poltergeists. They're physically violent because their anger is so strong that they can't even control it, half the time." She turns back to the living room. "I better get back, anyway. Have a nice time in the bathroom!"

Ava then proceeds to skip back into the room. Okay, that makes sense. Based on what Ava just said, it's controllable anyway. Just sounds like it may be a bit tricky.

Once I've been away long enough to seem like I relieved myself, I return to the living room. Tom, Ava, and Mosi are sitting in the same spots they were when I left, but plonked onto the floor with their legs crossed and hands linked are Carmen and Kato. I've either walked into a séance, or the whole world has turned batshit crazy. I suppose they're both the same thing, really. Tom spots me in the doorway and practically bounces in his chair.

"Kato's reading our auras!" he announces, as if it's the most exciting thing to happen since the reincarnation of Christ.

"Right," I mutter as I head back to my seat.

"Oh, groovy, hey! Could my mum try it on you, Felix?" Ava requests, her eyes boring into me. "See if she can figure out what I couldn't."

I stammer. "Uh, I dunno, I'd rather pass. I mean, I'm good, thanks."

As I speak, Annabel glares at me from her spot by the fireplace. "You might see Mum again, do it!"

Despite my protests, Ava continues to gaze at me expectantly. Annabel is right. There have been no images of our mother flashing through my head since that night, and amongst all the hysteria that's been going on, I almost forgot about it. If I do let Kato do this, will it even happen? Will I just see the same thing? Will I see something different?

Curiosity must get the better of me because moments later, I'm sitting where Carmen sat. Now that I'm directly opposite Ava's mother, it's difficult not to stare. She's beautiful. Her thick, curled hair frames her face in a way that makes it look perfectly oval, and her deep brown eyes are the biggest I've ever seen. She reaches her hands out, and after a brief hesitation, I take hold of them. They're cold.

Kato instructs me to close my eyes and clear my mind, just as Ava did all those weeks ago. I struggle at first, through nerves or anxiety, I assume, but eventually empty my mind as much as possible. A feeling of immense relaxation overwhelms me, just as it did when Ava tried to read my aura. Kato is saying something, but her voice is so smooth that all I hear is a gentle murmur.

As I find myself falling again, I picture how bizarre this whole scenario would look from an outsider's perspective, and a ringing sound begins filling my ears. I almost want to laugh at the predictability. Unlike last time though, the ringing sound vanishes as the images appear. And I feel sick.

I can't breathe. The woman--my mum--is crouched over me, and she's shouting the same words she shouted when I last saw her. I think it's raining. I can see behind her in this vision, and there are bright lights integrated within bouts of darkness so black that I feel like I'm suffocating by just looking at them. The entirety of my body aches. Last time, I couldn't feel anything. I was numb. I don't want to feel all this.

I can't breathe, my body is trembling, my head aches. My mother shouts again. I don't understand. Who am I not meant not look at? There's no one else here. I try opening my mouth, but I can't. I can't move any part of my body.

"Felix, baby, look at me. Nothing else, just look at me," my mum says, this time, her voice calm. Her gaze locks into mine, and I notice that I have my mother's eyes.

"Where's Annabel?" The voice is mine, but I don't say it. "Is she hurt? Is Daddy still in the car?"

My mother's eyes briefly glaze over. "It's fine, darling, everything's fine," she says, but despite not truly knowing this woman crouched in front of me, I know she's lying.

She keeps telling me to look at her and nowhere else, and she keeps telling me not to look at them, but I don't know who they are. I want to stand up, to look around, to figure out what's going on. My chest feels heavy and my limbs are throbbing, but I keep trying anyway. I don't move an inch. Instead, I move my eyes over my mother's shoulder, and I see a car. The bonnet is crushed, and strewn over it with her arms limply hanging by her side as blood seeps from her forehead, is Annabel.

Blackness returns, but this time, I can't open my eyes. I'm falling again, but it's not relaxing anymore. It's violent. My brain feels like it's rolling over inside my head, and the sensation of sickness re-mains in the pit of my stomach. I hear a voice and vaguely recognise it, but can't make it out through the ringing sound. Then, as quickly as it hit me, it all goes away. The pain disappears, and I'm left floating in a dark abyss.

Chapter 9

The first thing I see when I open my eyes is a perfectly white ceiling, and the only explanation for that is that I'm lying down. As I sit myself up, the image of the ceiling is replaced by one of a sagged face. Jamie's grandmother. What the--When did she rock up? She says something, but my disorientation is rendering me dumb and deaf.

I'm still in Ava's living room, except it's only me in here now, and I'm half-lying on one of the comfy sofas. The fire is still roaring. Where is everyone? What even just happened? I scan the room but still can't see anyone, and as my eyes turn back to what's in front of me, I'm reminded of the fact there's a dead old woman standing at my feet. I'd kill to have her plush dressing gown wrapped around me right now.

"Sorry," I interrupt her mid-sentence. "Not really a good time, I'm a bit out of it at the--Uh, what's wrong?"

"I just want to thank you for helping me with Jamie," she says in a voice far softer than I remember. Granted, last time I did see her she seemed to be having a mental breakdown. "I couldn't leave without thanking you."

I shrug in response. "Oh, it's cool, didn't really do much."

"Listen," she begins as her eyes dart back and forth. She leans in slightly, and lowers her voice as she continues speaking. "There is something going on, and it's getting bigger. I'm scared they're listening, I--I don't know what they're capable of, I'm scared of what they'll do if--" She freezes, glances around again, then lowers her voice even more. "They're watching you--they're watching all of us. You need to lose them."

"What?" I ask, unsure of whether what she's saying makes no sense, or if I'm still a bit delusional.

She says nothing, just stares, and small bursts of light begin to flicker around her. I don't have much time.

"Wait," I try. "What was wrong last time I saw you, when you said I wasn't safe? Is that what you're talking about?"

Jamie's grandmother still says nothing. The bursts of light surrounding her become more bright and frequent, and soon a ring of white light has formed itself around her entire body. I ask her to elaborate again, but I'm not even sure she can hear me anymore. As the frame of light around her becomes so bright that it almost blinds me, her lips part ever so slightly.

"Felix." She doesn't say it quietly, yet my name sounds like a whisper. "You have to remember."

The burst of light sheds itself over her whole body until nothing remains but empty space. This old hag loves a bit of melodrama, doesn't she? As if seeing what I assume was the corpse of my older sister sprawled across a car in some hallucinogenic state wasn't enough, now I have to deal with a load of mumbo-jumbo a dead old woman unleashed onto me. In fact, to top that off even further, where the hell is every--

"Felix?"

I lift my head and turn to the doorway, and see Carmen standing on her tip-toes looking over the sofa at me. Oh good, there haven't been any apocalypses while I was busy hallucinating then. Mind you, god knows where Annabel has gotten to.

"Hey, you all right?" Carmen asks as she treads over to the sofa, and I sit myself upright. "You scared the shit out of Mosi and Kato, pal, they thought you were possessed or something. Ava said you acted freaky when she did it too, what's that all about?"

I wave my hand in the air in an attempt to shrug the whole thing off, but when I try to stand, I trip over nothing and fall back onto the sofa. Why is my head spinning?

"Oi, take it easy," Carmen snaps.

"Sorry, I--I dunno. I get migraines a lot. I shouldn't have done that really; I felt one coming on, that's why I didn't really wanna do it at first."

That actually sounds pretty legit, doesn't it? I'm impressed with myself. I might roll with that one to explain my increasingly frequent bizarre behaviour. Carmen nods, seemingly satisfied with my excuse. My head still feels light, so I inhale a sharp intake of breath, and release it slowly. I figure I'll be fine now, so attempt to stand up for the second time. Turns out I was wrong because once again, I find myself crumpling back onto the sofa.

"For Pete's sake," Carmen groans.

My head is swimming again, so as she shoves my chest down to get me back into a lying position, I don't have the will or the strength to stop her. This does actually feel a lot better. Carmen sits down onto the laminate floor so that she's eye-level with me, and crosses her legs.

"You keep trying to get up too quickly, just shut your eyes and relax for a bit," she suggests. "I won't kiss you this time, I promise."

"Thank god for that," I mutter as I do as she says.

"Piss off!" Carmen smacks my arm, making me open my eyes again. "You hardly stopped me, and you weren't even drunk, mate, so shut it."

She has a point. I turn my head to the side to see her face inches away from mine. We're playing chicken again, and I refuse to be the one who turns away this time. Every troublesome thought, from the words Jamie's grandmother spoke to the image of Annabel's limp body now engraved in my memory, is drifting from my mind, and all I need to focus on are Carmen's pink lips.

I can feel her warm breath on my skin, and the flowery perfume she's wearing is making me even dizzier than I was moments ago. A strand of her dark hair falls onto her face, but she doesn't move it away. Who am I kidding? God, I fancy her.

"Food's ready," Carmen announces, suddenly standing back up. "Sorry, that's why I came in here. We thought you better eat because of the whole passing out thing, and y'know--Well, you definitely should if it was a migraine, food will be good."

I nod a bit too enthusiastically in an attempt to brush off any awkwardness, and lift myself up off the sofa, this time a lot more slowly. Other than asking me if I feel any better, Mosi and Kato don't address the fact that I just collapsed in their living room as I make my appearance, but I can feel their eyes on me throughout the whole meal. The warming smell of freshly cooked lamb circles the air, while I stare at the fungi on my plate and attempt to measure the degree of my self-loathing.

On the bright side, Annabel has finally decided to show up. She's sitting in a spare chair at the end of the long table, and the way in which she keeps sighing and playing with her hands suggests that she's eager to speak to me, probably to question me over the vision. I keep envisioning her fragile body dumped onto a car bonnet, and it's making me feel kind of sick.

As we arrive back at the flat, we pass Mason in the hallway. We've not seen him in at least a week, so expect some kind of acknowledgment, but he completely ignores us and brushes straight past without a word. What a sociable guy. As we walk into our kitchen, I can't really blame Mason for fleeing because while Katie has crumpled herself onto one of the sofas, Jamie's sitting on a plastic stool with his eyes fixated onto a box of cereal as if it just insulted him. Hardly party central.

Tom interrupts the silence with his booming voice as he blabbers on about lamb or something, but neither of them look up at him for more than five seconds. I was hoping there wouldn't be anyone in here so that I could access my secret stash of pork sausages, to be honest. Disappointed, I leave the kitchen and head into my bedroom, where Annabel is waiting for me.

"What happened? Did you see things again? Why did you pass out? Is it because you saw something? Why didn't you pass out last time? What did you--"

"Slow down, Jesus, you're giving me a headache," I mutter as I fall onto my unmade bed.

Annabel shuts her mouth, but continues to look at me expectantly. The image of her in my vision keeps flashing through my head, and it's making it difficult for me to look at her. I don't want to tell her.

"Felix?" she questions again.

I sigh. "I dunno why I passed out. I mean, what I saw this time round was way more... intense, but it was pretty much the same thing."

I shrug in hope of implying that the story finishes there. The expectant look remains in Annabel's eyes though, and she presses for more. Just tell her, it's not like she doesn't know she's dead, I try to reason, but I can't bring myself to do it. Annabel has always had this fascination with the person she was when she was alive, as if that person was never even her, and I wish I had something better to tell her other than the way her corpse looked strewn across a car. She asks me again.

"I saw you," I finally manage to mutter.

Annabel's jaw drops. "Seriously? Are you kidding? You saw me when I was alive? Oh my god, that's insane! What was I like?"

"No, you don't understand--"

"Did I say anything to you? Was I with Mum? Was I the same as I am now? This is--"

"Annabel, you were already dead."

She freezes. "Oh... I thought... Oh, sorry."

"I think I know what I'm seeing--I mean, I'm pretty sure it's the accident," I say in an attempt to get her mind off what I just revealed. "It just doesn't make sense though because Mum isn't dead in it, she's not even in the car. Neither am I, for that matter, but they found us all inside of it, didn't they?" I ask, to which Annabel nods quietly. "Maybe it's not actually what happened, maybe my mind's just trying to fill the empty space where the memory should be." I sigh as I lean my head back against the wall behind me. "Either way, I've still got no clue what the hell is going on."

Annabel nods again, and doesn't say anything. I was expecting more feedback, in all honesty, especially considering she's usually the type to have plenty to say. Then there's Jamie's grandmother and her dramatically vague announcements to worry about. I've no idea why this didn't occur to me before--probably because I'm a goddamn idiot--but I'm beginning to think that all this may be connected.

The images of the accident, the things Jamie's grandmother spoke about, her telling me to remember, the creature I keep seeing. In fact, is the car crash what Jamie's grandmother was referring to? Is that what I need to remember? I turn my attention back to Annabel to voice my thoughts, but she speaks before I can.

"Why do you think Mum saved you instead of me?" she asks quietly as she stares at the wall.

"What? Annabel, I don't think it worked like that, I don't think anyone saved anyone."

Annabel doesn't respond, and instead, just vanishes. Shit. She can't really think that, can she? I understand how the thought of your own mother leaving you to die while she saves your bratty eight-year-old brother can't be too heartwarming, but I really doubt that's the case. I call Annabel's name, but get no response. Shit.

I spend the next hour or so trying to move the same chewed pencil I'd tried shifting before we left for Ava's house. Not with my hands, of course, I've already mastered that skill. I initially attempt to move it off a whim, but with no luck, turn to Annabel's theory of it only being possible when I'm pissed off. The only issue is that I'm not pissed off. Monumentally confused and stressed, sure, but not pissed off.

Ava didn't specify angry energy when I asked her about it earlier though, so I decide to allow myself to get knee deep in this shit-pile of confusion.

As I try to focus that confusion onto the pencil though, all I get is a slight wobble, and that might just be from aggressively tapping my foot under the desk. On the bright side, it's becoming really goddamn frustrating, so hopefully that'll build enough for me to manipulate it. More time passes and it's still not working, and it's really starting to irritate me because what use is this bullshit ability if I'm too emotionally inept to control it?

I'm still glaring at the pencil as if it's committed the most heinous crime when there's a loud knock on the door. I jump, and the pencil shoots forward, bouncing itself against my bedroom window. Of course, now it wants to listen.

There's another knock on my door, so I leave the pencil where it landed on my desk, and get up to answer it. Carmen is standing there with raised eyebrows.

"You all right? Kinda look like you want to kill someone."

"Yeah, sorry, I just... Never mind," I reply. "What's up?"

"A few of us are watching some films in the kitchen, if you fancy it. Jamie's being his miserable self by locking himself in his room again, and Ava's getting some work done, but the rest of us are up for it."

"Even Mason and Katie?" I question, and Carmen nods. "Shit, yeah, can't miss that. I see unicorns more frequently than I do them."

Carmen laughs a bit too much for such a shit joke, but I kind of like it. Once I grab my phone, we head into the kitchen to join everyone. Tom and Mason are sitting beside the small coffee table in-between the sofas, while Katie and her boyfriend sit on one of the sofas with a laptop awkwardly perched on both of their laps. Tom and Mason are looking at something on the table, but I can't make out what it is.

Carmen sits down while I go to grab myself a drink of water, only to realise I've not cleaned any of my glasses. I take one of Jamie's from his cupboard.

"Where'd you get that?" Carmen's voice distracts me from what I'm doing.

I turn to the group, and I assume she's referring to whatever Tom and Mason have on the table, but I still can't see it. I quickly pour some water into the glass, and head on over to them.

"Some guy from the paranormal society gave it to me," Tom explains as I near them. "Cool, right?"

Once I reach them, I finally realise what it is they're talking about. Laid out on the small coffee table is what looks like a board game, but it doesn't take me long to realise what it actually is.

"Some random guy gave you a Ouija board?" I ask Tom as I sit down next to Carmen. "Sounds legit."

"You're not going to use it, are you?" Carmen asks.

Mason looks up from the table and rolls his eyes at her as if she's stupid. "Nah, just thought we'd stare at it and do nothing."

I personally want to hit the guy, but Mason's sarcasm doesn't seem to faze Carmen because he doesn't silence her. "They're meant to be really dangerous, I don't think--"

"If you're too scared to use it, babe, just say. It's all bullshit anyway," Mason retorts.

"You could always not be a dick about it," I interject.

"Bloody hell, calm down. You fancy her or something, Ferris?"

"It's Felix."

"Whatever."

I have to say, I can't quite remember Mason being this level of monumental dickhead during freshers' week. There's a bottle of vodka on the floor beside him and he's got a drink in his hand, so I'm not sure if he's drunk or just a general arsehole.

"I'm going to go and ask Ava about it," Carmen announces as she stands up.

I figure that's probably a good idea. To be perfectly honest, I also think it's bullshit, but after being stalked by some big gangly thing with black eye sockets, I'd rather be on the safe side. Mason laughs as Carmen leaves the room, and Katie begins reading off information she found online regarding Ouija boards. She's searched for safe ways to use one, so hey, at least the thought is there.

Katie is reading something out about cleansing the area, which in itself sounds suspiciously satanic, when Carmen returns. Ava follows suit, and I expect to see anger or concern on her face as she wanders in, but instead she's just humming a tune. Without uttering a word, she grabs the Ouija board from the small table, and heads back out the door.

"Hey! What are you doing?" Mason calls after her, to which she says nothing.

We follow Ava as she leaves the flat and begins skipping down our block's stairs. She's still humming something. Mason keeps calling her, and she keeps ignoring him, and for someone so small she sure is fast. Her pace seems effortless, yet we all have to jog lightly to keep up with her. Once she's left the building, she walks around it until we reach the path that runs alongside our block, and she stops at the riverbank.

"Ava, what are you doing?" Tom asks this time.

As expected, Ava says nothing. Annabel has joined us now, and she watches Ava with curious eyes. I figure it's a good sign. Maybe she's not so upset anymore. My attention is soon pulled away from her though because as Ava continues to hum an upbeat song, she drops the Ouija board onto the ground, snatches Mason's drink straight from his hands, pours its content over the board, then lights the corner of it with a lighter. It bursts into flames.

"That's not mine!" Tom yells as panic drowns his voice.

I am laughing so hard. I don't even know why I find it so funny, but as Tom dances around the thing trying to stomp the fire out, my stomach is literally aching from laughing so much. I catch Annabel's eyes to see her laughing too, and Carmen seems to find it pretty hilarious. Ava was so goddamn casual over it, it was brilliant. When I turn to her though, my laughter stops. She's stopped humming, and her face is blank. Cold even. She looks around the circle, her gaze lingering on each one of us for a few seconds.

"Don't ever touch one of those things again."

Chapter 10

The last week of term feels like it's never going to end, and we're all on our toes after Ava's ritualistic burning of the Ouija board. Everyone's heading off to some old country manor house to play Scooby-Doo on the weekend, and Carmen and Tom are currently in the process of trying to convince me to join them.

It's a trip organised by the paranormal society, and as Tom technically signed me up for it in freshers, there's nothing stopping me from going, apparently. I'm going to take a wild guess here and assume that the place isn't even haunted, as nowhere that's meant to be haunted ever really is, and even if it was, I'd rather avoid that potential trainwreck.

"C'mon, mate, you're the only one not going, you've gotta come!" Tom pleads as if I define his existence. "Carmen has promised you a quickie round the--" Tom's sentence is cut short by Carmen's elbow in his abdomen.

"We just think it'd be a fun thing to do as a group before we all go home for a month, y'know?" she says.

I guess she has a point. Considering the whole deprived orphan scenario, I'm staying in the flat over Christmas break because I don't have a home to go back to. I've only ever had brief stints living with foster parents, so I hardly have any ties anywhere. Not to mention the fact I'm paying a full year's rent for this place, so I might as well make the most of it.

"Felix?" Carmen says, reminding me of the current conversation.

I shrug as I stand up from the sofa. "Nah."

"What is it with you and ghosts, man?" Tom groans as I stop next to them beside the kitchen island. "Can't tell if you're scared of them, or if you are one."

I laugh as I steal a strawberry from the opened box sitting in front of Carmen. She swats my hand away, but it's too late. I wink at her as I leave the kitchen, and head into my bedroom.

Annabel is listening to an audio book when I enter, and she barely looks up at me as I wander in. She's been quieter than usual since the revelation of what I saw in my vision, and I wish I could promise her that my life isn't a result of a sacrifice of hers, but I can't. I mean, I don't really know that. I'm about to try and discuss that in some shape or form when I hear a knock on my door.

"Yep?" I ask as I open it, and I'm surprised to see Jamie standing there. He's barely left his bedroom since we were at the pub a while back.

"Um, sorry--I, uh, there's a lot of Maths on your course, right?" he enquires.

I wave my hand a bit. "Eh, sorta."

"I was just wondering if you'd be able to, uh, aid me in completing some coursework."

I tell him sure because hey, why not? Jamie briefly heads back into his room to grab some stuff, then returns with a pile of papers and a textbook in his hand. I've no idea where this sudden bout of sociability has arisen from because on the rare occasion he shows himself in public nowadays, all he ever really does is stare blankly at nothing.

I've tried breaking through to the guy, considering I'm the only one aware of his grandmother's death, but he's snubbed me off each time. I'm pretty sure I've developed a bloody soft spot for the guy, considering our matching home circumstances, which sucks balls. I hate it when I feel things.

I wave Jamie over to my bed as I slump myself onto my desk chair, then swivel it over to him. He's pulling a strained expression as I rest my legs on the end of the bed, but I'm not quite sure what's so distressing about my feet, so ignore it. It's probably the hole in my sock. I'm about to ask him what this coursework is all about, but he gets there first.

"Aren't you going to switch that off?" he asks.

"Huh?"

Jamie nods behind me, and I swivel back around to see Annabel sitting on my bedroom floor with her legs crossed. I experience what I can only assume is a brief heart attack because I think Jamie has somehow spotted her, but then I realise she's playing the audiobook out loud, so to him there's just some random audiobook playing on my bedroom floor. Annabel must have heard Jamie because she switches it off seconds after him commenting on it.

"Sorry, forgot it was on," I mutter. "What kinda maths are we talking here? I'm--"

"How did you do that?" Jamie interrupts, looking even more dis-
tressed.

"Do what?"

"Switch that off? You didn't touch it."

Oh, shit. I glance back at the floor, and shoot Annabel the hardest
glare I can muster up. She then conveniently vanishes. I swear to
god. She used to mess up like that a lot when I was younger and she
was new to this whole ghost thing; she once got extremely pissed off
at me when I was ten or something, and I was playing in my foster
family's garden at the time, so she decided to telekinetically throw
mud at me for fifteen minutes straight. My explanation to my foster
parents involved an elaborate tale about a stray dog trying to steal
the washing. This is easy compared to that.

"It's an app," I reply, waving my phone.

Jamie nods his head, but I'm not sure he's bought it as he continues to watch me suspiciously. We promptly begin discussing
coursework, which only contains pretty basic maths, to be honest.
There are a few tricky formulas, but after I explain everything once,
he clicks onto it immediately, as if he already knew the answers
anyway.

"Can I ask you something quickly?" he asks as we're mid-way
through a question, so I shrug. "What are your memories of your
parents like? I don't mean to pry, you don't have to answer, I just--I'd
just turned fourteen, and I've forgotten some things, and I'm worried I'll forget a lot more."

I scratch my head. "Pretty vague," I half-lie. "But, I mean, I was
eight so it is kinda different."

He nods. We continue with the question we're tackling, and we've
only just started the next one when Jamie changes the subject again.

"What happened?" he asks. "I mean, how did they, uh... you know."

I'm starting to get the feeling this visit isn't about coursework. The little shit is using it as an excuse to talk about dead parents. Classic move. He continues to ramble on about something or other, telling me I don't have to answer about a million times. I know it probably makes me a sick bastard, but I always want to lie and formulate some really bizarre story that makes their deaths sound like some kind of adventure film because the reality of it is such a cliché.

"Car crash," I say, "nothing interesting."

"Plane," Jamie replies, to which I raise my eyebrows. That's different. "Dad was a pilot; we owned a small plane. He misjudged the landing."

Bloody hell, someone must have a big inheritance. At the realisation of how inappropriate of a thought that just was, I apologise to Jamie as if he can read my mind.

"You going to ghost house?" I ask him in an attempt to change the subject, only to realise that what I just asked is probably even more inappropriate than my inheritance thought. "Uh, I mean, y'know, the trip everyone's going on."

Jamie shakes his head. He looks so damn deflated, and my sympathy for the guy is slowly melting my brain. I think he just really needs to get out, even if that does mean visiting some bullshit haunted manor that only remains standing thanks to the gullibility of the paying public. I lean back slightly in my chair, and say nothing for a while.

"You go, I go?" I offer.

"Pardon?"

"I'll go ghost hunting if you come with," I elaborate. "Carmen and Tom keep nagging me about it, plus I figure it's something we can all do as a group before we piss off for a month." I lower my legs from the bed, and roll my chair closer. "And no offence, mate, but you need to get out of this flat before you throw yourself out of it."

I assume Jamie will flat-out say no, and that this is going to take some hard-core convincing, but to my surprise, he nods. It's the subtlest nod I've ever laid eyes on, and he seems as excited as someone who's just been offered to watch paint dry for a week, but it's a nod nonetheless.

Chapter 11

Two days later, as I'm sitting on the minibus heading towards this so called haunted manor, never has regret raged so strongly inside of me. The president of the society is relaying to us what she refers to as the rules of respect, which apparently plan out how to behave in the presence of spirits. They claim we mustn't swear around them, which is as dumb as it is nonsensical. Annabel swears more than I do.

Mrs. President doesn't elaborate on why we can't swear around them, just that they find it offensive. Which they don't. The best rule is that communication attempts must only be made at night because only then do they feel comfortable, and I've no clue what section of her arse she pulled that out of. I realise I probably just sound like a cynical hag here, but these stereotypes have gotten pretty exhausting over the past ten years or so. No wonder there are so many poltergeists in the world. I'd be pissed off at the extent of this bullshit too.

Mrs. President must notice the sour look on my face because once she's finished her speech, she wanders over to me at the back of the bus. Her hair is dyed jet-black, and I can't tell if her face is that pale because it's her natural skin-tone, or because she's so busy hunting ghosts away from the daylight they apparently loathe. I keep imagining how funny it would be if we suddenly had to break, and she went flying down the aisle. Sadly, we don't.

"A sceptic, I see," she says to me as she stops beside my row.

"Two, actually," Jamie pipes up from the row opposite, and I want to high-five the guy.

Mrs. President turns to him and smiles, then glances between us. "You'll soon change your mind."

With that, she quickly turns back around--I assume to make the unnecessary lace cape she's wearing swish dramatically, and saunters back to the front of the bus. I turn to the row of seats behind me to slowly shake my head at Carmen and Tom, as if cursing them for dragging me into this pit of crazies.

I have to admit, I'm impressed when we see the manor. It's far larger than The Cavern, and while some of the bricks of that place look as if they're crumbling away, you can tell this is a tourist attraction. There isn't a blade of grass out of place. It's turning dark now, and based on the mindset of this lot, I assume we've come this late to avoid making the spirits uncomfortable.

There are floor lamps shooting white light up at the house, creating the illusion of it being mightier than it is. Oddly, I've never visited a haunted house before. I've been to places I was told were haunted, and they never have been, bar one with a ghost dog who was pissed at his owner for losing his ball. I've never been to a place like this though, where the entire reason for its being is harbouring ghosts. Whether there will actually be any is another story.

The tour begins in the main living quarters, which I think is old-timey talk for living room. I was never really into in history. Our tour guide is speaking in such a patronising manner that I can't quite tell if he thinks we're small children, or just idiots. Probably the latter. I would if I were him.

Annabel couldn't miss this barrel of laughs, of course, so she stands beside me uttering sarcastic comments about our tour guide, who she thinks resembles a mix between 90's John Travolta and this homeless guy who used to sell rocks he'd painted in an underpass in Sheffield. It's a pretty accurate comparison.

"The Lord and Lady, unable to produce children of their own, resorted to thieving street children in an attempt to mould them into perfect boys and girls. If a child dare step out of line, they would be no sooner banished from the house. Though we must bear in mind that those are the official claims..." Our tour guide pauses for what I assume is dramatic effect, and lowers his voice.

Give me strength.

"The truth may be far darker. Some reports claim that if the street child was anything but perfect, the Lord and Lady would murder it. Dispose of the child, move onto the next one."

"What reports are those?" Jamie demands.

The tour guide stammers slightly. "What do you mean, sorry?"

"You referenced reports, but didn't provide any sources. It's hardly believable," he replies in a tone that's effortlessly casual.

I love this guy, and one-hundred percent regret throwing him into a lake.

Our tour guide mutters something about checking later. Honestly, it's hard to take a guy seriously when he's dressed in a pair of tights. This is a seventeenth century building, and so while I understand why staff feel the need to dress up like they crawled out of their mothers' wombs during that era, I'd rather they didn't. If I was a seventeenth century ghost, I'd be offended.

Our guide has a brown cap on, and a puffy white shirt with strings dangling from the collar, and I can't quite distinguish whether he's trying to channel a chimney sweep or a pirate. I want to know the source of this guy's information too; sounds a bit shoddy to me.

As we move into the drawing room, I actually begin wanting to see some spirits. Our tour guide has moved on to patronising us with stories about the time this manor was used as a refugee house in the Second World War, and a genuine dead guy would really spice things up. The room itself is pretty impressive.

Four enormous sofas form a square in the centre of it, two of them a deep red while the other two are a dark green colour. The walls match the red sofas, though not much of them can be seen because similarly to Ava's house, they're filled with portraits of men and women from another era. Tall windows adorned with bold paisley curtains fill the left-hand wall, and the outside lighting seeps in to varnish everything inside with a white glow. Oak tables are placed beside each chair in the room, and the back wall is almost fully covered by bookcases. If that wasn't grand enough, hanging from the ceiling is an enormous chandelier.

I soon realise that this room is as good as it gets. The others are impressive, don't get me wrong, but nothing quite stands up to that drawing room. Things only go from bad to worse when people begin claiming to feel things touching them, or a strange sensation in their gut. One guy from the paranormal society even jumped into the air at one point, claiming that something brushed against his ankle.

"This is shit. Can I throw a book at his face," Annabel, who was lingering beside me at the time, muttered into my ear. "Give him something to really scream about."

I immediately laughed out loud, and got some real cold glares from the Paranormal Society clowns. Thankfully, the only one of my friends seemingly falling for this bullshit is Tom, but that was a given. Ava is raising her eyebrows each time someone claims they sense something, Jamie just downright opposes every single thing our tour guide says, and while Carmen appears interested in the history and legends of this place, she doesn't seem fooled.

I hold out hope for some dead folk, but the more rooms we enter, the more my hope shrinks. We enter the kitchen; bullshit, we head into the basement; bullshit, we go back up into the hallway; more bullshit, we go to the master bedroom; oh look, bullshit. Not even a dead cockroach. Of course, people maintain to claim feeling things, and I don't think they realise how ridiculous they look screaming and yelping at thin air.

But then Carmen shrieks.

We're walking through the second floor hallway at the time, and it's a rare but greatly appreciated moment of silence on behalf of the tour guide. Carmen lets out a shriek, and her body cowers against mine as her hand manically scrambles for my own.

People turn to her questioningly, and I spot a small shoe quickly disappear into the crowd, so I follow the direction it was moving towards until my eyes stop at the tour guide. Standing beside him, barely reaching his waist, is a scruffy-haired boy wearing khaki shorts, knee socks, and a woollen jumper. Well, I'll be damned.

Carmen realises she's grabbed my hand, and swiftly releases it as she stammers. "I swear to god something just touched me." She glances between Ava, Tom, Jamie and me. "Something pulled on my skirt."

I flash my eyes back to the front of the group, who have now paused, to see the kid grinning wildly. He starts giggling at Carmen's shock, and I've never seen anyone look more pleased with themselves. I turn away, careful to avoid any eye contact. Jamie raises his eyebrows at her, and she raises her shoulders in response as if to say I shit you not.

I glance at Ava to see if she's picked up on the small child now leading our tour group, but nothing in her expression suggests it. When I look back to the tour guide, the boy has gone. A girl a few feet away from me yelps, and the boy flashes past my eyes. I like this kid.

"Don't worry yourselves, ladies," our tour guide says as we enter a guest bedroom. "It's only one of the refugee children messing with you. He has a liking for women."

The little boy is back beside our guide, who's stopped at the end of the king-sized bed that takes up barely an inch of the massive room, and his face lights up at the acknowledgment of his existence. His small chest is puffed up with pride. Holy shit, this is the cutest kid I've ever seen. I turn to Ava again, and while she now seems to be paying close attention to what's going on, nothing suggests that she can sense this child.

I turn back to the bed, and the kid is still gleaming as our guide starts discussing his mischievous habits. One time, he apparently tugged someone's skirt a bit too hard, and it ended up around the girl's ankles. That one makes him laugh, and I'm so engrossed in his freckle-faced charm that I forget I'm staring. Our eyes clash, and his widen. Shit. His jaw drops, his entire body freezes, and he vanishes.

Partly because my curiosity has gotten the better of me, and partly because I feel bad for terrifying the kid, I mutter something about toilets, and tell everyone I'll catch up with them as they move onto the next room.

Once they're gone, I whisper into the air. "Hey?"

"You scared the kid half to death, you really think hey is going to work?" Annabel scoffs as she sits on the perfectly made bed.

"Negativity isn't healthy, Annabel." I tut.

"I'm already dead, what damage is there to be done?"

"Touché."

I call for the little boy again, but get as dead of a response as I did the first time. I try once more, and when that reaps no response, I consider moving back into the hallway to see if he's anywhere there. If this kid really is a refugee, he's been stuck in this place for around seventy-five years, and that's way too intriguing to leave be. I try once more just in case, but with no result, I make my way out of the room and back into the hallway where Carmen was picked on.

Once out of the guest bedroom, I turn to look down the hallway, and what I see at the end of it is so typical that I actually want to laugh.

Chapter 12

This time, I don't run away.

The creature stands taller than I remember, and I'd almost forgotten how black its eyes actually were. My instinct is telling me to run a mile, to catch up with the group, to get the hell out of here, but I don't let myself. I don't know if it's because I've officially turned insane, but I feel an urge to stand here and stare back at it.

Despite being partly hidden by the shadows, its broad frown is immediately detectable, and its face is still a washed out grey colour. The headache is beginning to creep in, and I'm losing the sensation in my fingers, but I refuse to budge. The creature disappears for a millisecond, then appears a few steps closer. Holy shit.

"Felix? What are you doing?" Annabel. "What are you looking at?"

I shift my eyes to my side, and see her staring at me with furrowed eyebrows. Can't she see it? I lift my eyes back to the end of the hallway in hope that maybe this is all in my head, but nope. It's still there. My chest is becoming tighter, and the pressure in my head is increasing by the second. The creature turns its head slightly.

"What do you want?" I try to ask confidently, but I sound like a timid child.

It doesn't answer. It doesn't even twitch.

"What? Felix, what the hell is wrong with you?" Annabel questions.

"Can't you see it?" I ask her.

She gazes at me and stammers. I point to the end of the hallway, directly at the creature that's now inched itself even closer. Annabel stares directly at it, but turns back to me and shakes her head. How can she not see it? She starts talking to me again, but the pain in my head is too distracting for me to pay attention to her. The creature's gaze lingers on me, weighing down my entire body, and I just want to stop it but I don't know how to, so all I can do is stare back. It vanishes, then reappears again. It's barely five feet away from me now.

My mind is screaming at me to get the hell out of here and never look back, but as my eyes lock with the creature's, I'm frozen. Its leer presses down against me, and all I can do is push against it. God, my head hurts.

"Felix, answer me!" Annabel's voice sounds distant.

I fight against the heavy feeling in my chest, as if doing so will force the creature's eyes off me, and I don't know if it's just some kind of placebo effect, but my breathing becomes less shallow. Annabel calls my name again, but I'm so focused on the pain that I couldn't respond if I tried. I keep pushing and pushing, so much so that the pain circling my body is gradually replaced by a weak numbness.

The creature is inches away from me by this point, and at least two heads taller, but I can't avert my eyes from its own. The pain is almost non-existent now, and it feels as if every flicker of my energy is racing through my blood, while my body stands as a shell. I don't even know if I'm breathing anymore.

The creature has stopped nearing me now, the sensation of numbness is turning into light-headedness, and it feels amazing. I feel invincible. I've not stopped pushing against the invisible force fighting me, but it's become effortless, as if it's simply human nature. My vision is blurring, but I don't feel weak. I can't hear Annabel anymore--I don't know if she's still here, I don't even know if I'm really here anymore.

This sensation of invincibility is exploding around me, and I'm so transfixed by it that I don't notice it coming to an end. As the sensation peaks, as I'm about to reach the nirvana of whatever this is, it shoots away from my body, and everything is replaced by darkness.

"... worth a try... recognise... voice."

"Oi... up... shithead."

"Watch... language, please, there... children present."

Voices mesh into one, and I can't make sense of anything anyone is saying. My head is throbbing. I try to lift my hand to it, but it's as if my body is disconnected to my brain.

"You wanted me... him up!"

Annabel? I try to speak, to say anything, but I can't move my mouth. There's something hard resting against my back, or am I lying on something hard? Am I lying down?

"Felix? Jesus, c'mon." Yep, Annabel.

I'm definitely lying down, and based on the subtle smell of dust and oak furniture, I'm still in the manor house. Why are my eyes shut? I try to open them, but struggle to even mange a twitch. What the hell just happened?

"I think... waking." Another voice. Who's that?

"Could slap his face." Another different voice.

Are they talking about me? I listen for Annabel's voice again, and soon hear her call my name. I still can't open my mouth, and the pain in my head is creating a low buzzing sound. I manage to flicker my eyes a little, then Annabel speaks again.

"Throw something... crotch, that'll work. I've done it before... pretty funny, when he... like fourteen. It made him cry and--"

"Don't!" I quickly interject without even realising I've spoken.

I couldn't be more relieved to have found my voice. I finally manage to progress from flickering my eyelids to opening them, and at first, all I see are a blur of colours. Three pairs of eyes gape at me, and I recognise the pale blue ones as Annabel's.

She says my name, and I mumble something I don't even understand in response. As my eyes adjust to being open, the blurred figures eventually shape into those of a small boy and a blonde woman with braided hair, and judging by her archaic choice of a puffy gown, she's not from this century.

By the time I've properly come to, I'm sitting up on the hallway's rug with my back resting against the pale wall. I wasn't out for long--barely a minute, apparently--but Annabel is as clueless as I am to what the hell is going on. No change there then, really. The small boy is the one I saw during the tour, but I'm yet to discover who the woman is. Her dress looks expensive, and I'd say she's no older than forty.

I've just finished describing the creature that was lurking here no more than five minutes ago to Annabel, and the woman is shooing the boy away.

"Aren't you freaked out by me?" I ask, looking up at her.

She smiles lightly. "No, it's a great pleasure. Only once have I been accompanied by another like you."

"You've met someone else who can see spirits?" I'm so shocked that the words only just about leave my mouth in the right order.

She nods. "A long time ago."

The woman kneels on the floor beside me, then gently rests her palm on my forehead. She shuts her eyes briefly, and there's a smile on her face as she removes her hand and opens them back up. Not quite sure what that was. My head feels a lot clearer though, and all traces of dizziness have disappeared. Hell, I feel better than I did before I passed out.

The woman's eyes are a striking brown, and despite her face being void of make-up and her hair being pulled painfully tightly into a braid, she's oozing with warmth and tenderness.

"Did you see that thing?" I ask.

"Yes," she responds. Annabel furrows her eyebrows, and the woman must notice because she releases a breathy laugh. "You are just a child, dear," she says, turning to Annabel. "Once you wander this earth for as long as I have, you begin to notice things others fail to."

"What was it?" I question her.

"Bad news," she replies simply, and I wait for elaboration. "I'm uncertain of what they are, but they were never in any way human, and they only bring darkness. Though never have I seen one vanquished by a human, certainly not a human child."

"I'm nineteen," I mutter.

"Pardon?"

"Sorry, nothing, I--what do you mean? What did I do?"

"You vanquished it," she says as if that explains anything what-soever. She chuckles again. "Killed it, in the sense that it will never return."

I'm slowly beginning to consider the possibility of me being the Anti-Christ. One second I'm throwing people into lakes, and the next I'm vanquishing demonic stalkers. It's a real party when I'm around.

"But they are not your danger," the woman continues. "They are controlled by greater forces, ones that only seek to destroy. To employ one against a human is..." She hesitates, and shifts her eyes from mine. "It's unheard of. They want something from you, and they will not ask nicely."

Annabel and I glance at one another, but as I turn back to this woman in hope of understanding more, she suddenly vanishes. What--

"Mate, what the hell are you doing?"

I hastily pull myself up from the carpeted floor to stand at the sound of Tom's voice, and it sure as hell isn't subtle. Thankfully, no one's with him.

I inwardly curse, and wish he could've waited just a few more min-utes. For once in my life, I'd found someone who actually seemed to know exactly what this whole dead people thing is about. I wander over to Tom with a shrug, as if that's a perfectly good response to explaining why I was just sitting on the floor in a haunted manor house. As it's Tom though, the weirdness doesn't really click.

"I told everyone you'd be fine, but no one ever listens to me," he says as he drapes his arm over my shoulder, and I can't really remember reaching a level of closeness to Tom that would make this normal. "Carmen was scared you'd been ghostnapped. You need to get in there, mate, she's thirsty for you. I dunno how much longer I can resist seducing her myself."

Tom's a weird one. What he's saying is gross, but he's kind of like a confused, excited puppy, so no one really takes him seriously. He doesn't stop talking as we make our way back to the group, and it gives me time to zone out and think. As great as it is that I apparently got rid of that thing, it would help if I knew how the heck I did it, especially now it sounds like that isn't the only one.

What are these forces that employ those things in the first place? What would they want from me? I fear I'm not going to get a chance to speak to that woman again, so as Tom and I join the rest of the group in one of the many bedrooms of this house, I make a decision. I'm going to tell Ava everything.

Chapter 13

From that moment onwards, intense anxiety floods my mind. The tour is finished within the next fifteen minutes or so, but I'm not paying much attention because I'm running over what to say to Ava in my head. I don't stop throughout the whole journey home, and even when the society's president starts berating Jamie and me over whether or not we're converted believers, all I can think about is what to tell Ava.

Do I tell her about my parents? Is that relevant? Do I just keep it simple and say I can see spirits? Should I mention Annabel? Do I give a full explanation, or just say I can see them and wait for the questions? How can I announce this to her without sounding like I'm taking the piss, or sounding downright crazy?

It's gone nine o' clock by the time we get home, and I must have been quieter than I thought on the bus because Carmen asks me if everything is okay. I shrug it off, and head straight into my bedroom. I pace back and forth. What should I say?

"What's up with you?" Annabel asks now that we're alone. She's taken her usual spot on my bed.

"I'm gonna tell Ava," I mutter absentmindedly.

"Seriously?" Annabel gasps. "Holy--Finally!"

I'd usually tell her to shut up, but don't have the energy. "What should I say? I don't know if I should just flat-out tell her everything, or just say the basics and answer her questions, or--"

"Whoa, relax for a second," Annabel cuts me off. "Listen, stop stressing. No matter how you do it, you'll get the same outcome, so just do what you feel most comfortable doing."

She has a point. It's just that other than the foster mother who kicked me out because of it, I've never uttered a word about what I can do to anyone. It's goddamn scary. I'm still not even certain Ava is genuine, but I don't think I'll ever stop doubting her until I confront her about it.

I turn to Annabel and nod slowly, then swiftly leave my room before I can stop myself chickening out. Annabel follows. I knock on Ava's door. I don't get a response immediately, and consider knocking again, but a voice calls from the other side as I'm about to lift my arm to knock for the second time.

"Come in!" Ava calls.

Here goes nothing. I take a deep breath and push the door open, but freeze within two seconds of being in the room. Ava sits cross-legged on her bed, while Carmen sits opposite her. Ah, shit. I can hardly reveal my mutant abilities while Carmen's here. I sort of just stand in Ava's doorway and stare silently as the door shuts behind me.

"Yes?" It's Carmen who asks.

"Uh, oh, sorry," I mumble. What do I say? "I'm just bored."

Really, Felix? Really? That's your genius response? Annabel, who's followed me into the room, laughs at my idiocy. If Ava and Carmen weren't here, I'd shoot her the dirtiest look. The girls are facing each other on the bed, and Ava is dangling her hands in the space between them, with her fingers spread out. There's a pungent chemical smell circling the room. What the heck are they doing? Dabbling in a crystal meth business venture?

"Join us," Ava eventually responds as she nods at her desk chair. "The more the merrier."

For the sake of awkwardness, I do as she says, and sit myself down onto the chair. Carmen shoots Ava a look I can't figure out as I wheel it nearer to the girls, and what they're doing finally clicks. Carmen has a small bottle in her hand, with a liquid that matches the colour of Ava's nails. Oh god, what have I gotten myself into?

As I take in Ava's impeccably clean room, which is a far cry from my own, I realise there are flowers. Everywhere. The layout of the room is an exact copy of mine, only mirrored, and in every empty space there are flowers. Some are in vases, while others sit alone on the windowsill and desktop. There's a slight hint of a floral smell emanating from them, and if it wasn't for the overwhelming chemical stench, I've got a feeling they would smell a lot stronger.

"What's up with the flowers?" I ask Ava, who's now painting Carmen's nails.

She responds by humming a nursery rhyme I can't quite put my finger on. My thinking face must be showing because Ava stops humming to laugh.

"Ring a Ring o' Roses," she explains. "Flowers and herbs warn off negative spirits. Why else would we place them on graves?"

As if that's completely reasonable, common knowledge, Ava turns her attention back to Carmen, who's apparently perfectly accepting of that explanation. How did me trying to come clean to Ava about my abilities turn into a girl's night in?

"I wasn't disturbing anything, was I? I can leave if you want, it's cool," I say in hope of them shooing me out.

"Whoa, no, don't be silly! Just girly talk," Ava replies, which gets her another brief glance from Carmen.

The girls start talking about their nails and some colour I've never heard of before in my life, which based on the bottle in Carmen's hand is red, but no, maroon apparently. I make a joke about it sounding like something you'd name a whale, but the response I get from Ava is a blank, arguably sympathetic, stare which screams you're a bit stupid, Felix. Carmen's just trying not to laugh at me, which is nice of her, I guess.

Annabel is sitting on Ava's desk, her legs dangling off the edge of it, giggling at my painful ordeal like it's the most entertaining thing she's ever seen.

"You're definitely the one with the spirit attachment," Ava says out of nowhere, and in the most casual tone I've ever heard. She looks up from Carmen's nails to focus on me. "It's not a dark one, don't worry."

It's like the world is trying to force me to become this crumbling mass of awkwardness. I don't really say anything in response, just mutter some inaudible disagreement, alongside a shrug of my shoulders.

"Can we do yours?" Carmen suddenly pipes up, a sly grin on her face.

"Huh?"

"Paint your nails," she explains. "Or is your masculinity too fragile?"

I shoot her a challenging look, but it barely shakes her. She raises one of her eyebrows, and I can tell she wants to laugh. Her usually plump lips are pressed into a thin line, and her eyes don't budge from mine for a second.

"Is that your big secret? Fragile masculinity?" she says with a smirk.

I remain silent, my eyes still boring into hers. She raises one of her eyebrows again, and waits expectantly.

"Nope, my masculinity is rock solid, so go for it. Paint them any colour you want," I finally reply, feeling proud of myself for winning our silent war, only to realise minutes later as my fingernails start turning purple, that I actually lost it.

With painted nails and lost dignity, I return to my bedroom half an hour later. I didn't achieve anything there, did I? I was hoping Carmen would leave at some point, but they were discussing watching films together until late, so I got out while I could. I'm going to have to try another time. I lie down onto my bed, shut my eyes, and sigh.

"Purple looks good on you," Annabel says from above me. "I swear that girl could ask you to punch yourself in the face, and you'd do it."

I open my eyes and turn my head to look at her. She's sitting on my desk chair with an amused look on her misleadingly innocent face. I promptly shoot her an obscene hand gesture, which is an atrocious idea because it only leads to more fingernail mocking.

"Nothing wrong with guys painting their nails," I mutter. "And you claim to be a feminist."

"Want me to speak to her?" Annabel says out of nowhere.

"Who, Ava?"

She nods. Shit, why didn't I think of that? I spent the entirety of tonight stressing over the unpleasantness of revealing all to Ava, when I could've just gotten Annabel to do my dirty work for me. Hell, better still, if Ava's abilities aren't what she makes them out to be, there'd be no risk on my behalf because she'd never know we tried to contact her.

"Why didn't you suggest this before?" I ask her, sitting up on my bed.

She shrugs. "I dunno, I think I just like seeing you in distress. It's funny."

She's so lucky she's already dead and I can't kill her.

We wait until two in the morning to make our move because that's when we finally hear Carmen say goodnight to Ava, and the room to her door opening. Carmen's in the room next to mine, so when I can hear her shuffling around the other side of my wall, I send Annabel away. My heart is beating hard against my chest as I wait, and Annabel returns a lot sooner than I thought. The second she does, I come down with a serious case of word vomit.

"What happened? What did she say? How much stuff did you tell her? Did she answer any questions about those creatures, or--"

"She couldn't hear me."

"What?" I ask, stammering. "Really?"

Annabel shakes her head, and furrows her eyebrows. "I even pushed one of her flowers off her desk, and she called out to ask if anyone was there, but she didn't hear when I responded. I really tried focusing on her energy, like I do with you whenever we talk, but--I don't know, nothing happened. Maybe she can do some minor stuff, but... but she can't communicate with us." She slumps onto the bed beside me. "I really thought she was the real deal."

If Ava's abilities are bullshit, then chances are everything I read in that book of hers is too. Shit. How the hell am I going to figure all of this out now?

Chapter 14

Within days of entering the Christmas break, everyone besides Jamie, Carmen and I have gone home. Jamie and I are both staying here over Christmas, except Jamie's going to some second cousin's uncle's brother's niece's house or some shit for the week leading up to Christmas, and the few days following.

Carmen's only here for the first week of holidays, and I'm glad because I'm not sure how almost four weeks alone with Jamie would affect my rapidly frazzling brain. She's leaving tomorrow though, so I better brace myself. I've hit a brick wall with the ghost business, and I'm a little worried I'm in no place to be wasting time.

I've reached the conclusion that the best thing for me to do at this point is try and return to the manor house to track down that female spirit. As I sit at the kitchen island with a bowl of cereal that tastes of soggy feet, I search the opening hours of the place. Of course, it's closed for Christmas.

There are voices in the hallway, and while I recognise the deeper one as Carmen, there's another that's so high-pitched I think it may be giving me a migraine. I check the opening hours of the manor house again as if they'll have magically changed, but just become increasingly frustrated at the world for not working in my favour.

I'm so engulfed in irritability that I barely notice Carmen entering the room, an older woman with Southeast Asian features by her side. I assume it's her mother. Carmen's speaking at an uncharacteristically fast pace, and as I glance at them, I can't help noticing that her mum is kind of fit for someone who's probably forty-something.

"...I just don't think he'd want to, y'know, it's not that serious and--" Carmen freezes as she spots me. Her eyes quickly scan mine, she turns to face her mum, and smiles. She gestures towards me. "This is him."

"Huh?" I question.

Carmen widens her eyes, but I've got no idea in hell what that's supposed to mean. A gigantic grin bursts onto her mother's face, and she starts telling me her name--Lily, apparently--and asking me for mine, and she shakes my hand vigorously, and I don't think I've ever been more confused in my life. She has a thick Welsh accent, which sounds as equally perplexing leaving the mouth of someone with her features.

I watch her, dumbfounded, while she stares at me expectantly. What is she--Oh, my name.

"It's Felix." Carmen gets there before me.

"Oh, like the cat?"

You'd think I'd be used to that comment after nineteen--well, eleven years, though I'm sure it probably pissed me off at eight-years-old and under too. I resist a roll of my eyes, and nod. Lily goes to open her mouth again, but she's quickly interrupted by her daughter.

"We're just going to grab some stuff, won't be long," Carmen says as she glides over to me. She grabs my arm and yanks me from my chair, then nods at the end of the room where the sofas are. "Make yourself comfortable, be back now!"

Still with no further insight into what's going on, and now being pulled away from my breakfast and out of the kitchen, Carmen drags me into her room. She moves so quickly that I've not even got time to ask her what's happening before we enter.

"Okay, please do me a massive favour," she says the moment her bedroom door closes.

Her room is unnervingly clean, and I wonder if it's a girl thing or if I'm just grosser than I thought.

"Y'know how I said my 'rents are obsessed with being the first ones to visit me at uni, and all that bullshit?" she says, to which I nod. "Okay, well I've decided to go straight to my dad's from here tomorrow, so Mum being Mum obviously wanted to one up the guy and decided to surprise me, as she put it, and rock up unannounced today. The thing is..." Carmen clears her throat.

Where is this going?

"Okay, right, well basically, I told them the reason I was coming home a week late was because I've got a boyfriend here, and I wanted to stay with him for longer, and--ugh, I know it sounds dumb as shit, but I needed an excuse to avoid home for as long as possible, but now she's suddenly appeared and she's demanding to meet this imaginary boyfriend, and bloody take us out so she can impress said boyfriend, and--"

"You want me to be your fake boyfriend?" I ask, trying not to laugh. Carmen shrugs an awkward yes, and I lean against her door. "My services come at a price, y'know."

She rolls her eyes. "Shut up! There'll probably be free food in-volved, and whatever else it'll take for her to impress you."

"I dunno, mate, I'm quite difficult to impress. She might have to buy me some new shoes or something too, I've been eyeing up this pair of--"

"Oh, piss off, yes or no?"

"You had me at free food."

As we leave the flat and make our way to the car park, I begin to understand Carmen's frustration with her mother. We've not even reached the car yet, and she's made two passive comments about Carmen's father, both in relation to a failed business venture he tried out when she was pregnant with Carmen. Seventeen years ago.

I don't think she understands my accent too well either, as I have to repeat at least half of what I say. Apart from the ex-husband bashing and communication struggles, she seems nice. A bit loud, but nice enough.

When Lily and Carmen start discussing food and places to eat, I'm a little perplexed at first because I was only just eating breakfast, but then it occurs to me that it's almost one in the afternoon. I didn't even get to finish that breakfast anyway, not that I'd turn down food if I had.

Lily says she's into pub food, so we decide on grabbing a bite to eat at Ava's family pub because despite only ever eating a bowl of chips there, they were damn good. Once we reach the pub, Carmen thrusts her hand into mine seconds after leaving the car, and it takes me a moment to remember the reason I'm here.

"Be convincing," she whispers into my ear as we lead her mum into the building.

As someone who's never had the emotional availability to reign in a girlfriend, I pretty much have no idea what to do. I just follow Carmen's lead and stay wherever she puts me, which is currently with my hand resting on her thigh, and I probably shouldn't like it as much as I do. We've found ourselves a table beside one of the small, square windows, and are analysing the lunch menu.

The restless sensation I felt when we visited this place originally has returned, but it might just be because I'm really damn hungry. I decide on a vegetable lasagne without even consciously reminding myself that I'm meant to be vegetarian, and it scares me slightly. Lily's ecstatic at that revelation, as she's veggie herself.

She's dragged Carmen's father's name through the mud approximately six times by now, and every time she does so I glance at Carmen expecting a wince on her face, but never see anything other than a smile.

"You're not Carmen's usual type," Lily says to me as we're still scanning the menus. "She likes blondes--baby face types, y'know? Nice to see her with someone who can actually grow a bit of facial hair. Ugh, and she's always going for those silly airy boys who care more about their hair than their brains. Her last boyfriend was a right plank."

"Mum!" Carmen hisses, and I hold back a laugh.. "I have to remind him to shave half the time as it is."

Does she? I mean, what? Is this meant to be couple banter? God, this is stressful. I laugh when Lily does, in hope that it's the correct response. My facial hair isn't even that bad, only a bit of designer stubble for that rugged look I go for. The fact I buy most of my clothes from charity shops probably doesn't help. Jesus, no wonder I'm single.

Once we've all decided on food, Carmen and I go up to the bar to order. Though not as hectic as it usually is in here, we have to wait a while until we're served. There's no sign of the spirit bartender today, and Mosi seems to be working it alone. He shoots us a big smile when he spots us, and calls over to say he'll be with us soon.

"You've never had a girlfriend, have you?" Carmen says, catching me off-guard slightly. She rests her elbows on the sticky bar, then looks up at me with curious eyes. "Are you a virgin? Is that your secret?"

"Nah, that ship sailed four years ago at a house party with Rebecca Thomson from the year above. On an air mattress in her little sister's room, if you want the juicy details."

"How romantic." She shakes her head. "Illegal too, considering you would've been fifteen. Pretty sure Rebecca Thomson could go to jail for that."

I flash Carmen a toothy grin, to which she laughs, and it isn't much longer until Mosi finally gets to us. I'm feeling generous, so pay for the three meals myself, which only comes to just over twenty quid anyway thanks to a buy one get one free offer. What are student loans for, eh?

As much as I love the prospect of free stuff, I can never actually bring myself to let other people pay for me. My kindness is a curse, really. Carmen grabs her drink, while I grab Lily's along with my own, but Mosi stops me before I can follow Carmen back to the table. I turn back around to see his dark eyes boring into me, as if trying to find something in my own.

"Everything okay since you were at ours? You gave my wife a real fright," he enquires, to which I shrug a yes. Mosi hesitates, then leans in a little. "Listen son, aura readings can have strange effects on some, and I'd never ask you to talk about it, but... it helps. Talking helps."

I don't really know how to respond to that, so I just say, "thanks."

Mosi gives me one last nod, then shuffles along the bar to serve a bearded guy who looks like he's already drunk several pints too many for mid-afternoon. Well, that was weird.

When I return to the table, Carmen and Lily are discussing the underground caves that lay beneath this pub. Lily suggests visiting them after food as the tourist entrance is in the building next door, and Carmen seems thrilled at the thought. When their eyes turn to me questioningly, I nod and say I'm up for it. Why not, eh?

Our food arrives within the next fifteen minutes or so, and Carmen gives me a peck on the lips once we're done eating, which makes me turn redder than the ketchup I drowned my lasagne in. I fidget a lot throughout the meal, as the restless feeling refuses to budge.

Food eaten, we head out of the pub and into the small building next door. For a tourist attraction, it's not at all flashy. The building itself is a renovated cottage, and as we wander in, we find ourselves in a small reception area. There's a queue of about four groups of people, who are being led one by one through a door just behind the receptionist's desk.

There's not much décor in the room; a stand of pamphlets advertising other tourist attractions on the reception desk, and some framed black and white photos of the city adorned with historical facts regarding the caves. I would read these while we wait, but I can't. I want to go down to the caves. I really want to.

The agitated feeling I get in Mosi's pub is stronger than ever, and all I can think about are these caves. I need to see them. I don't want to see them, I need to. I have to. I'm practically bouncing from foot to foot, and Carmen must notice because she raises her eyebrows at me. God, I really want to see these caves.

Tickets in hand, we're ushered towards the old wooden door others have walked through, and I only now notice that there are stairs at the other end of it. I charge ahead, bouncing down the stone steps, and I have to stop myself from running. What the hell is wrong with me?

Once we're at the bottom, there's a slight damp smell, and it's a bit nippy. My body is buzzing by this point. There's a tour guide waiting for us alongside a group of ten or so other people. The guide is a slender woman who's almost as tall as I am, and she's talking about health and safety or some bullshit, but I need her to hurry up because I have to see the caves.

"I can't tell if you're excited or super angry," Carmen whispers into my ears.

"Huh?" I question.

Carmen says nothing; just raises her eyebrows again, and glances down to my feet, which are tapping manically. I stop them. Carmen takes hold of my hand, and we follow the tour guide as she leads us through the dark, narrow hallways.

The strange sensation is growing the deeper we get into this passageway, and all I can think about are the caves we're about to enter. It's like I'm obsessed. Just as the restlessness is about to become too much for me to bear, we enter one of the underground rooms, and every trace of the feeling vanishes. Just like that. And I feel amazing.

My head is light and I can't stop smiling. It's suddenly so warm and snug, and I'm not quite sure why, but I want to pull everyone around me into the biggest hug I've ever given anyone. I look at Carmen, and goddamnit, I want to kiss her. So I do. I plant a kiss onto her plump lips, and linger there until it's more than just a peck. God, this is good. Everything is great.

Carmen's looking at me like I just decapitated her mother, who's listening intently to the tour guide as she talks about monks or some shit, and I decide I really like Lily. She's so cool. So, so cool. I think this was used as a religious room because the tour guide keeps talking about God, and he must've been such a great guy. Creating the universe would've been such head stress, man, but he's managed to keep it going for trillions of years, so fair play to the fella. I didn't even believe in God before, but now I do. I so do.

The room is quite big, but very empty. There's what appears to be a shrine in the centre of it, and there's some creaky wooden furniture dotted around the place, but other than that, it's pretty basic. Shrines are such nice ideas. I feel so damn good that I have to stop myself from humming as we continue on to the next room, which appears after we pass through another hallway lit up by small light bulbs stuck onto the low ceiling above us.

This room is enormous. It's incredible. Amazing. We're on a bridge, and underneath us is a big pool of water. We're underground but on a bridge! How crazy! It's awe inspiring, and so I let the tour guide know how beautiful her room is because it is. It's so beautiful. She shoots me a weird look.

We move on to the next room, then the next, then the next, and they're just all so fantastic. I can't really remember what they are or what they look like as we move on to each new one, but I just know they're wonderful, y'know? I just know it. As we enter the last room of the tour, I find myself feeling the most ecstatic I've felt all day.

There are ghosts! Loads of them! We're in a gigantic room with the longest wooden table I've ever seen in my life slap-bang in the middle of it, and sitting on each one of the chairs is a spirit. They're drinking and laughing and eating and chatting, and it's the most brilliant thing I've ever seen. They're so loud! They're of all ages, all decades, all shapes, all sizes, and it's honestly just the best. Wonderful. Amazing.

None of what they're feasting on is real food or drink, and to everyone in the tour group, there's not a sound to be heard or a thing to be seen. I can barely hear our tour guide over the dead's partying, not that I'd be listening anyway. I love this. This is incredible. This is the most fantastic thing I've ever experienced.

As we leave this room to return upstairs and back into the reception area, I take one last glance back at the spirits sitting around the enormous table. I'm about to wave goodbye to them because why the hell not, but Carmen grabs my hand and pulls me out of the room. Our group begins climbing back up the stairs, and while most people seem rather chilled, I'm still grinning from ear to ear. Did no one else realise how otherworldly that experience was? God, it was good. So good.

Chapter 15

I'm officially insane. It's happened, I've cracked. Do I need to be sectioned? Probably. Carmen, Lily, and I must have been outside the building for about ten seconds when I crash back to reality. As we climb back into the car, the women are discussing university courses or something, but I can't focus on them. Seriously, what is going on? I just saw about twenty ghosts all in one place eating dead guy food and drink, and reacted like it was normal.

I've never seen more than a few ghosts in one place, let alone a group of them having a goddamn party. Did any of them see me? I don't think so. What about the fact I apparently found some soggy manmade caves to be the absolute best thing since sliced bread? I mean, bloody hell. Despite my delirium having vanished, one thing that remains is my mood. I feel good. I feel really good.

Lily drops us back to the flat at around six in the evening. She says her goodbyes to us, tells me it was lovely to meet me, and then disappears as suddenly as she arrived. The second the door to our flat closes, Carmen releases the longest sigh I've ever heard.

"God, she really knocks it out of me," she mutters as we head into the communal area. "Thanks for rolling with this, seriously."

"It's cool, it was fun," I reply. "She's not that bad, c'mon."

We sit down onto one of the black sofas, and out of habit from today, I grab Carmen's hand and rest it on my lap. Realising what I'm doing, I'm about to let her go, but decide not to. I don't really want to. I don't know whether it's my good mood that's making me this bold all of a sudden, but I'm just rolling with it. It's not like Carmen is pulling away.

"No, I know, I am harsh on her. I just..." She laughs, and I don't know if she intends it to, but it comes out dryly. "I wish she could shut up about Dad for five minutes. Makes me wonder if she wants to see me, or if she just wants to beat him."

For the first time ever, there's a glint of something shaky in Carmen's voice as she talks about her parents. She must notice her slip up because moments later, she laughs and starts saying something about her parents being part of The Hunger Games--which according to Carmen is a book reference, as she soon explains to me when she notices my blank expression. Sounds like a rip-off of Battle Royale to me.

Before I can say much back, she jumps up from the sofa and starts talking about drinks, and if I want one. She's already pouring me a glass of wine as she asks, so I'm not sure I have much of a choice.

"This was a fiver from the booze shop round the corner, so it may kill you," she says as she hands me the glass and sits back down. She lifts her own glass. "Chin chin."

"A fiver? Jesus, don't spoil me," I reply sarcastically.

"Fine, I'll take it back," she replies as she reaches out to grab my glass of wine, which I quickly snatch away. "Yeah, I thought so, dickwad."

She lets out a laugh before taking a gulp of her wine, then places it on the floor below us. As I take a sip of my own drink, she turns around on the sofa so that she's hanging off it--her head dangling so that it's almost touching the floor, while her feet are in the air. Her dark hair is sprawled across the carpet like a splash of water, and she shuts her eyes. She moves her feet around in a rhythmic motion as she hums a tune.

"You smashed or something?" I ask with raised eyebrows.

"What? No, this is my first one. I just like sitting like this." She giggles. "And c'mon, if anyone's smashed, it's you. Did you not see yourself in those caves earlier? I'd swear you'd just popped a shitload of pills."

That's a fair point. I was hoping it wasn't that obvious. I'm about to give Carmen some sarcastic response when Annabel appears on one of the kitchen stools, and it bugs me a little. I kind of want to be alone with Carmen.

"Yeah, what the hell was wrong with you earlier?" Annabel questions me.

Carmen is still chuckling slightly, while Annabel manifests herself to sit on the arm of the sofa beside me. I give her a pleading look in hope that she'll get the message and go away, but she doesn't move an inch.

"What can I say?" I finally reply to Carmen. "I have a thing for caves."

"Did you even notice me there with you guys? You didn't acknowledge me once," Annabel continues, which I ignore. "It's fine, Carmen has her eyes closed, so just give me a thumbs up if you could see me." I still ignore her.

"Nah, I don't know, I was just in a really good mood," I say as I take another sip of my drink.

"I thought you were going to kiss the tour guide when you told her how lovely her room was, not gonna lie," Carmen replies as she sits back to an upright position on the sofa. "I'm fairly sure it's not actually her room, by the way, and am definitely sure she doesn't decorate it herself. Never seen a vegetarian get so excited over a tannery either."

That big room with a family sized swimming pool in it was a tannery? Hm. Goes to show how little I was listening.

"Hello? Earth to Felix? I know you can hear me because you keep looking at me," Annabel rambles on. "Why were you ignoring me earlier?"

"You don't know that," I reply to Carmen. "She might be chief interior designer. Stop discrediting her, it's mean--"

"Felix! Stop ignoring me!"

"I'm just gonna pop to the bathroom," I announce, shooting Annabel the most scathing look I think I've ever mustered up.

Carmen nods as she gives me a soft smile, and I'm on my feet in seconds The moment I'm out of the kitchen, Annabel appears in front of me. There's no bloody escaping her, is there?

"Why are you ignoring me?" Annabel pouts.

I rub my temples. "Look, Annie, would you please maybe leave me be for a bit? The cave thing was kinda weird, and I'll explain it to you later, but I just want to hang out with Carmen for a bit. Without you." I pause. "I mean, it's not you, I just want to speak to her alone and stuff with no distractions."

I've never seen Annabel look so dejected. She nods, and she tries to muster a smile, but it doesn't really work. Ever since my second vision, and since her belief that Mum saved me instead of her arose, I've tried my hardest not to upset her. It's just that she doesn't realise I have a life outside of her sometimes, and having someone constantly in your ear can get a bit much.

I'm about to apologise, but she disappears. I swear to myself, then head back into the kitchen. There's my good mood gone. Carmen has finished her glass of wine now, so she's pouring herself a new one. She tops mine up as well.

"You all right?" she asks as we sit back down, to which I nod, and attempt a smile. "That was the most unconvincing smile I've ever seen, Felix."

"I'm cool, seriously. Probably just a bit tired."

She clearly knows I'm lying, but doesn't pry further. It's nice that she doesn't. We chat about nothing for what feels like ten minutes, but when I check the time, over an hour has passed. I'm at a good level of tipsiness now, and Carmen is in the process of pouring us another drink.

"Tonight, Felix Reynolds, I will uncover your secret," Carmen announces as she leans against the kitchen island.

"You what?" I question.

"Ugh, you're so forgetful," Carmen says with a shake of her head. "Y'know, your big secret. I've tried virgin, I've tried gay, I've tried spy parents--I mean, what is there left?"

I don't know if it's the alcohol or the elevated mood from earlier returning, but I suddenly want to tell Carmen all about my parents. All about the accident and my memory loss. I mean, that is the secret, isn't it? There never really was one to start with officially, but whenever Carmen brings this up, my thoughts always creep to the accident and my non-existent memory. Well, that and the ghost thing, but that's a definite no. I know I'm being foolish, so I quickly discard the thought.

"It's really quite anticlimactic," I joke.

"Oh, c'mon, just give me a clue," she pleads as she makes her way over to me and hands me a glass of wine.

"Nah."

"I'm never going to get it without some kind of clue, vouch for me here!"

"Nah."

"Please! I'm not going to give up, y'know."

"Seriously, Carmen, it's nothing, just leave it."

"Pretty please?"

"I said no." I don't mean to say it as harshly as I do, and the moment the sentence leaves my mouth I regret saying it.

Carmen stammers a little. She's yet to sit down, and is standing a foot or so away from me. She opens her mouth to speak, but nothing comes out. She tries again, and this time, a quiet apology slips out, followed by something about feeling tired, and then a good night, and before I know it she's left the room. Fantastic. I've managed to upset two people I care about within the space of a few hours. Great going, idiot.

It takes me a few minutes to muster up the courage to knock on Carmen's bedroom door. As I stand outside her room waiting for her to answer, my blood is racing through my body at an alarming rate. I don't know why I snapped at her. I sure as hell didn't want to snap at her. I hear movement from behind the door, and as the handle slowly turns, I hold my breath. Please don't screw up this time, please.

"I'm sorry," are the first words either of us say, and they're my own. "I'm an arse, I'm sorry."

Carmen shakes her head, her eyes shying away from mine. "No, I'm sorry, I shouldn't have kept going on. I'm bad for it, I know, I just get ahead of myself and keep talking and don't know when to shut up, and I don't want to be annoying but it's like it comes second nature to me or something, and I always end up putting my foot in--"

"Carmen, it's fine, you didn't do anything wrong."

She blushes, then closes her mouth. Her eyes look a little blood-shot, and her make-up isn't as pristine as it was earlier. I think she might've been crying. Naturally, I begin hating myself more. The sound of a doorknob turning catches our attention, and so Carmen ushers me in before Jamie enters the hallway to find us having a heart to heart. She tucks her fringe behind her ear as she sits down onto her bed, and gestures for me to sit beside her.

"Sorry," I say again. "I'm just a bit stressed at the moment, y'know, with exams coming up after Christmas and stuff. I'm a dick when I'm stressed."

"When you're stressed? Sorry to break it to you, but..." There's a tiny smile on Carmen's slightly blotched face, and relief at the realisation that we're okay washes over me.

"I can easily change my mind, y'know?" I reply with narrowed eyes, and for a moment there's a flash of worry on Carmen's face, so I reassure her that I'm kidding by poking her in her side.

"Ow!" she yelps. "Mate, that legit hurt."

As she rubs the spot where I just poked her, I use that distraction as a way to poke her again, this time on her other side. She quickly catches on and begins nudging me back until it gets to the point where we'll end up leaving flesh wounds if we don't stop, and so we do, and then I kiss her.

I realise I'm acting like I'm trying to re-enact some shitty rom-com, but I'm at the point where I don't really give a shit. The kisses start off small and sporadic, but as we lie down onto Carmen's bed, they start becoming more intense. I know I probably shouldn't do this, but I don't really care.

I'm not sure what time it is, or if I've slept at all, or if Carmen's even awake when I break the silence that's been lingering for a while. The room is dark, and I can only just make out Carmen's silhouette lying beside me. Despite sharing a single bed, it doesn't feel cramped. Her skin is cool and smooth against my own, and her hair smells of something sweet.

"There was an accident," I say, and it's barely even a whisper.

Carmen doesn't reply, but her breathing stops for a millisecond, so I know she's awake. I could stop now if I wanted to. There's no real need to tell Carmen anything, and if she questions me on what I just said, I can blame it on sleep talking. I want to though--I'm going to. I'm fed up of trying not to slip up and reveal anything. It's exhausting. I just hope I don't regret it.

"A car accident, when I was eight," I continue quietly. I can already feel myself backing out, and I know that unless I get it all out now, it's not going to happen. "No one but me survived it. My parents and sister were killed, and it wiped my memory completely, so I can't remember anything that happened before the accident. I--it's okay, I mean, I don't remember them or anything so I don't miss them--not like that, I mean, of course I want to remember them, I just mean I feel okay and not to worry... uh, y'know, yeah."

I speak so quickly and so quietly that I'll be amazed if Carmen understood a single word of that, and when she doesn't respond, I think she might not have. I'm about to say something--anything--when I feel the mattress dip. Carmen turns around, and it's too dark to make out the details of her face, but I can feel her eyes looking up at me.

She finds my hand under the duvet as she pulls me closer towards her, and entwines her fingers in mine. She lifts herself up slightly to plant a kiss on my cheek, then tucks her head under my chin. All the tension in body deflates, and I let out a quiet breath. And just like that, the only regret I have is keeping it a secret for so long.

Chapter 16

Jamie's face is a picture when I walk into the kitchen the next morning. He doesn't say anything, but he doesn't stop scowling at me as I open my cupboard to find some bread. I'm ravenous so there's no time for toasting or any other strenuous activity. Instead, I bite into a dry slice. I turn back around to face Jamie, and his eyebrows are raised as if he's waiting for me to say something. What exactly, I don't know.

"Just a quick reminder," he eventually says. "There are other people living in this flat, most notably, in the room adjacent to Carmen's."

"Huh?" I ask as I go to grab another slice of bread. "Oh!" I exclaim, finally catching on to why he's got a face like a slapped arse. I try, and fail, to hold back a laugh. "Yeah, sorry about that."

"It's not funny," Jamie mutters. "Where is Carmen anyway?"

"Showering. I was gonna go first, but I'm going to the gym for a bit, so I'll just shower after that," I reply before taking another bite of my bread.

"You've not showered yet?" he asks blankly, to which I shake my head. He looks at me as if I just told him I'd slaughtered a kitten.

"What?" I question.

"You're disgusting." He stands up from his stool. "And for the love of god, please clean your dishes."

With that, Jamie leaves the room. Geez, someone's in a bad mood. Granted, said dishes have been sitting next to the sink for about two weeks now, which has resorted me to eating out of takeaway boxes, but he could at least ask nicely. I will do it, just not right now. Sometime later probably.

Carmen is busy packing by the time I'm home from the gym, and there's no sign of Jamie, so I decide to head back to my room for a bit. After spending the night in Carmen's immaculate living space, it occurs to me how shabby mine actually is. Annabel is waiting for me on my bed when I get in, kind of like a mother waiting for her teenage kid to return home from their first wild house party. She looks a little chirpier than she did last night, which I guess is a good thing.

"Ugh, finally!" she whines. "C'mon then, the hell was up with you at the caves? Jamie's right, by the way, you're gross."

After everything that happened last night, I completely forgot about that. I try to look on the bright side; at least whatever happened in the caves was a good weird, least in the sense that it made me feel good. It could be even more evidence supporting the theory that I'm suffering from severe psychosis, but hey ho, it was a nice feeling.

I shrug at Annabel as I sit down beside her on the bed. "I dunno. I just felt really good, and I guess it showed. I don't think I could not see you or anything, I think I was just distracted by everything else going on. Did you see all the ghosts sitting at that huge table?"

Annabel nods. She fiddles with the sleeve of her oversized jumper, and her dark eyebrows furrow. I understand that look of confusion. There's been some really weird shit happening to me since I arrived at uni, and I'm beginning to wonder if I ever should've come here in the first place. I don't ask for much. I just want a life where I'm not bombarded with demonic stalkers, and to be able to enter a cave without falling in love with it.

"We're probably overthinking it anyway," I continue. "I doubt the cave thing is even related to the paranormal, I was probably just in a really good mood or something. There's nothing out of the ordinary about seeing all those ghosts, either. I mean, non-dead folk have parties all the time, so why can't your lot? Bit random, bit weird, but still."

Annabel nods again, but I don't think she's convinced. She lets out a sigh. "I guess so. We've got more important stuff to sort out anyway, mainly the fact that some evil, psychopathic force is apparently out to get you."

"All I know is that I've got five exams to revise for at the moment, so it would be just swell if all this shit could give me a break for a bit," I mutter as I lie down and shut my eyes. "I don't think I see dead people can pass for extenuating circumstances."

"Things have to calm down eventually," Annabel replies.

"Pfft. I don't think that'll happen, somehow."

Funnily enough, that's exactly what happens. Over the next few weeks, as if every spirit within a ten mile radius received a memo about my upcoming exams, nothing unusual happens. It's quite unnerving, actually. I don't go out much, and other than Jamie, there's not really anyone around to speak to. Once Jamie's gone, I barely leave the flat. It's times like these I relish Annabel's company because the reality is that if I didn't have her, I'd have no one. God, I'd forgotten how much I hated Christmas.

Carmen offered for me to spend time in Wales with her over the holiday at least ten times; she even invited me to have Christmas dinner with her family, but I declined each time. I'd only end up becoming an inconvenience, and don't really want to be the sad little orphan tagging along to another family's holiday. It can just get a tad bit lonely is all, although it doesn't bother me half as much as it used to.

When I was younger I used to keep a box full of spare change that I'd saved throughout the year, so that I could buy Christmas cards and address them to myself. I'd buy as many varied designs as I could, and write in each one with different handwriting so that when I put them up in my bedroom, I could pretend they were from my family. Looking back, that's probably the most depressing thing a ten-year-old can do.

I spend a lot of the holidays in bed. Some days, I don't even leave my room because I don't feel like eating, and sleeping is easier than staring at four walls. Some days I don't even see Annabel. It's not because she's not there, I just can't see her. It happens sometimes, and she thinks it's related to my mood, but I don't know. Whenever I'm at the point where I can't see her, I don't really care either. I don't care about much when I'm like that.

It's just frustrating because all I can focus on is my non-existent family and the fact they died, and I didn't. It makes me feel like the worst person to ever exist. When I manage to crawl myself out of that hole, I realise how nonsensical that is because I had no control over what happened, but I always manage to convince myself that it was all my fault when I'm in that headspace.

Christmas day is inevitably the worst. I wake up late morning to silence, and if it wasn't for the fact it's Christmas day, I wouldn't leave my room. I force myself out of bed, all the while wishing for the night to come so that I can go back there. Our flat's group message is filled with everyone wishing each other a merry Christmas, which I guess is nice, and Carmen sends me a message separately. That helps.

She did try to call, but the last thing I felt like doing was talking, so I made up some story about being busy with some course friends who are here over the holidays. I'm not sure she believed me. We talk most days, and if ever we don't, it's only because I can't bring myself to get out of bed to do anything.

I throw a supermarket pizza into the oven for my Christmas dinner, and drink some wine Jamie left in his cupboard in an attempt to spice things up. It doesn't really work. I can't see Annabel today, and that's probably the worst thing about it. I'm completely alone.

When I head back to bed at around seven, I'm feeling the worst I've felt in a long time. I don't know why it's bothering me so much this year. Last year was fine, and I was living alone in a flat then, so I don't know why this year is any different. I guess I had Annabel then.

A few hours pass, and I can hear a rattling sound. I ignore it at first, assuming it's an animal outside or something, but then there's a quiet thud as something drops to my bedroom floor. I sit up in bed, but can't see anything. I hear the rattling once more, and spot one of my pencils moving on the desk.

"Not now, Annabel," I mutter as I lie back down.

This time, she throws the pencil at me.

"Piss off, I'm not in the mood!"

She throws another one. I grunt as I jump out of bed, and swear under my breath. I stand over my desk where Annabel was shaking the pencil, and notice that one of my notebooks is open. I switch my desk lamp on to inspect it.

On the first page of lined paper is a badly drawn snowman that honestly looks more like a deformed horror villain than anything at all Christmassy, and written underneath is a small message. The writing is awful, and resembles that of a five-year-old writing a full sentence for the first time, but I'm just about able to make out what it says.

To Felix,

Merry Christmas

Lots of love,

Annabel

P.S. That's meant to be a snowman

I smile, and for the first time in days, I feel okay. Annabel has never been able to write before because she says controlling the movement of a pencil while using the correct amount of pressure is near enough impossible to do with her mind. This really must've taken some effort on her part.

I rip the page from the notebook, and grab some Blu Tack from my bedside cabinet. I decide to stick it on the wall opposite my bed, and it fits in perfectly amongst the posters I already have up. Once it's on the wall, I head back to bed feeling a lot better than when I left it. As I lie back down, I know Annabel's here. I can't see her or hear her, but I can feel her warmth all over my body, and I know tomorrow won't be so bad.

It's New Year's Eve, and I'm sitting on the sofa in the communal area feeling sorry for myself while Annabel practices her writing skills beside the kitchen island. Since she wrote me the Christmas card, she's become obsessed with learning to write. I hear the notebook slam shut, and when I turn towards her, her eyes are on the doorway.

Moments later, Ava walks into the flat for the first time since she left four weeks ago. I stammer a little at the sight of her, having barely spoken to a soul since Jamie left over a week ago. Her family went skiing or some other shit rich people do over Christmas, and I didn't even realise she was home yet. An enormous grin grows on her face when she spots me moping on the sofa.

"Groovy, hi Felix! Carmen said you're, like whoa, festering in the flat all day every day," she announces in a sing song voice. "So I'm taking you out."

For a moment, I worry that Carmen has told Ava everything about my parents and the accident, but I dismiss that thought. I trust Carmen enough not to do that. I flash Ava an unimpressed look, but she pays no attention to it.

Instead, she laughs, waltz over to hand me a flower--some purple thing--then skips out of the room. I forgot how weird this girl was. I leave the flower on a countertop, then go after her to find her standing outside my room. Once she sees me, she wanders in as if it's been her home since birth.

Once inside, she begins cleaning up. Is that normal? Is it some weird girl thing? My room's not even that bad. My curtains are closed, and have been for a few weeks, so she swishes them open to reveal the extent of the mess I've collected over the past month or so.

Ah. Okay, it's worse than I realised.

I'm only now noticing its slightly putrid smell too, and I'm suddenly kind of embarrassed about Ava being here.

"Uh, no," I interrupt her mid-tidy. "I mean, it's okay, thanks. I'll sort that out later, I've been meaning to do it."

She shrugs, immediately stops clearing things away, then sits on my bed with her hands placed neatly on her lap. "Okay."

Oh, okay, that was easy. I don't actually know why she's here. She wants to force me out of here, I get that, but why she's sitting on my bed, I don't know. I'm about to ask her when she turns to me and tilts her head slightly.

"Who's Annabel?" she asks, and I stop dead in my tracks.

What? I dart my eyes around the room in search of her, but she's nowhere to be seen. Does Ava know something? Have I said something? She must notice the startled look on my face because she soon elaborates.

"That paper," she explains, lifting her arm to point at the wall opposite the bed. "The one with the snowman on it."

"Oh! Uh..." I'm not sure what to say, so I just tell her the truth. "My sister."

Ava nods. "Oh, groovy, I didn't know you had a sister."

I don't know what to say to that, so I just reply to her with an awkward shrug. She doesn't pry further, and instead, informs me to get ready because we're going to her family's pub. On one hand, I really don't want to get drunk with a load of middle-aged people in a pub on New Year's Eve, but then on the other, I really want to get drunk with a load of middle-aged people in a pub on New Year's Eve. What the heck, eh?

We've not been outside for ten seconds when I take that back because holy shit, it's cold. We're on our way to our halls' car park as Ava's driving tonight, and we must barely be outside for three minutes between the time we leave the building and get into her car, but I'm fairly certain I've reached the initial stages of hypothermia by that point.

More surprisingly, I actually feel a lot better. Simply coming into contact with fresh air clears my head. Annabel is already in the car when we get inside it, and I don't think I've ever seen her so excited. I guess me not leaving the flat means her not leaving the flat either, least not properly, so I shoot her a tiny smile through the rear-view mirror.

"Would you like me to try and contact your spirit attachment?" Ava asks me as she starts the car in the kind of tone you'd ask someone how much sugar they want in their tea.

"Uh--I.. uh, I don't think I have one, it's okay," is all I can muster as a reply. I don't think I've said a single sentence to her without stammering yet.

"I could help him or her move on to The Beginning," Ava continues, as if she didn't hear a word I just said. "Sorry, I mean what most people would refer to as heaven. Every pure spirit deserves it. Yours is very pure. Probably young."

I want to tell her that Annabel is happy where she is, and to leave us be, but hold my tongue for obvious reasons. Annabel herself grins at me through the rear-view mirror at the mention of her apparent purity, the cocky little swine.

We're speeding down the main road now, and for some reason, Ava has rolled down the window on her side of the car. She drives with one arm dangling out of it, and the winter air gushes into the vehicle in a flurry. Thank God I brought a jacket.

"Nah, seriously, it's fine. You've got this spirit attachment thing confused, I think," I say to Ava without looking at her.

I expect her to argue back or something, but she says nothing. She just nods, and continues driving. She doesn't say anything else for the next ten minutes or so, and the only sound to be heard is Annabel's quiet humming alongside the sound of the car's engine. We can't be more than a minute away when Ava speaks again.

"You're not a very good liar."

We've stopped at a red light, and her eyes are piercing into me. In the darkness of the night, they look black. She watches me with something I can't quite put my finger on. It's not expectancy as if she's waiting for me to confirm her statement, it's more like curiosity. When the light we've stopped at turns green, Ava turns away and continues driving without another word.

Chapter 17

As we walk into the pub, I'm surprised to see Jamie sitting at one of the tables near the bar. I can't focus on him for long though because the place is rammed. Within moments of stepping into the building, I'm sweating from places I didn't think I could sweat from. Laughter booms from all corners of the building, cheesy Christmas songs blast through the speakers at the bar, and I've never seen so many god-awful Christmas jumpers in my life. I kind of love it.

Ava grabs my arm and yanks me towards Jamie, and we sit down at the table with him. His hair is in its usual slicked back style, and it looks more like a dead animal than ever. He's dressed to the nines, suit and tie and all. I feel a little underdressed in my unwashed white t-shirt and secondhand jacket.

"Since when did you get back?" I shout to him over the noise.

"About half an hour ago, my aunt dropped me straight here," he explains. "Carmen's not coming, is she? I'd rather not repeat the trauma from last time you two were together in the flat."

Ava laughs, and I figure Carmen must've told her about that night because she struggles to hide the knowing smile that lingers on her lips. I've not really put much thought into what'll happen when she does return, and I don't even really know what I want to happen. I just hope it's not weird between us.

Jamie's still looking at me like he's eaten something sour, so I give him a wink, then say, "nah, we're saving that for another time to give you something to look forward to."

Jamie tells me I'm not funny while Ava and Annabel, who's found herself a stool beside Jamie, laugh at his blatant horror, and I'm questioning why I ever thought tonight would be a bad idea. Ava mentions drinks, and I briefly glance at Annabel to gauge her reaction, but she just shrugs. Go for it, she mouths. Well then, in that case, it would be rude not to.

Three hours, five vodka shots, and several beers later, the three of us have been joined by a group of Ava's family friends. Annabel's either disappeared or the alcohol has kicked in, and everyone's singing their best rendition of Fairytale of New York. I've always fancied myself as a bit of a singer, especially when I've had five shots of vodka, but the only spare person available to be my Kirsty McColl is Jamie.

"Mate, c'mon, it's literally our song!" I exclaim to him over the hustle and bustle of the pub. "They hate each other, that's the point--Well, I think it is. It doesn't matter anyway, it's fate, it's the universe binding us together! You get to call me a scumbag, and a maggot! I realise I'm more vocally suited for Kirsty's part, but I sound really northern when I sing and it just won't work, man, it just will not work."

"I swear to god," Jamie groans, leaning his head back against his chair.

"Aw, c'mon Jamie!" Ava interjects, having picked up on our conversation. "I did it with Steve."

Steve is her dad's friend. I like Steve, he has a beard. He told me food gets stuck in there sometimes.

"C'mon, be my Kirsty," I plead to him with big eyes.

"No."

"If you don't do it for me, do it for the Ghost of Christmas Past." I pause. "Oh! Ava, is there actually a Ghost of Christmas Past? I've never seen one myself, I have to admit, but there was this one who said he could predict the future. Ugly bugger he was, face looked like it'd been through a blender, but it was a boating acci--"

There's a sudden smash, and there's cold liquid running down my leg, and Ava's friends are saying something about napkins, but I'm confused. It's only when I look down to see beer seeping through my black jeans and a smashed glass on the table do I realise what's happened. Shit, did I do that? I don't think so.

Something flicks the back of my head, so I go to rub it, only for it to be flicked again. Someone hands me a tea towel--not Steve, but another guy with a beard--but it's too crowded in here to use it, so I step outside.

I know it's cold because air gushes out of my mouth when I breathe out, but it doesn't feel it. I don't even have my jacket on, and I feel all right. I sit down onto one of the wooden picnic tables outside the pub, and as I begin rubbing at my jeans, there's another flick at the back of my head.

"Annabel?" I question, but get no response. "Stop being annoying."

"What?"

I turn to the pub entrance to see Jamie standing there with an irritated expression still on his face. I wave my hand in the air to shrug it off, and continue working on my jeans. They're not really getting any drier, and the beer has reached my crotch by this point, which isn't the best feeling in the world.

"You do realise you're rubbing your dry leg, right?" Jamie asks, moving towards me. "You're without a doubt the most annoying drunk I've ever met."

"Aw cheers, that means a lot to me," I reply, genuinely proud.

"Right... Yes, anyway, the countdown is happening soon, so I was ordered to come and collect you," Jamie states extremely unenthusiastically. "Well, and to check you're not passed out under a table or any--Ow!" he suddenly yelps as he rubs his arm and looks down at it. "What the--Something just scrammed me."

I laugh at the guy because he's such a dramatic little bastard, but when he moves his hand from the spot on his arm, I see that it's red. It's bleeding a tiny bit. I stand up from the table to inspect it, and there are four fresh scratches on it.

"Annabel?" I mutter aloud.

"What?" Jamie asks, to which I shrug off.

Why did she just do that? Sure, she does annoying shit sometimes, but only ever to me. And never anything harmful. Jamie's still rubbing his arm, so I take it as a chance to scowl into the air in the hope that Annabel will notice it.

"What?" Jamie asks again.

"Nothing, I was thinking aloud, Annabel's just this--"

"No, not that, you said something else," he interrupts.

I gaze at him and shake my head. "Mate, I haven't said anything else. I don't--"

"There! Listen!"

I clamp my mouth shut and listen, but all I can hear is the distant sound of a motorbike. Just as I'm about to speak again, the chequered tea towel I left on the picnic table flings off it and smacks into my side. That definitely wasn't the wind.

Jamie stares at the towel as it lies in a heap on the damp concrete, and begins stuttering. I'm starting to feel the cold now. I think I'm shivering. There's another movement; one of the pub's wooden deck chairs, and this time it's definitely not the wind. It falls backwards into the wall of the pub, one of its legs snapping in the process.

"What the... Felix, did you just see that?"

I stare at the broken chair, and only then does it hit me. This isn't Annabel. This is something dark. Shit.

"That's our cue to head back in," I mutter, more to myself.

Within seconds, I'm trying to push the pub door open, but it's not budging. I ram it a little with my body, but there's still nothing. I bang on it, but no one inside must hear me because it's so goddamn loud in there.

"What's happening?" Jamie's breathing is heavy. "Why have they locked it?"

There's a swishing sound. Something hard strikes my ankle. I lose my balance, and only just manage to stop myself from falling. On the floor beside my foot is the chair's broken leg.

Jamie starts banging on the door now, but I know it's a lost cause because there are too many people in there for them to hear us, and the door isn't going to unlock itself any time soon. We're going to have to run.

I turn to Jamie, who's still hopelessly trying to shove the door open, and I have no idea what to say with no time to figure it out. So I don't say anything. I grab his arm and pull him away from the door. I'm much stronger than him, so when he pulls back, I barely budge.

"What are you doing? We can't stay out here, we need to get back in!"

"Jay, we're not getting back in, and we can't just sit around here, so do you have any better suggestions?"

As if on cue, an empty glass that was left on the picnic table I was sitting at minutes ago is thrown onto the floor with an ear-shattering smash. What remains of it rolls towards us, stopping at Jamie's feet. He stares at it for a few seconds, then looks back up at me with his eyes wide.

"Yes, okay, we'll go."

If I wasn't shitting myself right now, I'd probably find it hysterical how matter-of-factly he just said that. This isn't just something dark, this is a poltergeist. It has to be. I grab Jamie's arm and we sprint towards the road opposite the pub as if either of us have any idea where the hell we're running to.

I've only ever dealt with a poltergeist once before, and that one was much weaker than this. It could only just throw a pillow at me, for starters, let alone break a chair. All we can do is run and hope for the best.

Chapter 18

We're trying to lose it, but it's proving useless. Panic and adrenaline have overridden my drunkness, and anything left over is just making me unsteady on my feet. I've been scratched by this point, and there's a constant stream of rocks being thrown at us. Jamie's rambling on about something as we run, so I tell him to shut up because he's going to make himself out of breath.

After a while of aimlessly sprinting around the local area, I begin to notice streetlights flickering, and after another five minutes, I begin realising that they flicker every time there's a turning. It's far too controlled, and definitely too clever of a move for a poltergeist. It's Annabel. It has to be.

"Turn the direction of the street light that flickers!" I call back to Jamie, who's increasingly lagging behind.

"What? I don't--what do you mean?" he shouts back.

"Just follow me!"

My legs are beginning to ache, and my throat stings. The street-light to my left flickers. We turn left. My ankle hurts from where the chair leg hit it earlier, but I grit my teeth and ignore it as best I can. Something smacks into my arm. A stone, I think. Another light flickers, and we turn left again.

I don't recognise this part of town, and the streets are empty. Where the hell is Annabel trying to take us? We take the next right. Jamie swears. I glance backwards to see him almost trip, but he just about saves himself. I think something hit him. We turn left again, then right, then another right. Something scratches my arm again. This is useless. This isn't working.

I turn to Jamie, and I don't think he's going to be able to run for much longer. There must be something we can do, somewhere we can go. A streetlight on the left flickers, just as I spot a concrete bus shelter to the right. An idea hits me. I run towards the shelter as the streetlight to the left flickers again.

All sides bar the front of the shelter are covered, but there's a concrete panel extending from the roof of the shelter to the ground in the middle of it, so Jamie and I stand in line with the panel, ensuring that no part of our bodies poke out.

"What is going on?" Jamie practically screams, despite there being barely any sound around us.

"Bad stuff," I manage to say through gasping breaths. "Mind you, I don't think I've ever sobered up so quickly in my life."

"Now's not the time to try and be funny!" he snaps back.

I slowly poke my head around the concrete panel, but there's nothing to see. The road is empty, and it's too dark to make out much anyway. The streetlight I ignored is flashing manically now. I'm about to move further out when I spot something heading straight towards me, so I quickly step back behind the safety of the concrete. There's a smash. I think it was a glass bottle. I have an idea, but I need Annabel to execute it.

I need to speak to her. Out loud.

I turn my eyes to Jamie, who's still trying to get his breath back. I can't do it in front of him. How the hell is this going to work? Now we're under shelter, we're at an advantage. We need the poltergeist to try and attack us. Their power is formulated entirely by energy, and the more they use up, the weaker they become. Or at least according to Ava's book.

There's no way we can taunt it safely though, it's too risky. Annabel, on the other hand... I really need to speak to her. I have to speak to her. I glance at Jamie again. I don't have a choice, do I? I shut my eyes and take a deep breath. I'm going to regret this.

"Annabel, I've got an idea!" I call out.

"What? What are you--" Jamie.

"We need to drain its energy! Distract it, taunt it, throw things at it so it has to fight back! Make it--"

"Felix? What--Who are you--"

"Make it throw big things at us that'll take a lot of energy, and just tell me which way to dodge if you have to! No idea how, but--but we'll figure it out."

It's silent for a minute after that. Jamie's too busy gawking at me to say anything, and I begin wondering if Annabel is even here. Maybe the streetlights weren't her. Maybe the poltergeist was leading us on a wild goose chase.

Just as I'm about to lose all hope, something smashes into the concrete panel we're hidden behind. Then something else, then another, then another. There's banging and smashing and swishing sounds, and while they do eventually turn less extreme, it's too slow.

"This isn't working," I mutter under my breath.

"What?" Jamie, who's regained the majority of his energy, asks.

I peek out from behind the concrete again, and the first thing I see is the streetlight flickering even more frenzied than before. Maybe Annabel was onto something. I glance down to see a spilled bin on the floor, but the moment I look back up, something hits me just under my left eyebrow.

"Shit!" I yelp, immediately sheltering myself back behind the concrete.

I lift my hand to my eye, only to feel something sharp snag my skin. When I bring my hand back down, it's covered in blood.

"Oh god, is there glass in your eye?" Jamie shouts more loudly than necessary, which doesn't exactly calm the situation.

"No, it's--it's just my eyebrow, it's fine, I'm fine." I lift my hand back to my wound to try and keep the blood off my face. "Is the streetlight still flashing?"

"What? I don't know if I should check, what if--"

"Is it?" I roar.

"Yes, I think so, I can sort of see it from here, I mean--"

I take Jamie's arm with my free hand before he can finish his sentence, and pull us both out of the bus shelter. Once I let go of him, Jamie follows me like a lost toddler, and I look up to see the streetlight to our left switching on and off. Annabel better know what the hell she's doing here.

Within seconds, it feels like we're back to square one, except this time, I'm trying to keep blood from running into my eye. The light to our right flickers, so we turn right. Then the one to our left, so we turn left. Then left again, then right, then left, then left. Another stone is thrown at my legs.

I can hear a crowd in the distance, but the blood rushing in my head is too loud for me to be able to make out where it's coming from. Another right. Jamie is shouting something behind me, but I can't understand him. A right again. Another glass bottle is thrown in my direction, but I dodge it. The streetlight to our left flickers, and I slow down for a moment. It's an alleyway. I don't know if this is a good idea.

Without much else to choose from, I risk it.

"Don't go down there!" Jamie cries out, but I ignore him, and he follows me anyway.

It's pitch black now. I can barely see my hand in front of my face. There are no streetlights left, and I get the sinking feeling that Annabel has gotten us lost. The crowds sound louder, but we're so enclosed in this alleyway that it's blocking out too much noise to be able to tell how close they actually are. Jamie's shouting something again.

Then all of a sudden, as if by magic, we emerge into the largest crowd of people I think I've ever seen in my life. We're on the high street. We're in the city centre, slap bang in the middle of the busiest street possible, on the busiest night of the year. This is perfect. Holy shit, no wonder Annabel was leading us here. No way can the poltergeist track us among hundreds of people.

Drunkards scream and sing and stumble around the cobbled street, and every single person has a smile plastered on their face. I laugh. I'm not quite sure why, but I start laughing and I can't stop.

By the time Jamie and I have found our way back to Mosi's pub, I've managed to control the bleeding on my face, and there are people sparsely gathered around the outside of the building. Jamie's not said a word since we left the crowds of the high street, and his face is as pale as a ghost--no pun intended. I can see Annabel again now, but I've barely had time to stop and think, let alone a chance to speak to her.

"Whoa, guys!" I instantly recognise the voice as Ava's, and manage to spot her emerging from one of the groups. "Where have you been? Do you know what happened outside here? One of the chairs has broken, and the--Felix? What happened to your face? Are you okay?"

"Yeah, no, it's fine, I just--"

"Dad!" Ava calls behind her. She takes my arm and yanks me towards the pub. "Dad! We need the first aid kit!"

Once inside, we see Mosi clearing away some glasses behind the bar. He looks up at us with a smile, only for that smile to quickly disappear. Is my eye really that bad? I briefly turn to Jamie for his opinion, but he doesn't even look like he knows where he is.

"What happened?" Mosi questions as he motions for us to sit down at one of the tables.

We do as we're told, and it's only now that we're in the light of the pub that I can see how much dried blood there is on my hand. Bit gross. On the bright side, I'm pretty sure I managed to pick out most of the glass from my eyebrow when we were walking back here.

Mosi places a stool beside me to inspect my wound. Ava has disappeared somewhere behind the bar--to get a first aid kit, I think--and Jamie sits silently on one of the chairs while Annabel watches from the booth next to us.

"Did you get into a fight?" Mosi asks, his deep voice vibrating in my ear.

"Sort of," I reply, being half honest.

"It looks a lot worse than it is, but it will need a few stitches." He looks up, and I follow his gaze to see Ava returning with a small, green bag. "I'll do that for you now. Don't worry, I am trained."

To be frank, he could be one of the drunk partygoers I picked up from the street, and I'd probably still let him do it for me. I'm too tired to care by this point. The quicker this is done, the quicker I can go to bed and pretend that none of this ever happened. Mosi zips open the small bag Ava handed him, and begins to work his magic.

A pint of orange squash, and twenty minutes of me pretending having a sharp thing digging tiny holes into my eyebrow isn't painful for the sake of reputation later, Mosi and Ava disappear behind the bar to finish clearing up.

Jamie's still said nothing, and now it's just the two of us, his silence is making things awkward. Annabel is still in the booth, but she's just as deep in thought as Jamie is. I can't believe I'm saying this, but I actually want the guy to say something. Eventually, he does. And the moment he does, I regret ever wishing it.

He lifts his eyes to my face, and speaks in a deadly flat tone. "I am not leaving here until you tell me what the hell just happened."

Chapter 19

Thankfully, I didn't end up having to tell Jamie what the hell just happened. Ava interrupted to take us home before I could answer, but I know the inevitability of having to explain myself to him is fast approaching. As such, I've been avoiding him all morning. It's not even eleven yet, and he's knocked on my bedroom door about five times, and when I headed into the kitchen for my hangover bread, I ordered Annabel to check it was empty beforehand. I know I can only ignore him for so long, but I've got no goddamn clue what I'm going to say to him. The fact my eyebrow feels like it's falling off isn't helping.

I've managed to escape the flat unnoticed to grab a well-needed full English breakfast at one of the uni cafés. Annabel and I are about to go over the shitstorm that was last night, which I refused to bring up until I had some food in me, much to her annoyance. Considering the alcohol rendered my abilities non-existent last night, I've got nothing to give anyway. We're sitting in the corner of the café, and I'm facing the wall so that no one thinks I'm having an in-depth conversation with myself.

"Right, okay, hit me with it," I say as I take the first bite of my breakfast. I go for the bacon, and it's good. It's so, so good. "What dead bastard is after me now?"

"This isn't a joke, Felix." Annabel's voice is the most serious I've ever heard it. "You've had a spirit warn you you're in danger, you're seeing flashbacks to the moment our parents died--the moment I died, you're being stalked by something demonic not even I can see, you've had your brain turned to mush by underground caves, and now you've almost been killed by a poltergeist. Something really, really bad is happening."

Jesus, way to kill the mood. I don't really know how to respond in a way that won't piss her off, so I just take another bite out of my breakfast and shrug. Turns out that's the perfect response to piss her off.

"Felix!" she snaps. "Why is everything a joke to you?"

I drop my knife and fork onto the plate and sigh. "It's not, I just--Look, let's start with last night. What happened?"

Annabel tucks her hair behind her ears and clears her throat. "Well, you were being an idiot and almost revealed to everyone that you can see spirits, so--"

"What? No, I didn't."

She shakes her head at me. "You asked Ava if there was such thing as the Ghost of Christmas Past, then proceeded to tell a story about that spirit--David, I think his name was--we ran into a few years back."

"Oh, yeah! I remember David. God, he was an ugly shit." I laugh, but Annabel just glares at me. "Oh, so was the spilled drink your doing?"

"Yeah, and the head flicking. Everything else... wasn't." I nod for her to continue. "The poltergeist was already outside when you left the building, but it wasn't... it wasn't random. I think it had been waiting for you. It wasn't in a human form or anything, just a pool of darkness like the one we saw a few years back, but I could sense it come to life when you stepped outside. I don't know why, but it didn't start attacking until Jamie appeared, it's like it... it--I don't know, wanted something from you, and then Jamie interrupted it."

"You sure?" I ask. "It might've just been a coincidence that it started attacking then."

Annabel immediately shakes her head. "It's a poltergeist, it's their instinct to mess with the first breathing thing it sees, and it didn't bother you straight away. It wanted something."

"You don't reckon it has something to do with my gangly stalkers, do you?" I ask with a mouthful of toast, to which Annabel nods as if I'm stupid. "Alright, alright, sheesh. Everything has to be connected--it has to be. I just have no idea how. Maybe we should try Ava again. She knows when you're around, so she must at least have some kind of--"

There's a tap on my shoulder, and I turn my head to see Jamie standing above me. Oh, shit.

"Who are you talking to?"

"No one..." I say far too slowly for it to sound genuine.

Jamie scoffs. Without any invitation on my part, he pulls up a chair at my table. It's the one Annabel was using, so she has to swap to another. Once he's sat down, he doesn't say anything. He just stares at me expectantly. When I ignore him and continue gnawing the hash brown I was in the middle of devouring, he scoffs again.

"You want my black pudding? Never been into that shit. Grimey as hell," I say, my eyes still fixed onto my plate.

"What happened last night?"

Straight to the point then. I ignore him.

"Maybe you should tell him the truth," Annabel pipes up, to which I shoot her a look of I'd rather chew my little toe off.

"What are you looking at?" Jamie again.

"Nothing," I reply.

"Yes you are, you just looked at that chair."

"Nah."

He bangs the table. "What happened last night?"

I groan. "I'm just as clueless as you are, mate, I don't know why you're asking me all this."

"You're lying. I'm not an idiot," he snaps. He glances at my food. "I thought you were vegetarian."

Ugh, this again. "I'm having an off day," I mutter.

Jamie scoffs. Again. "Sure you are. Last night, you knew what to do, you knew what the streetlights meant, you started talking to someone who wasn't there, and then as though there was someone there, it did exactly what you told it to." He pauses, quickly scans the room, then turns back to me. "Was it a... you know, was it a ghost?"

I stare at Jamie silently. This is one mess I'm really not sure how to get out of. I glance back to Annabel with pleading eyes in hope of her knowing what to do, but she just shrugs. She thinks I should tell him. She doesn't have to say it, I can just tell. The only other time she's given me this look is before I told my foster mother about my abilities because y'know, that went so brilliantly.

Shit, what do I do?

I doubt Jamie would believe me, come to think of it; the guy's the biggest sceptic I've ever met. I'm nineteen now too, not twelve. It's not like he can ship me back to a kid's home if he doesn't believe me. I could tell him it's a joke.

"Felix," Annabel says quietly from across the table. "Just tell him. It won't be like last time."

"Please tell me what happened." Jamie speaks up again, and there's desperation in his voice.

I take a deep breath. "It was a poltergeist," I say into my food.

"A what?"

I lift my eyes to his face. "A poltergeist."

Jamie's staring at me now. I can see a million words running through his head, but he can't get any of them out. His mouth is moving slightly, but he's making no sound. Annabel gives me an encouraging nod. Screw it, there's no turning back now. I take another deep breath, and shut my eyes as I speak because if I don't, I'll realise what I'm doing.

"I've been able to see ghosts since my parents died, the person I was speaking to last night was my sister--she's dead--and because I know you'll want proof, I can tell you that your grandmother died wearing a red dressing gown and white slippers, and she was found in her house because you tried calling her but got no answer." I open my eyes, then turn to Annabel. "And that salt shaker is going to fall over."

As if perfectly rehearsed, Annabel knocks over the salt in the middle of our table. Now Jamie really looks scared. All I can do is wait. Adrenaline is shooting through my body, and I'm rhythmically tapping my foot under the table. What the hell am I doing?

"Was that why you told me to call my family the day she died?" is all Jamie says. He's not looking at me; he's staring emptily at the table.

It takes me a moment to realise he's talking about his grandmother. I say yes.

"You saw her that day." He says it as a statement, but I can hear the question in his voice, so I say yes again.

Finally, Jamie lifts his eyes to my face. He remains silent for a while, and he's gazing at me like he doesn't want to miss a single move I make. Annabel's watching him, and she looks just as anxious as me. He's not told me I'm wrong, or that I'm a liar, or that I'm insane. I think that's a good thing.

He's still not saying anything. I've lost my entire family to a car crash, been left to deal with the fact I see dead people alone since I can remember, spent the past few months being stalked by evil entities, and been attacked by a poltergeist, yet this is the most scared I think I've ever felt. Say something, I repeat in my head over and over again. Say something.

Finally, Jamie speaks. "I think I believe in ghosts now."

Jamie doesn't say anything else for the remainder of the time we're at the café. He's not left my side, but his mouth has stayed shut the whole time. It's a nice change, really. When I mention going back to the flat, he still says nothing. He just nods. Ava's moving back in for good in a few days, and no one else is returning for at least a week, so it's just Jamie and me in the flat.

In ways, I'm pleased because at least I know he's not going to be able to run around announcing my confession to anyone. Nonetheless, this is the most awkward thing I've ever experienced in my life because he's not taking his eyes off me for a second. I could probably go for a shit, and he'd follow me. I'm trying to revise in the kitchen, but I can feel him staring at me.

After about an hour of pretending I don't notice him stalking me, Jamie finally speaks.

"Does Ava know?" he asks quietly.

I shake my head.

"Have you told Carmen?" is his next question.

I shake my head again.

"How about--"

"I've not told anyone else."

Jamie's quiet again, but not for long. "Was your sister killed in the same accident as your parents?"

I sigh. I think I preferred it when things were awkward. I close the textbook I was reading, then swivel around on the kitchen stool to face Jamie. It's not like I was getting anything done anyway. I nod at him with a shrug. He nods back, slowly.

He's about to open his mouth, but pauses briefly as his eyes narrow. He eventually remembers how to speak. "Is your sister here now then?" He says it like he's scared Annabel is going to lob him at a wall or something.

Annabel, who is indeed here, and is currently lying on the sofa opposite him, perks up at the mention of her existence. She's trying to downplay it for my sake, but I can tell she's ecstatic at the prospect of someone else finally becoming aware of her. She's asked me if I want her to do anything spooky around Jamie at least five times since we left the café. She's saying it's to convince him further, but she knows as well as I do that he doesn't need any more convincing.

"Yeah," I mutter with another shrug. Still need to work on my shrugging problem.

Jamie stammers. "Can she see us? Is she watching?"

It's hard not to laugh at him, so I do. Only a tiny bit. It's kind of like when you play peek-a-boo with a little kid and they think that if they can't see you, you can't see them. It just sounds like such a dumb question to me. Annabel finds it just as amusing as I do, and turns to me with a mischievous look in her eyes. I hesitate, but eventually roll my eyes and nod. Go hard or go home, and all that.

Before Jamie can process why I'm pulling faces into thin air, Annabel grins in glee, jumps off the sofa, skips over to him, then flicks him hard on the back of his head. I'm laughing before he even feels it.

"Ow! What--what did you do?"

"Hey, I didn't do anything," I reply, still snickering.

I'm rapidly warming to this whole idea of revealing my darkest secrets. This is great. As Jamie continues stuttering like a fish having a stroke, it slowly occurs to me what I've done. I don't know what I expected to happen if I ever told anyone about this stuff, but it wasn't this. We're still in shallow water at the moment, I'm not ignorant of that, but I feel okay about it. Hell, I feel kind of good about it.

Part of me wants to sit down with Jamie and tell him everything; about Annabel, about all the ghosts I've encountered in the past, about my visions that accompany aura readings, about the creatures that have been stalking me, about the ghosts I saw at the haunted manor we visited, about the weird experience I had in the underground caves.

I've never been able to utter a word about any of this to anyone, so knowing that if I wanted to now, I could, is a surreal feeling. I know I'm getting carried away with these thoughts, so I don't allow them to spill out of my mouth. It's just weird. I've never experienced this situation, and I'm at a loss with what to do with it. My train of thought is interrupted by Jamie, who's finally recovered from Annabel's abuse.

"When are you going to tell everyone else?" he asks.

Now I'm the one looking shit scared. This may have gone better than expected, but no way in hell am I ready to do that. I need at least another ten years.

I manage to convince Jamie to keep my secret to himself. Mainly through threats. I told him I'd instruct Annabel to summon evil spirits to curse him if he told a soul about what I can do. He shit himself. So that was funny. He's asked some pretty dumb questions so far. Do they float and walk through walls? being one of my personal favourites. I didn't realise people actually thought that shit. Messing with him is the best, though. He asked me something about if spirits can read minds, so I told him they could, just for the shits and giggles. He constantly looks like he's on edge now, it's brilliant.

It turns out he's actually quite a valuable asset. I've not revealed everything, but I've hinted that there may be something weird going on, and that our run in with the poltergeist isn't the first shady thing to have happened recently. He read Ava's book on spirits within three days, and is on a constant internet search to find out more about life after death. He even thinks he's found what my stalker friends are, and he might be onto something. He reckons they're these things called Trackers.

Their appearance isn't known, so we can't guess based on that, but the online forum post Jamie found defines them as creatures formed of the remnants of disfigured souls created to locate stranded spirits and/or enemies in order to aid in furthering the agenda of dark forces, and eliminate potential interferences. Their name is literally a synonym for stalker, which they one-hundred percent are, and the spirit at the manor mentioned their usual task being locating spirits, so it sounds close enough. Plus I've always been a bit of an interference.

I'm silently hoping that the so-called dark forces consist of the one poltergeist we ran into the other night, and that it stops there. This poltergeist has a vendetta against me because I was rude to it five years ago or something, so the bastard has sent out some Trackers to find me. It finally got to me, and we evaded it, and we're all going to live happily ever after.

I'm about ninety-nine percent sure that's utter bullshit, but that's the theory I'm rolling with to make myself feel better about the probability that something is out to murder me. The fact it didn't immediately attack me outside the pub suggests something more complex, and as Jamie pointed out the other day, one of the first things Ava noted about the paranormal is that even those with abilities can't physically see the dead. The fact I can might spell bad news for me.

But I'm remaining optimistic. I'm sure everything is fine and I'm definitely not going to be dead by the time my first year of university is over.

Chapter 20

I've been so wrapped up in all this ghost drama that on the day of my first exam, I forget it's the day of my first exam. It's not until Tom asks me if he can borrow a pen for his own exam that I remember. He lost all of his over Christmas, apparently. Not quite sure how that happens, but I didn't dare question it because I'd only be bombarded with some weird, elaborate story.

He dyed his hair red over the holiday, which he explained to me was in honour of the festive season, despite the fact he did it about a week after Christmas. It's better than the badly bleached blonde it was before, I guess. Sort of. Everyone has moved back in now other than Carmen, and maybe Mason. He's not made an appearance, but he doesn't show his face during term time either. He could've been home all through the holidays, for all I know.

I don't even really think about the exam much while I'm taking it. It's for my hydraulics module, and thankfully, I find this crap quite easy. Annabel offers to cheat for me a few times throughout the hour and a half, and while I appreciate the gesture, I decline.

I got her to check through my notes, which contained the answer to a question I was stuck on in my Spanish GCSE exam once, and I've felt like a fraud ever since. I feel confident enough with how it went without Annabel's aid anyway. I don't think I've gotten a first or anything, but I can't see me having failed. I can't say I really care, to be perfectly honest. I've got a fair few distractions at the moment.

I go to the student bar at The Cavern after the exam, and order myself a whisky and coke. I've only been to this place three or four times, and I'm not really sure why. There's a really chilled atmosphere, and the booths they have here are the comfiest things I've ever planted my arse on. The music played is based on request too, and because it's pretty quiet here at the moment as it's still morning, I'm basically choosing every song. It smells slightly of syrup and stale beer mats, and the colour theme centres around a blinding hot pink and purple, but I guess it adds character to the place.

There should probably be some alarm bells ringing in my head over the fact I'm in a bar drinking alone at eleven in the morning, but hey, we all have our flaws. I promise Annabel I'm not getting drunk or anything, but based on the fact she's sitting opposite me with a face like thunder suggests she doesn't completely trust me.

It just feels like I've hit a brick wall, like I should be doing something about all of these weird occurrences, but what? It's not exactly something you can just Google. The only option I can think of is to return to the haunted manor and find that female spirit. She seemed to have a decent idea of how things work in the afterlife. I groan as I lower my head onto the sticky table, and become one with the peanut crumbs and beer stains.

"Exam went well then?"

A voice startles me, and when I lift my head back up to see Carmen standing over my booth, I start stuttering like a deranged broken record. I don't know if I'm only noticing this because I've not seen her for over three weeks, but she has a glow about her. Her hair is pulled up into some kind of ponytail or braid or something, but a strand has fallen out and is tucked messily behind her ear. There's a dimple in her cheek as she smirks at me. I forgot how much I fancied her. Well shit. Another thing to add to my current car crash of a life.

"If it's any consolation, the inevitability of my exam failure is driving me insane. Turns out putting up Christmas decorations and getting drunk on toffee cider most nights is far more fun than revising Portuguese grammar," Carmen says as she sits down opposite me.

"Sounds better than my holiday of not trying to murder Jamie in his sleep," I argue.

"Touché. I'm surprised you both made it to January alive, actually." She reaches over to my drink, then takes a sip, only for her face to contort into a look of pain. "Holy--You do realise it's not even midday yet, right?"

"I have sorrows to drown," I mutter. "You owe me five pence for that sip, by the way."

She raises her eyebrows at me challengingly as she bites her lip to fight a smile off her face, and I don't know if it's because I've not had any female contact for several weeks, but it's kind of hot. Not wanting to show any sign of weakness, I raise my own eyebrows in return and reach my hand out to Carmen. The grin that's been trying to break itself onto her lips finally appears, and she reaches into her jacket pocket to bring out a ten pence coin. She drops it into my hand.

"Keep the change." She winks.

"Hey," Annabel says out of nowhere, and I glance at her. I forgot she was sitting with us. "Yeah, hey. Hi. I'm here, just to remind you. I'd rather not watch you blatantly flirt with each other over the table, thanks."

I ignore her, then proceed to throw the coin Carmen gave me back at her. She manages to smack it away, and it rolls onto the floor, but neither of us bother to pick it back up. Annabel groans, then swiftly vanishes. She's such a prude. I'm about to ask Carmen what time she got here when a waiter approaches the table with a basket of chips, and places them in-between us.

"Feel free to take some. I figured you needed some food in you considering you looked on the verge of a breakdown when I spotted you in here," Carmen says to me after thanking the waiter. She grabs a chips and throws it into her mouth. "D'you know why this place is called The Cavern?" she asks, to which I shake my head. "The city's underground caves run underneath the uni, and apparently, there's an entrance to them in here somewhere."

"Really?" I ask, genuinely interested. "That's pretty cool."

"You and your caves," she says with an eye roll. "My mum sends her love, by the way. I think she fancies you. Our pseudo relationship can't break down, she'll be ruined. Well, either that or she'll use it as her opportunity to nab you while you're on the market."

"That's cool with me, she's hot," I reply as I grab a chip from the red basket.

Carmen smacks my hand away, but it's too late. I throw the chip into my mouth and flash her a cheesy grin, accompanied by a mouth full of food.

"You're actually disgusting," she says as she fights back a cringe.

I'm kind of over the moon that she appeared this morning. Without even being aware of herself doing it, she has this faultless ability to de-stress me, which temporarily fools me into thinking I'm not some mutated dead person therapist when I'm around her. I take another chip from the table because I can feel a headache creeping on, and I figure it must be because I've not eaten yet today. They're kind of soggy, and are a little too much on the salty side, but I'm too hungry to care.

"You all right?" Carmen asks me as I'm finishing off the chips, to which I respond with a questioning look. She nods at my hands. "You keep moving your hands about."

Do I? They do feel a little weird, like I have pins and needles. I must be doing it subconsciously or something. I brush it off to Carmen, but she doesn't look completely convinced. The food hasn't improved my headache much either, but it's hardly unbearable, so I just ignore it. It isn't until Carmen is in the middle of a story about how her uncle got really drunk really early on New Year's Eve, and ended up passing out in their local pub's bathroom by seven, that I realise what's going on.

Please no.

My eyes are on Carmen, and I really don't want to look outside the booth, but I'm going to have to. Besides, I might be wrong. I might just be paranoid. I swallow, then turn my head, and standing solitarily against the wall opposite us is a Tracker.

Nah, screw this guy. I'm not dealing with this right now.

"I'm just gonna pop to the toilet," I say, interrupting Carmen, only to apologise for interrupting her and looking like a dick in the process.

I rush to the toilet at the other end of the bar with my head down. I doubt avoiding eye contact makes much of a difference, but I'll just pretend it does to make me feel better. Even if it does, I've already looked directly at the thing. The gents is empty when I enter. The Tracker doesn't seem to have followed me, so that's something.

I have a pee I don't even really need to try and calm myself, only for a guy to come in and use the urinal right next to mine. There are plenty available at the other end, which just makes things worse. I'm gazing at my reflection in the mirror when my new friend leaves, and I'm deathly pale. My vision is a little blurry from my headache, but even then, I can see how crap I look.

I'm in dire need of a shave and a haircut, and the artificial lighting in the bathroom seems to highlight the only scar I have from my parents' accident. It cuts through my left eyebrow, stopping any hair from growing there. I've still got a mark on my other eyebrow from the New Year's poltergeist assault too. God, I look rough.

As I lift my eyes back up from washing my hands, I jump. It's there. Behind me. I can't be arsed for this anymore. I really, really can't. I inhale a sharp intake of breath, briefly shut my eyes, then turn around to face the creature. It's about five feet away from me.

"What d'you want?" I ask dumbly. It says nothing. Just stares at me with its black irises. "Look, mate, can we just cut to the chase here? I can't be bothered for your creepy arse anymore, and to put it bluntly, you're annoying. Really, really annoying."

It tilts its head, then manifests closer to me. Not by much--no more than a foot. It doesn't say anything. Surprise, surprise.

"If you want something, you can ask me, y'know. It'll save us both a lot of stress," I continue, to no reply.

The Tracker shifts forward again. It's pretty much standing right in front of me by now. I'm not sure if it's because I'm used to the feeling, but the pain that usually comes with these things is nowhere near as strong as it was before. My head still aches, but it's more of a numb throbbing now.

I stare at the creature, and push against it with my mind like I did at the manor house. That's easier now too. As the need to give one more push niggles at the back of my neck, I stop myself. I don't want to vanquish this thing. I want an explanation.

"Look mate, I'm pretty sure I can get rid of you easy, so let's compromise here," I announce. "You give me some idea of what the hell is going on here, and I won't send your arse back to where it came from. Deal?"

My headache subsides briefly, and I think it might have finally gotten its thick head around what I'm trying to say, but it doesn't speak. It does nothing. Just keeps staring. If anything, its unnaturally downturned mouth lifts the slightest bit. Then its arm shoots out, touches my shoulder, and it burns. It's like a knife has been thrust into my collarbone, as shockwaves of pain tear down through the rest of my body, and before I even realise it's happening, everything is black.

When I wake up, I'm not in the bathroom anymore. I'm somewhere familiar. There are arms around me, hair in my face. I can't see anything. I don't know how I know I've been here before, I just do. It smells of sweat and perfume, and the scent is so familiar that it almost winds me, but I don't understand what it is. There's screaming. There's a voice in my ear, a voice trying to soothe me. It's muffled, but I know I recognise it. I know this situation; I just can't remember it.

After a few minutes, I manage to poke my eye through a gap in the arms around me. I see leaves, branches. We're in a bush. Are we hiding? What are we hiding from? There's a lot of flashing light, but there's darkness. Deep, black darkness. They're both appearing in bursts. I shuffle around to get a better look, but the arms around me hold me still.

"Felix, just stay! Don't look at them!"

I know that voice. I know whose arms are wrapped around me. Annabel. I say her name but the words aren't leaving my mouth. I can't make any sound. I try again, and nothing. It's like I'm stuck in a body I have no control over. Just as it's beginning to feel like I'm trapped in a recurring nightmare, a sudden flurry of blackness is shot in our direction.

Annabel picks me up, and we run out of the bushes onto a road, barely missing the attack. I'm momentarily confused. How is she holding me? She's almost a foot shorter than me. Then I remember this isn't real, and when it was real, I was an eight-year-old kid while she was a sixteen-year-old girl.

We're crouched behind a car now. Our family car. There's a man sitting in the driver's seat, and his eyes are open but I don't think he's alive, and I think he's my father because he's wearing a jacket I've seen my father wear in photos, except its bloodstained now and he's not smiling like he does in the photos.

I can barely breathe, and I don't think it's eight-year-old me who's struggling. Where's our mother? Is this before my past visions? It has to be. Annabel is alive. We're still crouched behind the car, and there's more light than dark now. I think that's good. I don't know. Annabel doesn't let go of me.

I'm looking up at my dad. I don't know why, but I can't stop, and I don't know if it's present or past day me gazing at him. He looks so real.

"Felix! Run!" Annabel suddenly screams, her voice breaking.

It all happens before I can even process it. I snap my head to my sister, and Annabel pushes me away from the car. She pushes too hard, so I stumble to the ground, and when I look back at her, all I see is darkness where she was, and then her body is being thrown into the air like a rag doll, and she's lying on the car bonnet and her eyes are open, but she's not there.

Hands grab me from under my arms, and I'm flying. Then I'm back on the ground, and it's damp and cold, and I'm looking into my mother's eyes. She's crying. She's telling me not to look at something, and it's like a sick game of déjà vu. This is where my visions usually start.

I need it to keep going. I want it to end, I don't want to see this anymore, but I need it to keep going. I need to understand. I'm watching Annabel. Her eyes are parted open slightly, but she's not moved. I can't see my father from here. The bright lights are increasing. If this is some kind of battle, I think they're winning.

There's a light-headedness buzzing through my body. My eyelids feel heavy. No. No, no, no. I have to stay here. I try to force myself to stay present, but as each second passes, I can feel myself slipping out of this dream. Everything becomes more and more distorted and hazy, and there's nothing.

Moments later, I'm back in the bathroom. I'm on the floor, and my back is leaning against the tiled wall. There's a guy crouched over me, and he's saying something but my ears are ringing, so I can't hear him. I think he's asking me for my name. I say it anyway, then mutter something about a migraine. He looks like another student because he has a young face, but he's got the bar uniform on. I think he's a waiter here.

The guy nods. "Are you with anyone here?" he asks, to which I nod, then mutter something about Carmen. "Ah, I know, table fourteen. Wait here."

I don't even notice him leaving, but the guy's gone. My head is throbbing, and I feel sick. I'm shaking. I blink my eyes to clear my vision, but it doesn't help much. There's a female voice, and I assume it's Carmen, but quickly realise it's not. It's too high-pitched.

"Felix? Hey... Hey, say something." Annabel.

The image of her on the car bonnet flashes through my mind.

"Felix? You're freaking me out now, what happened? Did that thing hurt you?"

She touches my face with her palm, and it's warm and soothing. She gives every other living thing a shiver down their spine, but to me, she's always warm. I immediately feel better.

Her wide eyes are boring into mine, and she looks older than I've ever seen her. Her dark hair frames her oval face, and I have this overwhelming desire for her to look after me. I've not properly seen her as my older sister for a long time, but right now, that's exactly what she feels like.

"Annabel," I finally manage to say quietly. "Mum didn't sacrifice your life for mine. You did."

Chapter 21

By the time we arrive back at the flat, I feel like a spring chicken again. That was by far the most extreme reaction I'd had to one of those things--I assume because I had physical contact with the creep--and I was a little anxious I'd end up maimed for life. But hey, I feel fine.

Carmen's eyes were glued to me the whole walk home, and I almost had to physically restrain her from calling a cab to take us back because she was worried I would, I don't know, start foaming from the mouth or something. Once we're inside I flop myself onto one of the sofas, which is now ten times lumpier than it was at the beginning of the academic year, while Carmen stands over the kitchen island. She's still watching me carefully.

"I'm not gonna die, I promise," I joke, to which she rolls her eyes.

"Have you been to the doctors about these migraines?" she questions, half ignoring my comment.

I shrug, but follow it with a yeah because I figure that's probably the best response to give. Carmen nods, but her lip twitches slightly while her eyes narrow. I'm pretty sure she doesn't believe me, which unnerves me a bit because I'm usually quite the liar.

After pouring a glass of water, she wanders over and sits beside me on the sofa, then gestures it to me. I raise my eyebrows at her, which she challenges with a smirk and another shove of the glass in my direction. I decide to humour her, so take it from her hands, and down the water in the matter of seconds.

"You should've done a medical degree, you're on the way to curing cancer here, mate," I say with the cheesiest of grins, ensuring to make my sarcasm obvious.

"Oh, piss off." Carmen punches my side.

"Hey, screw you, I take that back," I mutter, rubbing my ribs.

"Seriously, Felix, you should get it checked out," she replies, the joking tone in her voice having disappeared completely. "Even if you have genuinely been before. It's not right."

Annabel has appeared by now, and probably for the first time ever, I actually want Carmen to be the one to leave. I say something about going to have a nap, which seems to please Carmen, and head into my bedroom. Once inside, Annabel hits me with the avalanche of questions I expected.

She asks what I saw in the vision, if what was happening was before or after my previous visions, how she saved my arse, what I saw of Dad, of Mum. Everything, really. Once answered, Annabel is quiet for a long time. So long, in fact, that by the time she speaks again, I'm lying on my bed on the edge of sleep.

"Good and bad spirits," she says, snapping me out of my doze.

"Huh?" I question, still lying down.

"The light and darkness you see in your visions. It's obvious. We're imbeciles for not realising it before."

"What, you think it was some kind of battle between good and bad dead guys?" I ask, to which Annabel nods. "That's some Harry Potter type shit. Why though?"

"That I don't know."

Annabel opens her mouth and looks like she's about to say something else, but quickly snaps it shut. Her eyebrows furrow, and her thinking face is switched on. I'm still feeling kind of hazy after my partial nap, so shut my eyes again without really thinking much about what Annabel just said. In fact, after a minute or two, I start forgetting what it was she even said. Something about dead people, I don't know.

"What if you could always do this?" she pipes up again, and this time, I sit up.

"Huh?"

Annabel rolls her eyes at me. "See spirits," she replies like I'm dumb. "We've always assumed the crash is what sparked your abilities, but what if it's your abilities that sparked the crash?"

I stare at Annabel then, for a while. No, that can't be right. People can't just be born able to do this shit, surely? Well, according to Ava they can, but we've kind of disproved the accuracy of her claims. This crap being bestowed on me after a life altering accident just seems like the obvious answer.

I shake my head. "I dunno, Annie, seems a bit far fetched, doesn't seem--"

"Felix, you see dead people, is this possibility really that hard to believe? Think about it," she says, her voice tinted with what I can make out to be either excitement or anxiety. "If your abilities were a result of the crash, how come you can see these spirits in your visions? I know these visions are technically after the crash, but I think it's obvious by now that the accident didn't just knock us all out, and bam, dead--or in your case, unconscious. Surely your abilities wouldn't have magically appeared midway through the accident, y'know? It just--"

"Yeah, but in those visions, I see things as present day me... I mean, I'll have the desire to say something, or move, or whatever, but I can't, so consciously it's me now, and present day me has this mutated ability. It's probably just that," I reason, but Annabel begins shaking her head aggressively. She's pacing around my room now.

"No, no. The only thing that's said throughout your whole vision is don't look at them. I say it to you, Mum says it to you. You can obviously see the spirits, and it's obviously something you've always been capable of because if it happened as a result of the crash, Mum and I would have no idea about what you were seeing."

Hm. She kind of has a point there. What if the things I see in my vision aren't spirits, though? This theory is based entirely around that, and they don't look like what I'm used to seeing. What else could they be though, realistically? Before our conversation can develop any further, there's a knock on my bedroom door. Begrudgingly, I lift myself off my bed to answer it. Standing there is Carmen, with a somewhat confused look on her face.

"So I was just talking to Adam--a friend of mine on your course, not sure if you know him--and you do know you have an exam in twenty minutes, right?"

Oh, shit.

I completely forgot I had two exams today, holy shit. In a mad dash, I scramble my stuff together as Carmen watches from the doorway. Bloody hell, I'm an idiot. I shove the stuff I need into my bag, probably damaging half of it. Crap, where is my student card? I search my desk but find nothing, so hastily scan the rest of my room in hope of it appearing, only for my eyes to stop in the doorway to see Ava now standing with Carmen.

"Ava said she'll drive you, don't worry," Carmen quickly explains, to which Ava shoots me a smile. "But, I mean, if you're still not feeling great, maybe give it a miss. You can apply for extenuating circumstances, or just take a resit or--"

I shake my head and wave it off. "No, it's fine--I'm fine, just literally forgot."

Carmen doesn't look convinced, while Ava hums beside her, twirling her car keys around her pinky finger. After finally locating my student card under my bed, I hurry out of the flat into Ava's car, and already know this exam is going to go badly.

Once I'm in the exam hall, I realise it's not just going to go badly, but horrifically because all I can think about is the conversation Annabel and I had before leaving. If she's right--if those things in my vision are spirits, and if I could see them regardless of the accident, I really am the reason my whole family is dead.

The exam goes as predicted, as does the next one. And the next one. And the one after that. I'm not even relieved once they're all over. I don't really care enough about them, to be honest. After Annabel's revelation about my visions, I don't have much interest in anything else. It's all I can think about, day in, day out. I killed them. It's that simple. If I could see spirits before the accident, I killed them. My family are dead because of what I can do.

I know things are bad because throughout the exam period, I have some days where I can't see Annabel. I become a bit of a recluse in general, really, initially blaming it on the need to focus on exams. By the time we're halfway through February though, I can't really use it as an excuse, and people are starting to notice.

One thing I can't ignore is that either my telekinetic abilities have increased, or my mood swings are messing with them completely. I've gone from struggling to nudge a pencil on a desk to sitting in bed feeling like the biggest sack of shit, when all of a sudden, my chair violently wheels across the room.

One time, I was even in the kitchen with a few flatmates, and in my mopey mood, made a cupboard door that was open slam shut. That scared them shitless, except for Ava, who just looked amused. She didn't seem to suspect anything, though. To think, I'd almost given up on the whole telekinetic thing. It's just a shame it seems to have sparked up when I couldn't give less of a shit.

I'm meant to be going to a house party at Ava's house tonight, and the only reason I agreed to it was to get my flatmates off my case. I've not socialised much outside the flat since New Year's, and I've been asked if everything is alright several times by most of them--even Tom, so I'm pretty sure they think I'm depressed or something.

It's starting to irritate me, so hopefully showing my face at this party will get them to quit it. Exam results were released today, so it's meant to be a celebratory party for that, but I've not looked at mine. Don't really want to. I can see Annabel all okay today, so I'm not planning on drinking tonight--don't want to ruin that.

Ava, Carmen, Tom and Jamie share Ava's car, while I somehow end up lumped in Katie's boyfriend's car with the infamous couple. Well, in fairness, I volunteered in the sense that the last thing I'm in the mood for right now is Tom's over excited rambling. Katie's boyfriend is blasting chart music while she takes hold of his hand that isn't on the wheel, so naturally, I assume we're going to crash any second now. At least I have some practice in that department.

Katie begins singing along to the music, and it's awful. Really goddamn awful. I still don't even know this guy's name. Midway through the drive to Ava's house, Katie throws a tantrum over her boyfriend's refusal to play a certain song, and stops speaking to him until we get there. So that's nice.

I'm so eager to escape the couple that I practically fall out of the car once we arrive, and Annabel stands beside me grinning madly at my displeasure. She's lucky; she can escape this kind of shit without question whenever she wants. As we enter Ava's house, I notice it's busier than I thought it'd be.

It's all Ava's family friends at the moment, but we've all invited a few coursemates and crap like that. Well, except for me. I couldn't be arsed to ask anyone, and don't tend to socialise with them outside uni anyway. Two of the downstairs bathrooms, the living room, the kitchen, and a second lounge area are open for party guests, so to begin with, we all awkwardly stand around the unnecessarily large kitchen while Ava greets all of her family friends. I'm already wishing I'd not come.

Chapter 22

B y the time nine rolls around, the house has filled with a lot more people our age. Carmen and Ava are having an in-depth conversation about who knows what with some old guy who's friends with Ava's dad, Katie and her boyfriend are probably off sucking face somewhere, Tom is god knows where speaking to god knows who, while I'm sitting on one of the living room sofas as Jamie rambles on about something to do with dead people. I'm not really listening.

Annabel's with us, and she's processing every word he's saying, so I'm sure she'll keep me up to date on any revelations. Despite its impressive size, the room feels cramped, and the heat from the roaring fireplace opposite me is just making me feel tired, so I excuse myself and make my way towards one of the available bathrooms. Annabel goes to follow me, but I subtly shake her away.

To my dismay, both bathrooms are occupied, so as I pass the living room Jamie's not in and spot a pair of patio doors, I decide to just head into the back garden instead. It's not like I actually need to go, I just want some peace and quiet for a bit. Obviously, the garden is something out of Alan Titchmarsh's wet dreams.

It's enormous, to begin with, and if it wasn't dark, the bushes and flowers that fill the place would be bursting with colour. There's a cobbled path swerving in and out of the shrubbery, which is highlighted by small lamps running alongside it. In the centre of the garden is a large, wooden gazebo, which casts a big shadow over one corner of the garden.

Sculptures adorn the place, popping up randomly with no obvious pattern or shape, just the odd water feature here, the odd cherub there; one of which is positioned in a way that makes it look like it's pissing into one of the flower bushes. I probably shouldn't laugh at that, yet here I am smirking to myself, alone in the darkness of Ava's garden.

"In need of some fresh air?" a voice suddenly asks from my side, and I almost wet myself.

I turn to my right to see four sofas--actual sofas, not garden furniture--facing each other on a wooden patio area, one of which is being used by Kato, Ava's mother. She's sitting on it, her legs crossed, with a cigarette dangling in-between her fingers.

I stammer. "Uh, sorry--I, yeah, sorry, I felt a bit ill," I lie.

She waves me over, and being the absolute idiot I am, I glance around to check it's me she's gesturing towards. Of course it's you. There's no one else here, you idiot. I sit beside her on the long, plush sofa as she shoots me a soft smile, and offers me a cigarette. I don't smoke, never have unless I've been mindlessly drunk, but agree out of what I perceive to be politeness.

I pretend to know what I'm doing and light it, then proceed to pretend it's not making me want to choke. I hate myself. So much.

We both sit in silence, and I'm not sure if it actually is uncomfortable or if I just think it is, so I avoid any kind of eye contact with Kato as I silently will my cigarette to burn out.

"There's a great deal concerning you at the moment, isn't there?" she asks with no pre-warning, as she exhales a breath of smoke.

Naturally, I don't reply as any sane human would with a no I'm fine, or a shake of the head, or a shrug. I just do nothing. Literally just look at her.

Kato smiles softly. "My guide--guardian angel, if you will. It's not quite as accurate as it would be if I were to do it, but he can see auras." She takes a drag of her cigarette. "Yours concerns him."

I'm really not in the mood for this mystic bullshit right now. I don't know what I expected, really, attending a house party at Ava's house. I take a drag of my own cigarette in hope that I've gotten used to the taste, but I haven't, so try my best not to outwardly gag. Being well trained in the art of sniffing out ghost-related conversation, Annabel is soon beside me.

"I'm a bit stressed with uni, I guess, it's probably that," I say in an attempt to shrug it off. "What's--I mean, what do you mean, guardian angel?"

"Every human is born with one; it's exactly as you see it in films and literature, really. They're spirits who dedicate their existence to protecting and caring for a member of the living."

"And you can see--I mean, communicate with them?"

Kato nods. "Everyone with abilities can to a degree--though we can't communicate with the guides of others."

I smell bullshit. I've never spoken to some spirit guide in my life. The only possibility of that is Annabel, and she provides about as much protection as a pair of armbands in the middle of a tsunami.

Not forgetting the fact she was still alive herself for the first eight years of my life.

"Cool," I say with a nod, finally stubbing out my cigarette.

Can't help but wonder where the hell these guardian angels were as my parents and sister were brutally murdered. Annabel seems fascinated, though. She asks me to question whether or not regular spirits can see guides because she can't see Kato's, apparently. If Kato wasn't sitting opposite me, I'd tell Annabel that's because it's total bullshit. It may partially be because I've been in this shitty mood recently, but I'm beginning to feel a little irritated by Ava and her family's fantasy stories.

"Please do look after yourself," Kato says as she turns her body to face me. "The one thing our guides can't protect us from is our own mind."

She flashes another gentle smile, squeezes my hand, kind of just stares at me for a few seconds, then stands up and makes her way back into the house. I'm pretty sure she just told me to see a therapist. I watch as Kato's long, airy skirt disappears into the house, then sit back into the sofa, willing it to eat me alive. I sigh.

"She's right, you know," Annabel says in a tone that's way too serious. "I really do worry sometimes, Felix. With all this stuff crazy stuff recently, and you seeing what happened during the crash. It sounds horrible."

I shut my eyes and sigh again. "It's not--I'm fine, honestly it's not a big--"

"Felix!"

Great. I turn my attention towards the patio doors, and Katie is standing there with an enormous grin on her face as she lifts her arms into the air, a glass of wine in one of her hands. I don't think I've ever seen anyone so excited to see me. She squeals--literally makes a noise that sounds like a mouse's mating call--and runs towards me to sit on the sofa, spilling half her wine in the process.

"Oops! Oh shit, sorry!" she exclaims right in my ear, momentarily deafening me, as she wipes my arm where some of the wine has spilled. "How are you? You okay? How come you're not drinking? Jakey is being such a dick tonight, did you see him in the car? All I wanted was a song!"

I'm really not in the mood for this right now. I'm really, really not. Also, Jakey? I'm a little sick in my mouth. Annabel is laughing at me from the sofa opposite as Katie continues speaking at a pace I can barely keep up with.

"He doesn't like my hair tonight either, he's so fussy. I wish he was more relaxed like you. You're relaxed, aren't you? Yeah, you are, you so are. I didn't even try super hard with it--my hair, but that's not what matters, y'know?" Give me strength. "Do you think it looks nice? Do you think it's pretty?"

"Uh, yeah, sure," I mutter through a shrug, in hope it'll contribute to her not talking so loudly in my ear.

A grin bursts onto Katie's pale face. "See! You're so, so, so much nicer than Jakey, I wish I had a boyfriend like you!"

For some bizarre reason, she then proceeds to wrap her arms around me in a hug that, for a small, skinny girl, is considerably constricting. Annabel is laughing like crazy by now, and I'm glad that at least someone can see the light in the situation. I try nudging Katie off me, but it just makes her squeeze tighter, and she rests her head on my shoulder.

"You're so nice," she says into my chest. "Jakey won't even have sex with me unless I have some make-up on, he's so mean. I bet you wouldn't do that, would you?"

Okay, I really don't remember reaching this degree of closeness to the girl. Before I have the chance to inform her that no, I'd not have sex with her with or without make-up because among other things, she clearly has some deep-rooted issues, she suddenly shoots her head back up off my chest, her eye make-up now smudged from burying herself into my jumper, and quite literally smashes her face into mine.

I would say that she kisses me, but when I immediately pull away, she just goes in for a second try while tightening her grip on me, so it's honestly more of an assault than a kiss.

"Do you guys want any--"

At the sound of another voice, Katie finally lets me free, and I'm so busy trying to compose myself and get my air back having had it all sucked out of me just then, that it takes me longer than it should to realise who's interrupted us.

"Uh, sorry--Yeah, uh, do you want anything to eat? Kato and Mosi have opened the buffet." Carmen.

Her eyes are locked in our direction, but they're focused solely on anything other than my face. She's biting the inside of her cheeks, and I don't think I've ever heard her voice sound so robotic. Katie squeals. Again.

"Oh, yes please! I'm starving!" She giggles, then turns back to me briefly. "Don't tell Jake!"

She spins back around, jumps up, skips past Carmen, and heads back into the house without another word. Before returning indoors herself, Carmen stands there for a few seconds with a look on her face that makes me feel like what would happen if Satan and every serial killer in history had a love child.

Chapter 23

I t takes me longer than it should to get up and chase after Carmen. There are a lot less people in the lounge area now because
I'm assuming most have headed into the kitchen to get food. There's
no sign of Carmen in said kitchen though, so after quickly scanning
it, I try the main living room. Jamie and Tom are in here, the latter
of which shoots me a grin and hurries towards me. I don't have time
for this.

"There you are!" he exclaims, the dark liquid in his cup almost
tipping out of it and onto the perfectly cream carpet. "Jamie was
worried you'd fallen off the roof or something, but I--"

"Yeah, hey, have you seen Carmen?"

Tom responds with a pout. "Dude, c'mon, lighten up a little," he
says through a groan as Jamie joins us in the doorway. "You've been
way too serious lately, almost as bad as him." He jabs his finger
towards Jamie, who responds by muttering something under his
breath.

"Sorry, exams probably," I mutter, "have you seen--"

"Mate, they finished, like, three weeks--"

"Have you seen Carmen?"

"I just saw her with Ava in the hallway, I think," Jamie pipes in, finally providing me with useful information.

I thank him, then leave the room. If Ava and Carmen were in the hallway, they're definitely not anymore. I scan the kitchen and then the lounge area one more time, but there's no sign of Ava, let alone Carmen. Finally accepting that I've astronomically failed in my attempt to redeem myself, I head back into the lounge area and leave the house via the patio doors again, and there she is.

Shrouded by a hooded jacket ten times her size, Carmen sits on one of the sofas with her phone in one hand, and a half empty wine glass in the other. Being the imbecile I am, I don't say anything, I just stand outside the patio doors in silence. I'm not sure if she's seen me.

"You going to say something, or?" Annabel chimes in beside me, scaring me half to death.

I shoot her a glare, and am about to grow some balls and indeed say something when Carmen speaks.

"I figured you'd not think to come back outside." She doesn't lift her head to look at me, and her voice is barely audible over the music playing in the house. "Didn't quite work, obviously."

I go to speak, but apparently have forgotten how to, so kind of just stand there gormlessly while willing the ground to open up and eat me whole. Carmen's still not looking at me. What do I say? How can I even crawl back from this? If it wasn't my own life I was screwing up here, this whole situation would be hilarious.

Finally, Carmen looks up at me, and the blank expression that had been plastered on her face turns into something more strained. For the second time tonight, I feel like the worst person to ever set foot on earth.

Carmen places her glass of wine onto the table in front of her. "Look, it's fine, it's cool--it's really cool, seriously, I mean, we're not even anything. It's fine, honestly--I mean, she has a boyfriend so it's not fine, but it's cool with me--as in, you know what I mean, yeah, it's fine."

"In case you can't tell, it's definitely not fine," Annabel pipes in. I shoot her the most scathing look I've ever given anyone. She shrugs. "Just saying."

I shake my head and swear under my breath as if that's going to help anything.

"No, it wasn't--I wouldn't..." I take a breath, trying to conjure up something that'll fix this shitstorm I've created. "It's not how it looked, which I realise is the most cliché thing I could've possibly said, so as you can tell, I've already screwed this up, and there's probably no point trying to explain because it'll just sound like excuses." I sigh. "I'm sorry. Just please believe me when I say I'd never do that kind of shit with someone who's got a boyfriend. Please don't think I'm that kind of person."

Carmen's still looking at me, but she doesn't say anything. Her eyes glaze over for a minute or so until eventually, she nods slowly--to herself more than at me, I think. I'm about to try pleading my innocence again, but she gets there before I can say a word.

"Could you leave me alone for a bit?"

As she speaks, I feel myself deflate. All that did was make myself look like a blathering idiot. I apologise again before granting Carmen's wish, and step back inside. I can't be bothered for this anymore, I just want to go back to the flat. If it wasn't over an hour's walk away, I'd leave right now.

The house is a little emptier now, with most of the older attendees having gone home, so it at least feels a little less claustrophobic. As I pass the front door on my way into the kitchen to grab whatever food is left, I pause. Screw it, an hour isn't that long.

I've only been walking along the deserted country lanes for around ten minutes when I realise that actually, when it's pitch black outside, zero degrees, and drizzling slightly, an hour is kind of a long time. The fact I left my jacket at Ava's probably isn't helping, either.

On the bright side, at least I have some company in the form of Annabel. On the not so bright side, she's spent this whole journey nagging at me to go back.

"At least go back to get a jacket, you're shivering," Annabel whines. "You'll catch a cold."

"Fun fact," I say, spinning around to face her, briefly walking backwards in the process. "Catching a cold from being outside is bullshit. If you're carrying the virus, it might bring out the symptoms, sure, but it can't literally cause--"

"Oh, shut up," Annabel snaps.

I shoot her a toothy grin, and continue forward. I'd rather die than admit it to her, but she's right. I'm freezing. I'll be fine so long as I keep moving, but walking home probably wasn't my wisest idea.

"So, anyway," Annabel says about five minutes later. "When are you going to talk about it?"

"What?"

She groans. "Oh, I don't know, maybe the fact you're blaming Mum and Dad's death solely on your eight-year-old self, over something you have zero control over?"

"I'm not talking about this now," I mutter.

"Yes, you are."

"No, I'm not."

I halt in my tracks, and turn to face my sister. Despite the rain, her dark hair remains perfectly dry, her pale pink jumper as loose as it's always been, while I stand with my hair flat against my forehead and my clothes sticking to my skin. She doesn't get it. She'll never get it. She doesn't remember what it's like to be alive, she doesn't realise what I took from her.

Annabel is staring at me in silence, but as I'm about speak again, I realise her eyes aren't focused on me, but on something over my shoulder. I turn around. Standing a few hundred yards away from me in the centre of the road, his hands in his trouser pockets, is the figure of a tall man. The dead kind.

The man smiles. "Ah, so the rumours are true."

"Felix, don't," Annabel says quietly. "He's dark."

"No shit," I mutter back.

I continue forward, keeping my head down to ensure I don't make eye contact with the thing.

"I know you can see me."

I hesitate for a millisecond, but ignore it and keep walking.

"Even if I'd not just seen you speaking to your sister, I'd still know."

This time, I stop completely. How does he know who Annabel is?

"What?" It's she who responds.

"Ah, my little lady, it's nice to make your acquaintance." The man bows, and it churns my stomach a little.

"Don't speak to her," I interject, looking straight at the bastard.

He grins. "There we go. That was easier than anticipated."

We're a lot closer to him now, and he's older than I first thought. He's a little shorter too--a good few inches shorter than I am. There are wrinkles crawling from the corners of his eyes, and his hair is an off-grey colour. He's dressed in a glaringly bright striped shirt with cord trousers, and there's a dried, bloodied wound where his right eyebrow should be. I'd guess a gunshot. Everything from his hunched posture to sinister grin makes me feel uneasy. I keep my eyes locked on him.

"How's the home life?" he asks, taking his hands out of his pockets, the eerie smile still intact on his face. "The 'rents good? Phoebe and Daniel, right?"

"What do you want?" I ask, but Annabel interjects before the spirit can answer.

"How do you know their names? Who are you?"

"So many questions!" He laughs loudly, and if it was the laugh of a living man, it would echo around these lanes.

He says nothing more, just stares at us. Annabel is right; how the hell does this guy know all that? He might've overheard us discussing our parents earlier, but there's no way he can know their names. While I want answers, I don't want to take this guy's bait. Instead, I stare back at him, refusing to back down. I'm not letting this freak scare me.

I can feel Annabel's gaze on me, waiting for me to make the next move, when the god-awful smile returns to the spirit's face.

"What did it feel like to kill them?"

My mouth falls open a little, and out comes a stammer. My posture falters slightly. Thoughts of how to respond race around my head, but none of them leave my mouth.

"I killed my brother, see. Shit of a human being, you should've seen the bastard begging for his life." The spirit's laughter booms once more. "But two in one night? And of course, not forgetting this bitch here." He nods at Annabel. "That's impressive, kid."

"Shut up," Annabel snaps.

"If only your folks had stopped after your sister, eh? I bet they regretted that as the air seeped from their lungs." He sniggers, and Annabel yells again, but he just continues. "Oh c'mon, relax. Don't tell me you feel guilty. Trust me, if they knew you'd kill them eight years down the line, they would've had you aborted in the first place anyway. Tit for tat."

"Shut up!" Annabel again.

The spirit laughs for the third time. "Oh, honey, he killed you. Are you so deranged that you don't see that? Or are you just dumb?"

Despite the freezing temperature and heavying rain, I'm sweating. It feels like my whole body is on fire. My mouth is dry, and my stomach is flipping. I can't keep my breath steady. I try to focus on it, to bring it back to normal, but all I can think about is Annabel's limp body being flung onto a car bonnet while my father sits lifelessly inside it, his eyes gazing into a world he no longer exists in. My teeth are chattering, but I don't feel cold. The spirit is laughing again.

"It was such a waste, wasn't it?" He's right beside me, whispering in my ear. "You're a bit of a shit reward, aren't you? For the sake of three lives."

I turn quickly, but he's gone again.

"Especially when the one who lived is their murderer," he hisses, this time in my other ear.

"Leave us alone!" Annabel.

Where is she? I don't know if it's the rain, or the cold, or the exhaustion, but my vision is turning patchy. I can't see her. I call her name, but all I hear in response is the spirit's ugly laughter. I look around, and I can't even see him anymore. I can't see anyone. I can't breathe.

"Struggling a little, hm?" The voice is in my ear again. I clamp both my hands over them, but it doesn't work. "A bit pathetic, don't you think? Imagine the pain your family felt as they died, watching each other getting killed off, one by one. And here you are, getting worked up over this. Reality hurts, kid."

"Stop," I mutter. "Stop, stop stop."

I press harder against my ears, but it's not working because I can still hear the spirit's voice. It's in my head, it's seeping into my bloodstream.

Annabel is screaming manically at it, shouting so hysterically that she sounds possessed, but I can't see her. I shut my eyes but instead of darkness, I'm welcomed by the image of my mother's panicked face. I shoot them back open, but the image remains etched on my brain. Why won't it go away? Why won't any of this go away?

"They regret saving you, you know." The voice sounds like it's behind me this time. "It wasn't worth it. They resent you for it. They really, really resent you."

My mother's image flashes in my mind again, and I see Annabel's limp corpse on the car bonnet. Is this real? Is this happening now? Stop. Make it stop. I can't catch my breath, I feel sick. My legs are shaking so much I can't stand, let alone try to walk away. I stumble to the floor and it's damp and cold, and for a moment, it's refreshing. I can't do this anymore. Why can't I make it stop?

I lift my knees up to my chin, and finally remove my hands from my ears. All I can hear is laughter. My father's empty stare pierces into me. Annabel is still on the bonnet, but she can't be because I can hear her shouting from somewhere. I don't understand what's happening. I smack myself in the head. It leaves me dazed for a few seconds. I do it again, and again, and again.

"Felix, stop! Stop it! You'll hurt yourself!" Annabel's voice sounds like a gospel choir in the middle of hell.

"Pathetic!" The spirit.

"Don't listen. Felix, look at me, don't listen!" Annabel. "He's messing with you on purpose, he's trying to hurt you, don't look at him. Look at me."

I look around in hysteria, but there's nothing there. Just an empty road. I can't see her, why can't I see her?

"Don't look at him, look at me. Felix, don't look at him."

She keeps telling me not to look at him, and she sounds exactly like she did the night she died, and it's making it worse, and I keep going over it in my head, over and over again, and it won't stop, it won't leave my thoughts. The spirit is laughing and laughing and laughing. I can barely see anything anymore, let alone Annabel. Why is it so hot? I think I'm going to be sick.

I push everything away as best I can--the sound of the rain, the feeling of the damp concrete underneath me, the remainder of what my eyes can make out--and lie down on my back. I shut my eyes. I keep trying to push it away. I focus on my breath, on my hysterical heartbeat. It's working. I think it's working. I'm not sure how long it takes, but eventually, it all goes away.

Chapter 24

- -

It's not wet anymore. Has it stopped raining? For a moment, I think it might be daytime because it's warm, but then I realise everything is dark so that can't be right. Or are my eyes just closed? I can't remember. God, I feel tired.

"Felix?" There's a voice, but it's not Annabel's and it's not the spirit's. "Hey, can you hear me? Felix?"

Carmen? I try to shift my body up, only to realise I'm half-smothered in something. What the hell? My eyes are droopy, but I force them open. Blankets. I'm smothered in blankets; a mountain of them. I think I'm on a sofa. Footsteps near me, and I turn my eyes towards the sound to see Carmen approaching me. She sits down beside me, but I'm not sure what on. Why can't I focus properly?

"What? Are we in Ava's house?" I manage to say. "I can't--I don't remember how--What happened?"

As I sit up, I realise I'm not on a sofa. I'm in a large double bed, and Carmen is sitting on the unoccupied side next to me. She's biting her lip.

"You disappeared," she explains. "We--we tried calling you, but you weren't answering, and it was pouring with rain and I was worried you'd gone outside because of what happened and gotten lost, and--sorry, I'm rambling, I just--Jesus, I was so worried." She lets out a breath. "We found you passed out just off the road about twenty minutes away, and you were freezing. We couldn't get you to wake up for ages, you weren't responding to anything." Carmen's voice cracks a little. "When you did come to, you were confused. You kept mumbling something about a man following you and..." She hesitates. "Your parents, and something to do with ghosts."

"Hey, maybe one of Ava's ghosties possessed me," I joke, but quickly get the impression now's not the time.

"The girl who'd found you didn't have a phone with her," Carmen continues, ignoring my poor attempt at humour. "So I called Mosi and Ava to come pick you up. They were--They'd been driving around looking for you."

"Oh," I reply simply. "I mean, sorry for doing that, I didn't--I don't know what happened, I can't remember anything," I say, half lying.

"We're pretty sure you were hypothermic, or at least getting there, hence the..." she nods at the blankets stacked on top of me. "Your clothes are in the wash, by the way."

I hadn't even noticed I wasn't wearing them. I shove myself out of the blankets a little further, removing all but one completely because it's kind of boiling, and can finally take in my surroundings properly. I've never been in this room before--it must be a guest bedroom or something. It's decorated much like the rest of the house, in an old-fashioned but perfectly kept style.

"Thanks," I finally say. "For finding me and, y'know, preventing my death. Mind you, I'm a bit of a ball ache, so it could've been a blessing in disguise. I'll hide a little better next time, eh?" I joke again, but receive an even more unimpressed look from Carmen than before, so follow it with a "I'm only joking, sorry, I didn't mean to scare you like that."

Carmen shakes her head. "Thank the girl who called me over to you. I never would've found you in the first place otherwise."

"Who was that?"

"I'm not sure, I think she's on your course," Carmen replies. "She said she'd been to the party anyway. A girl called Annabel?"

"Pardon?"

"Annabel? She said she knew you from uni. She lives in one of the houses around here, said she spotted you on her way home from the party."

Carmen keeps talking, but I zone out completely. What the actual shitting hell? I ask Carmen if she's sure, to which she nods. I ask her what she looked like. Long, dark brown hair, blue eyes, and wearing a pair of dark jeans with a velvet jumper. I gaze at Carmen, and I'm completely gormless. I don't--How can--What? She described Annabel perfectly. It was Annabel. She saw Annabel.

"Are you okay? Let me fetch you a hot drink," Carmen says as concern returns to her soft face, probably at the sight of what my own face is doing right now.

Before I can even try to conjure up words, she's left the room, and the sound of footsteps echo through the hallway outside. I scan the room like a crazed animal, but there's no sign of my sister anywhere. I call her name, but hear no response. Is she okay? Am I still asleep? Am I dreaming all this? I don't have much time to ponder because before long, Carmen returns with a mug in her hands.

"What time is it?" I ask as I take it from her. It's hot chocolate. Score.

Carmen takes her phone out of her pocket, and glances at it. "About three."

"In the morning?"

She laughs a little, and I can't begin to explain how good it is to hear a laugh that makes me feel better, not worse. "Yes, in the morning."

"Oh, what--Why are you up? Aren't you tired?"

"Couldn't really sleep. I think I was just worried about you," she replies as her familiar smirk spreads onto her face. "Even if you are a cheating arsehole."

"I didn't--I mean, I--"

"Sh, it's fine," Carmen replies, waving her hand in the air. "Katie explained it. I think she felt bad because she thought it was the cause of your suicide mission."

To be fair, it pretty much was, but I'm too embarrassed to say that out loud. Instead, I reply with an awkward nod. Perfect response. Well done, mate.

As I take a sip out of the hot chocolate Carmen made me, I feel something nudge my leg, and look up to see Annabel. She's gazing at me, wide-eyed. Oh good, she's okay. I flip my eyes to Carmen as subtly as possible in hope of an explanation of how the hell she could see my sister, and Annabel shrugs with the most clueless expression I've ever seen appear on her face.

"Uh, you okay?" Carmen asks, reminding me of where I am.

I turn to her, and she's staring straight in the direction of Annabel. Well, she obviously can't see her anymore.

"Yeah, sorry, I feel a bit out of it."

Carmen smiles. She stretches her legs out on the bed, the slides down a little so that she's lying on her back. She turns her head, which is now level with mine, and sighs.

"I don't know if I've ever told you this, but you do some really weird shit sometimes."

I laugh, relieved that the atmosphere has relaxed a bit. "Well, I can't argue that."

She responds with her airy giggle, while her eyes remain on my face. They move around slightly, as if scanning every corner of it. Annabel has sat down on the end of the bed now, and she's oddly silent. Her eyes aren't focused on anything, and she looks as though her entire world has been split open. Rather ironically, she kind of looks like she's seen a ghost.

"What's wrong?" Carmen's voice catches me surprise. She's still looking at me, except the smile on her face has vanished.

"Huh? Nothing, I'm cool."

Suddenly, a loud sigh emanates from the end of the bed. It's nice to see Annabel's returned to the present.

"Don't try to bullshit me, I know something's up," Carmen replies. "You've barely left the flat since exams ended, you've been acting way more reserved than usual, and you almost just got yourself killed trying to walk five miles in the pouring rain in the middle of the night, so if you even try to bullshit me, I will grab your clothes from the utility room right now and strangle you with your own shitty t-shirt."

"Graphic," I mutter in response, but Carmen's face stays stern. I sigh. "It's just a rough patch. Exams went shit, uni's generally stressing me out, y'know, just that kind of stuff. I'm fine."

Carmen nods. "Hm, okay. Would you rather be strangled by your shirt or belt? I imagine a shirt will be less painful."

Annabel laughs, and if Carmen's eyes weren't locked to my face right now, I'd probably give her the dirtiest look possible. Or throw something at her. Not that there'd be much point in that, but it helps release anger. Carmen opens her mouth to speak again, but it takes a few seconds for her to speak.

"Is it to do with your accident?" She stammers slightly. "I mean, it's just I know everyone going home for Christmas sucked for you, and I know you said it doesn't bother you, but it just seems like since then you've been... off. I just--I get it if you don't want to talk about that stuff with me, but please talk about it with someone."

"It's not--I..." Great explanation there, Felix.

Carmen's eyebrows are furrowed, and there's a hint of desperation on her face, and I don't know why, but I feel guilty.

"You don't..." She bites her lip. Her eyes close for a moment. "You don't blame yourself for any of what happened, right? Or feel bad about surviving it? I know that's the most stereotypical assumption ever, but I just... I don't know, talk to me?"

Chapter 25

I shake my head, and am about to deny the whole thing when I stop myself. This is all just going to keep replaying until I grow some balls and face it. I can feel Annabel's eyes on me, willing me to say something other than I'm fine.

I raise my shoulders. "Kind of."

"Seriously?" she asks, to which I nod. "Felix, how can an eight-year-old child even be half responsible for something like that?"

"It's a weird situation, I can't--It's hard to explain." As I speak, I can feel my heart rate increasing by the second. "Just, for argument's sake, think of it like I had a problem, and the sole reason we crashed was because of them trying to deal with that problem. That problem literally led them to their deaths."

"Was it a problem you could control?"

"Well, no, but--"

"Then it's not your fault. Even if you could control it, you were eight. It still wouldn't be your fault."

I shake my head aggressively. "Yeah, but, they--they were okay at first. It's hard to explain, it's... It only happened because they wasted their energy on me, to make sure I made it through. They shouldn't... It's hard to explain."

Carmen nods. "Okay. That was their decision. That had nothing to do with you." I go to interrupt her, but she stops me. "Look, I don't exactly know the situation, and that's okay; I don't expect you to tell me every little detail, but if what you're saying is right, then they clearly chose to save you. That's what they wanted. They wanted you to live, and they didn't care if that meant they didn't."

"Listen to her, Felix," Annabel speaks up, her voice quiet. "Please. If we'd have wanted to survive over you, we would've. I know I can't remember it, or anything before it, but whoever that version of me was chose things to happen like they did. We could've thrown you to whatever those things were and ran, but we didn't. You had no control over the situation. We did, and that's what we chose. It was our fault we died, not yours. And we were okay with that." She pauses. "I'm still okay with that."

I know what they're saying makes sense, and I know it's illogical for me to take full responsibility for what happened, but it's not easy to see it like that. Not if my abilities were the cause of the crash, not when that banished spirit stood there and told me my parents regret ever saving me. I know he was trying to get into my head, and the likelihood is that he's never met my parents in his wasted life, but what if he has? What if that's exactly what they told him?

I don't know if it's the enormity of this conversation, or the events of tonight, but I'm starting to feel exhausted.

"I know, I just... Even if that's what they wanted then, they might regret it if they were still around to be able to," I say, rather pathetically.

Carmen sighs as she manoeuvres her hands under the pile of blankets, eventually finding my hand. Hers is cold against mine. "No parent would ever regret choosing their child over themselves, Felix, and I would bet you anything that if given the option to come back, they'd do it all over again."

"I would." Annabel again. "And that's as your big sister, let alone as a parent."

I don't say anything back. I'm not sure what I would say. She hesitates slightly, but after a minute or so of silence, Carmen shuffles a little closer to me. I lift my blanket for her, and she shuffles towards me again until her body is touching mine, and her head is just under my chin. I drop the blanket but keep my arm around her, pulling her nearer again. Her hair smells a little of alcohol.

I'm really shattered now. We both lie in complete silence, but it's not the uncomfortable kind, and it's not long until I feel myself drifting. I look down at Carmen, and it occurs to me that she must actually be insane to want anything to do with me, and it makes me want to trap her in this moment before she realises she can escape at any time.

"Thanks," I whisper, but I think she's asleep.

My eyes are on the verge of closing when I realise the bedside lamp is still switched on. I look at it, focusing my attention on the string dangling from the lampshade. With whatever energy I have left from today, I envision it being pulled down. It does what it's told, and just like that, the room is pitch black.

Either I was a lot worse off than I thought last night, or everyone I know is ridiculously melodramatic because the second Carmen and I step into the living room, everyone's eyes turn to me with a look that screams he's alive! Ava was originally driving us all home last night, but after my escapade, everyone other than Katie and her boyfriend ended up staying the night. In fairness, there are more than enough beds.

Mosi and Kato fuss over me, offering me everything imaginable to eat and drink, which kind of makes me want to smack myself in the face because this is the second time I've pulled some inconvenient shit at their house--the third, if you count Mosi having to clean my face up at their pub after mine and Jamie's poltergeist adventure. I don't even want to imagine what they think of me.

Everyone is talking about last night as we snack on a late breakfast of bacon and sausage sandwiches, but I'm not really saying much. I've got a vegetarian sausage sandwich, of course, which is shockingly satisfying, though that might just be because it's lathered in ketchup. Plus, I am starving.

"It's a good thing you had your guide with you last night, Felix," Kato says, forcing me into the conversation.

I look up from my breakfast to see everyone's eyes on me. In fairness, I don't really think anyone's eyes have fully left me since I entered the room. Kato has a knowing smile on her face, and my thoughts shoot back to our conversation last night. I flash what I imagine to be a very unconvincing grin at her in response, then take another bite out of my sandwich. It was a good thing I had Annabel and Carmen, more like. This results in Jamie questioning what a guide is, and Kato explains to everyone what she explained to me last night. It's a bit repetitive, really.

By the time the afternoon arrives, I've returned to the guest room I slept in. I wanted some peace, but Jamie followed me in like a lost puppy. Then there's Annabel, of course, although her presence is welcomed because I want to know how the shitting hell Carmen interacted with her last night.

"Was it something paranormal?" Jamie asks the second the bedroom door is closed.

I jump onto the bed, and nod. I'm guessing he's talking about last night. Oh well, even if he's not, I've already nodded. No turning back now. He responds by staring at me expectantly.

"Well?" he questions. "What happened?"

"Kinda weird, not gonna lie," I say. "I was being a moody bastard so left the house to walk home--nothing paranormal there, I'm just a twat--and I bumped into this bad spirit. He was saying weird shit about my parents, like he knew their names and about the accident and all that."

"Did you know him? The ghost?"

I shake my head. "Nah. I mean, he could've been someone from my childhood--didn't actually think of that possibility until now, but I don't think so," I explain, and Annabel nods on the bed beside me. I guess she'd not thought of that either. "But yeah, I started feeling weird, all faint and shit, and I don't really know... I must've just passed out. The weird thing is that y'know the girl who called Carmen over when she was out looking for me?" I ask, to which Jamie nods. "It was Annabel."

He stares for a while. "What, as in your sister?" I nod. "How? What?"

"You tell me," Annabel responds.

"What, you mean you don't know?" I ask her.

"Nope. No clue."

"Oh, well you're bloody useless then." I groan. "Could she have abilities? Even if she doesn't realise it... I don't know, is that a thing?"

"No," Annabel says with confidence. "It was different, it was like... I don't know, like it was me, not her. Like I did something... It's hard to explain. It felt like I was dreaming, like I was talking and moving and physically there, but not present."

"Shit," I say, basically summing up the past five months or so in one word.

Throughout our conversation, Jamie has been gazing at me with a weird, and notably unattractive, look on his face. I think he still finds me speaking into thin air weird.

"Yeah, we got nothing," I say, turning back to him.

Jamie's thick eyebrows furrow, and I don't know how I've never noticed before, but the guy sort of has a monobrow. I mean, his eyebrows aren't literally connected in a solitary line, but if there were a few more hairs to thicken the thing up, it would definitely be one.

"Perhaps we should consult Kato and Mosi? Or even Ava? This is all beginning to feel unnervingly dangerous."

"Tried that." I click my tongue. "It's all bullshit; they can't do all this ghost malarkey. Annabel tried talking to Ava, but she could do sod all."

"Seriously?" Jamie seems genuinely shocked. "Well, I don't think that renders her, Mosi and Kato invaluable. They're certainly aware that there's something odd about you, which suggests they have some degree of ability."

"Are they?"

Jamie stares at me dumbly. "Felix, you reacted extremely abnormally to Kato's attempt to read your aura, had your eyebrow sewn back together by Mosi the night we were attacked by that evil entity, and displayed extremely bizarre behaviour last night."

"Yeah, but like, none of that shit is ghostie, more like heavily problematic."

Jamie sighs and rolls his eyes. He does that a lot. We're leaving in five minutes or so, but before we head back downstairs, Jamie forces me to promise I'll consider speaking to Ava's parents about the whole numerous ghostly murder attempts situation, but have no intention on actually doing so. This has nothing to do with them, and everything to do with me. All I need to do is remember.

Chapter 26

It turns out I didn't do as shit in my exams as I'd assumed. I didn't manage a two-one, but passed with a high two-two. Considering I entered uni determined to achieve a first, that's appalling, but considering I thought I'd literally failed, I've got no complaints. Besides, first year doesn't count. The only painful drawback of my grade is the awkward meeting I had to endure with my personal tutor, who always has to look at his computer screen before acknowledging me because he never remembers my name.

I achieved all A's at A-Level, so me getting a two-two in first semester is the equivalent of satanic kitten torture, if my tutor's reaction is anything to go by. I assured him it was just a rough patch aided by a mental breakdown, and I think he thought I was kidding, but I'm not sure I was. The meeting is over and done with anyway, so I just want to focus on not screwing up this semester quite so badly.

A week has passed since my dramatic performance at Ava's party, and having just finished a session with the boxing society, Tom and I are currently sitting in a booth at The Cavern reading up on some uni work. The original plan was to do this at the library, but Tom started whining about it being too quiet there which, I mean, is kind of the point, but whatever. I don't think either one of us is actually doing anything uni-related anyway.

Tom's spending his time staring at his laptop screen and giggling to himself, so it's probably fair to assume he isn't, and I'm spending it searching up my parents on the internet. I've been trying to find information on them all week, and holy shit is it difficult. There's just nothing anywhere. I was hoping researching them might spark some memories, or even just hint at what the heck they have to do with what's going on at the moment, but it's been an enormous failure so far.

Finding stuff on my mum has been easier than my dad, but none of it is especially extraordinary. It's all stuff I already knew, really. Finding something on my dad--literally anything--is like looking for polar bears in the Sahara Desert. It's like he never even existed. Part of me thinks that's a massive alarm bell because that's not normal, right?

I realise that there are varying degrees of information available about people on the internet, but that side of my family has always been a weird one. When my grandmother was still alive for the few years after my folks died, she always claimed not to know much about my dad's family. She'd met them before, but hadn't seen them since I was around three or four-years-old. She thought they were a bit weird, and my dad disagreed with the way they wanted Annabel and I to be brought up, which caused tension, and eventually es-trangement.

As an eight-year-old kid who couldn't remember who the heck anyone was anyway, I didn't care enough to ask her to expand further. I've no idea if by my dad's family she meant his parents, or his parents, brothers, sisters, aunties, uncles, cousins, dogs, and fish. I have no clue how big that side of my family is, let alone if anyone from it is still around. I sure don't know where the hell they were when I was left orphaned before I'd even reach double digits.

Regardless, my research seems to be getting me nowhere, and it's beginning to piss me off so I shut my laptop, sit back in my chair, and sigh. Tom finally looks up from his own screen, and it seems to take him a while to remember where he is. And probably who he is. I mean, it's Tom.

"Not going well?" he asks, to which I respond with a questioning look. "Work?"

"Oh, yeah," I mutter. "Not really."

"Same. I was just watching this video where a guy put wellies on his dog, and then threw it into the snow and it started going mental and running headfirst into massive snow piles. It was hilarious, man."

I'm pretty sure that's animal abuse. It's definitely not uni work, anyway. I don't think Tom quite catches my disinterested vibe because he's soon joining me on my side of the booth with his laptop to show me this apparently hilarious video. Yeah, definitely animal abuse. Once I've finished humoring him, I go up to the bar to buy us a couple of drinks, and return to find Tom sniggering at more animal videos.

"You decided on tonight yet?" he asks me as I hand him his half pint.

"Yeah, I'll come," I say with a shrug. "Could do with some comedy for the evening."

He's referring to a ghost hunt--sorry, a spirit walk--the paranormal society are organising. A few months ago, I would've preferred to drink my own urine than participate in this kind of bullshit, but I figure why not? In all honesty, I think I've just reached the point of desperation where I'm willing to try anything that gives me any remote chance of figuring out what the hell is going on at the moment. A tour of the city and its alleged most haunted places seems like it could be relatively useful, so I'll give it a shot.

"You need to embrace ghosts, man," Tom says as he shakes his head at me. "I feel way more connected to my grandmother since I got into all of it; it's like she never died."

"The one with the towels?"

Tom nods eagerly, and I still don't think he quite grasps how difficult it is to take his bathroom haunting grandmother with a towel fixation seriously.

We're not even ten minutes into this ghost hunt, and I can honestly say it's one of the most boring, uncomfortable experiences of my life. I don't know why I expected any different, really. I knew this lot had some screws loose from my last outing with them. To begin with, they're still wearing capes. Okay, I'm being a bit mean; in fairness, most are reasonable enough, it's just that the ones who aren't quite so down to earth are in another solar system all together.

We're doing this as part of a tour, so it's at least not wholly unprofessional, but everyone from the society are getting over excited over nothing. We've only visited one 'haunted' attraction so far, and that was a well that was used back when the city was just a village, and I was hoping for some kind of demonic girl climbing out of it scenario, but sadly there was nothing. The second stop happens to be Ava's family pub.

At the news of this, our tour guide becomes especially excited, and questions Ava on pretty much everything. It's quite intrusive, really. In fact, Ava herself seems a bit miffed, which is something I can't say I've ever seen in her before. As Ava answers the guide's questions while we stand outside the pub, I try my hardest to look enthusiastic about this whole experience.

For late February, it's not too cold, especially with our group being huddled together as we gaze at the old building. Ava mentions an elderly barman who haunts the pub, which catches my attention because I've seen the guy. Other than that, it's all stuff she's said to us before.

As we move on, it occurs to me that this city is filled with more hidden side streets and alleyways than I realised. I've generally ever only wandered the city's main streets, minus the time Annabel led Jamie and me through an unknown route in an attempt to escape a murderous poltergeist, so had no idea its side streets were this complex.

As I continue going through the motions of the ghost hunt, nodding and looking impressed where nodding and looking impressed is expected, I notice Ava still has a slightly soured look on her face.

"You all right?" I ask her when we've stopped for the fifth destination on the tour--only one has actually been haunted so far, minus Ava's pub, and the spirit there was an old woman who just looked bored.

"Something is wrong," she replies simply.

I wait for her to expand, but it's Ava, so she doesn't. "What d'you mean?" I question.

She sighs. "I don't know."

She says nothing more, and I don't think there's anything more to get out, so I don't press further. Strange. Jamie's been nagging me to seek Ava's, or least her family's, guidance with my recent paranormal predicaments ever since my freak out last week. Naturally, I've refused.

I've come to the conclusion that there is definitely something different about them, and that there are at least some paranormal bones in their bodies, just not anything that would be of any use to me. What's going on with me is personal, something they wouldn't have the answers to. As I'm running through these thoughts in my head, I feel a tap on my shoulder, and turn to see Jamie eyeing me. Speak of the devil.

Chapter 27

"Hey, something has just occurred to me," he utters, rather excitedly. He glances around the group to check no one's listening. "The scenario with Carmen last week, with her obtaining the ability to see and communicate with Annabel. Perhaps Annabel had slipped into her open state. I've not quite read as far as--"

"Her what now?"

Jamie grunts, then glances around the group again. We're currently on our way to a haunted wall. Yes, a haunted wall. As in bricks. Haunted bricks. Ever the eavesdropping type, Annabel has joined Jamie and me. I was a little surprised she wasn't here for the tour initially, but I think even she's bored of these crazed ghost hunters by now.

"You know," Jamie continues in a hushed tone. "Considering you're the one with the abilities, you've not exactly read up on the topic, have you?" I'd argue back, but it's a fair point. I'm horrifically disorganised. Jamie rolls his eyes. "When regular people communicate with the deceased, it's believed to be due to that particular spirit entering an alternative state of being to the one they generally reside in."

"Oh wait, yeah, I remember reading something about that, so anyone and everyone can see them, right?"

Jamie nods. "I've not found anything stating how a spirit achieves this state quite yet; I'm not entirely sure it's known, but it seems logical as Carmen is no longer able to communicate with her."

I nod back in agreement. "C'mon, give us your theory," I say, turning to Annabel as we finally arrive at the infamous haunted wall.

She doesn't say anything in response, but her eyes are glazed over, so I know she's contemplating the whole idea. She mentioned a similar idea to me a few days ago, probably because she also reads up on this shit, suggesting the whole scenario could be to do with her accidentally making herself visible to Carmen. Considering no one else had the chance to see her that night, as she slipped away as help arrived, we don't know if everyone could see her, or just Carmen.

"It makes sense," she finally says. "I just want to know how the hell I did it."

"Oi!" a voice calls, forcing the three of us to shoot our heads up towards the group of people crowding the wall. "What are you two doing lagging behind, keep up!" Carmen calls, a wicked grin on her face. "You're missing out on some major wall action here, guys!"

Jamie and I catch up to everyone, and slip back into the group. The wall ghosts have a relatively interesting story--something to do with execution, I wasn't fully listening--but I'm still bored half to death. This is the last attraction, so I'm willing for the whole thing to end. We're in the city's main square, and I'm able to find a bench to sit on, so I can at least pretend to listen in comfort. Well, it's slightly damp, freezing cold and made from hard metal, so hardly luxurious, but at least it's something.

As the tour comes to an end, a confusing mixture of relief and disappointment spreads through my body. The last trip with this society was so eventful, what with the Tracker, the little spirit boy, and the wise female ghost. This one being the complete opposite is kind of gutting, I guess, especially when I'm so desperate for answers.

I'm so wrapped up in my thoughts that it takes me a while to realise there's someone sitting next to me on the cold bench. The crowd has dispersed slightly now, with individuals having separated into smaller groups to discuss the snooze-fest that was the spirit walk. I lift my gaze to see Ava sitting beside me, but as I look around the rest of the square, I can't spot anyone else from the flat.

Annabel's sitting on the concrete ground in front of me with a somewhat dejected look on her face, but that's it. She's probably just as disappointed by this as I am. I turn back to Ava. She still looks on edge. If anything, she looks even more uneasy.

"Do you feel ill?" I ask her, remembering what she said to me earlier.

She shakes her head rather aggressively, but is looking at the floor. "No, it's not--It's just... hard to explain." She lifts her head to look at me, and I'm not sure if it's a result of the artificial city lights clashing with the sky's darkness as it tries to seep through, but her eyes look such a deep brown they're almost black. "Something just doesn't feel right."

"Something does feel kinda off, Felix," Annabel interjects, making me glance at her. The strained expression remains on her face. "I feel weird."

Really? Her too? Not being funny, but these two must be baked or something because I feel fine. I try to reassure Ava that everything is okay, but she just violently shakes her head again. I can't recall a time I ever saw Ava unhappy--well, minus the time she and her father trekked into their local country lanes to find me lying unconscious on the side of the road with Carmen, I imagine, but I can't remember that so it doesn't count.

"It doesn't matter," she suddenly announces, perking up. "I might just be sensitive at the moment. It's a strange time of the month."

"You sure?" I ask, not quite understanding her quick change of mind, or the comment that followed.

"Yes. So, whoa, I've been meaning to speak to you actually, alone," is her reply, to which I wither inside a little. Please don't be ghost related. "Do you actually like Carmen, or are you just messing her about?"

Oh, okay. Not really what I was expecting. Also not much better than I was expecting. If anything, worse than what I was expecting. Naturally, I just stammer. Annabel laughs. Ava's eyes are digging into me, and though the concerned look from earlier still lingers on her face, it's slowly being replaced by a look of accusation. For someone who's almost a whole foot shorter than me, she sure can be intimidating.

As I've apparently forgotten how to speak, Ava tries again. "If it helps, I think you're genuine and can really be quite adorably clueless, but whoa, you can be a bit of a dickhead." Her voice is sing-songy, and it's throwing me a little. "You know, with the inconsistency, the flip-flopping, etcetera. But then you're, like, totally all over the place as a person, and should probably consult a therapist, so I don't think it's your fault."

Well that's a backhanded compliment if I ever heard one. I mean, at least it started with something nice, sort of. Sure, it ended with being called a dick before being told I should seek professional help, but it's something. She's probably right though. I mean, I did put Carmen through finding me on the verge of death, alone in a dark country lane just the other day. Not too smooth, that.

"I'm not messing her about," I reply rather dumbly. "I mean, I don't mean to, I just--I don't know. I like her." Wow, great answer, Felix, ten out of ten for insightfulness. I quickly try to save myself from sounding too dumb by asking, "why's that anyway?"

"Jesus Christ." Annabel groans from the ground.

What? What's wrong with that question?

Ava simply smiles. "See. Adorable."

Huh? What the hell? Ava tries to keep the smile on her face, but it's soon wavering, and the strained expression returns. Before I have the chance to respond to her, she's on her feet. Most people have left now, and so I follow her as she wanders towards those who remain.

"Why's that anyway?" Annabel says in a mocking tone as we walk ahead, which I respond to with a look of confusion tinted with a slight glare. "Because she fancies you, you idiot, like proper fancies you. She's obviously worried you're going to break her heart, and all that melodramatic stuff you non-dead people stress over. I know guys are meant to be bad with this, but holy shit, you take oblivious to another level." She sighs. "God knows why she does, mind you. I'd rather lose all four limbs than want to go anywhere near you if I were alive, and well, not your sister."

She's not exactly boosting my self-esteem here. I can't respond to her properly considering Ava is right beside me, so rely on bitchy stares. Don't get me wrong, I realised Carmen and I had this thing, but I didn't exactly know what it was or what should be done about it. I still don't, really. It's all a stark reminder of why I've literally never had a girlfriend before.

We're still following Ava, who's now on the phone to someone, and we're heading away from the city's square and into a side street. I sigh. Ava's right though, I've not half messed Carmen around. One moment I'm falling asleep with her after she saved me from hypothermia, and the next I'm barely acknowledging her for days because I'm so wrapped up in all this ghost crap. Holy shit, I am a dickhead, aren't I?

"Don't you feel that?" Annabel asks, catching my attention.

She's looking at me with wide eyes as we follow Ava across a road, but other than the recent realisation that I'm an arsehole, I feel fine. Nothing out of the ordinary, anyway. I shake my head to her, and she bites her lip. I turn to Ava, and I don't know if it's because I've just not been concentrating, but she doesn't look on edge anymore. She looks angry.

Just as I'm about to ask her what's up, we turn a corner that leads to a small grassed park, and she comes to a halt. Hell, she stops so suddenly that I almost trip over her, but when I turn my attention to what she's fixated on, it makes a lot more sense. Sitting on a patch of grass are Tom, Jamie, and Carmen, and in the middle of the circle they've created is a Ouija board. My attention doesn't stay on them long though because lingering above one of the small trees of the park is a large, black mass.

Chapter 28

I take back what I said about only ever seeing Ava angry once--I'd completely forgotten about the Ouija board incident before Christmas. Although compared to this, that was child's play. Ava's jaw is clenched, and she's grasping her mobile phone tightly in her hand. I don't think I've ever seen anyone trying to not break into a fit of rage as much as she is right now.

Carmen jumps up immediately when she spots us, and I notice she has her phone in her hand. She must've been the one calling her. Tom stares in our direction with wide eyes and an expression that screams oh shit, while Jamie just looks irritated. I, on the other hand, am trying not to stare at the big black cloud of I don't even know what.

"Did you stop them, or have they already started it?" Ava asks before anyone can speak, and despite the obvious physical frustration, her voice is as calm as ever.

Carmen sighs. "Take a guess, they're idiots."

She continues with something else, but I miss it because Annabel turns to me with wide eyes, and asks, "Felix, are you seeing that?"

She's gaping at the black mass I'm trying to pretend isn't there, which isn't going too great because despite the fact it's night time and the park is poorly lit, the thing is so dark that it stands out like a splash of colour in a black and white film. This can't be good.

"It's fine," I hear Jamie say as I tune back into my flatmates' conversation. "Sorry, we'll just leave it." He goes to pick up the board, but Ava shoots her hand out to stop him.

"We can't just leave!" she snaps for the first time, well, ever. "You've released spirits--dark spirits into the world! We need to end it appropriately, not just cut it off. I mean, whoa, for someone studying at university level, you're not very clever."

Despite the bleak situation, I kind of laugh a little because I know insulting Jamie's intelligence will have pissed him off majorly. Without any prior warning, Ava grabs my arm and pulls me towards everyone. She tells Carmen to sit back down, then orders me too as well. The grass is wet, and I must be sitting on a rock because there's something digging into my leg. The black mass remains, probably proving Ava's point. I avoid looking at it.

"So what, do we need to sign off? Oh, can we sign off as Tom and the Ghoul Patrol," Tom jokes, evidently not catching on to the serious tone lingering.

Ava ignores him. She orders us to all place our hands on the planchette, to which I'm naturally perplexed by, but no one else is because they're all such committed paranormal society members. I'm quickly told it's the teardrop shaped piece of wood that's meant to move around the board.

"I don't--Why do we need to do it? We didn't start it," I question, desperately attempting to avoid joining in on a séance as the local ghost whisperer. I can't imagine it's a good mix.

"We interrupted it, so we're a part of it. The spirits will have latched onto us now as well," Ava replies, her voice still calm and controlled. When I still don't touch the thing, I notice her eye twitch. "If you don't participate, every spirit that has been released from Tom and Jamie's actions will not only be unable to be banished, but they'll latch themselves onto you."

Screw that shit. I sell my soul and join the others in placing a finger on the planchette. Annabel, who's now sitting beside me, is glancing between me and the black mass I continue to ignore. She's huddled up close, her shoulder brushing mine. I think she's scared.

"What have you asked so far?" Ava asks, focusing on Jamie.

"Uh, just if there's anyone there. Nothing responded though, I really don't think there's anything to worry--"

"Is there anyone there?" Ava calls into the air.

There's no response. Well that's bullshit because there's some shady black fungus right above us. Ava asks again, but there's still nothing. On the third go, she says something a little different.

"I can feel you. Stop hiding."

At that, the planchette moves. I assume someone's moving it, probably Tom because that's something he'd do, but everyone other than Ava seems stunned. I don't know why I'm so sceptical; I can literally see there's something here. Annabel nudges closer. Slowly, the planchette spells out the word quack.

The temptation to laugh arises again because there is no logical correlation between anything going on here, but no one else does so I keep my amusement internalised.

"What? What does that mean?" Tom asks, panic finally settling in.

"It's a nickname," Ava mutters with no further explanation. She looks up to the sky. "You're pathetic, and you're not wanted here. Return to the filthy dwelling you crawled out of."

Correct me if I'm wrong, but I feel like insulting an evil force isn't the best way to get rid of it. I gaze at Ava, slightly perplexed. She continues to shout insults into the air, and the trees are beginning to rustle, but I'm not fully sure it's the wind. My head is still down.

"What do you want?" she asks.

On cue, our fingers begin moving again. The planchette is slower this time, but eventually, two words are spelled out.

"The child?" Carmen is the first to say it out loud. She glances around us, finally making me look up. "What?"

As I lift my head, I spot the black mass in the corner of my eye. It's moved. It's nearer, and lower. I don't like how close it is to Carmen. Ava is asking another question, but I don't listen. I'm fixated by the dark cloud over Carmen's shoulder because there's something different about it compared to before. Among the blackness, I can make out a shape. I can make out a human figure, and just as I do, I realise I've let my eyes linger too long.

The mass vanishes. Suddenly, there's a snap. A twig falls from one of the small park trees, and just like that, all hell breaks loose.

A powerful gust of wind sweeps through the park, the trees and the bushes rustle loudly, and before anyone has a second to realise what the hell is happening, the Ouija board flies across the grass. Holy shit. Ava is yelling at everyone to grab it, and Tom is the first to respond. He jumps up and dives onto it, just as small flashes of blackness burst into the air around us as if the original black mass has exploded into a million pieces.

Within seconds, we're on our feet. Jamie's dashing out of the park, Tom's frozen with a stunned expression on his round face, Carmen's pushing herself against Ava as if doing so will keep her safe from anything and everything, while I stand in the middle of it all willing for a normal life more than I ever have in my nineteen years of being. Screw this shit. I pull a Jamie and head straight for the park's exit.

Unlike Jamie, I do acknowledge the existence of everyone else, and furiously grab Carmen and Ava as I pass them. The trees are swaying now, and leaves flurry around us in a mad dance. I don't think Ava knows what to do anymore, so as I yank them, she and Carmen follow me. I do the same with Tom, and we're all quickly sprinting away from whatever the hell is happening. That's always been a life strategy of mine; when your problems get too big, run away and hope for the best.

"What's happening?" Tom yells, I assume at Ava, but he screams it into the air at no one in particular.

He's running with the Oujia board under his arm, and I'm momentarily impressed by his pace considering it's quite the inconvenience, but then remember there's something trying to kill us right now. Ava doesn't respond to Tom, and nor does anyone else. A flash of black shoots past my peripheral vision, and my heart drops. Shit. This isn't good. This really isn't good.

Another burst of blackness whizzes by, this one in my direct line of vision. Jamie's a hundred yards or so ahead of us, but he's not exactly a prime athlete, so we soon catch up to him. If we weren't trying to outrun a demonic cloud right now, I'd be so pissed at him for bolting without us. Another shadow zooms past.

"Follow me!" Ava yells, and considering none of us have any idea of where we're going, we let her lead.

We follow her into a side street as more bursts of blackness explode around us. It's in that moment I realise there's no sign of Annabel. Shit. Shit. I fight myself from calling out for her. She's done this before; she can escape a situation like this easily, but it doesn't mean she's safe. More bursts of black. Shit, shit, shit. I'm assuming I'm the only one who can see any of this, and the others' panic is based on a violent wind following us, throwing rubbish and debris all over the place.

My breath is turning short, and my head is aching. A shadow appears in my peripheral vision again, but I quickly realise it's something else. Something tall with gangly limbs, a grey face and a frown. Nah. Piss off. I must stall for longer than I realise because someone grabs my arm, and yanks me forward. Carmen has hold of me. I snap out of the brief daze, and sprint on. Ava leads us into another street, and I think I know where we're going. Something dark passes right in front of my face. She's taking us to her pub.

If I'm right, we're about five minutes away, and I'm slightly afraid that's not enough time. The bursts of blackness are becoming more frequent, and the wind is getting stronger. As we pass a doorway in a narrow alleyway, I spot another tall figure sporting a cartoonish frown. I don't hesitate for so long this time. Then I spot another one in the distance as we emerge from the alleyway. Then more black flashes. Then another Tracker.

We're two minutes away now. My legs ache and it feels like my whole body is on fire. My head is throbbing by this point, and I know the last thing I need now is to pass out because of these freaks. I push all my energy against any of their attempts to dizzy me, but if we don't get to where we're going soon, I'm going to start stumbling.

Finally, we arrive. Ava leads us in through the back door of the pub, which has a shorter doorway, so we have to duck as we stagger in. We emerge into a small storage space filled with boxes and cleaning equipment, and as we stand around like lost children, Ava bends down to the floor and begins moving some boxes. As I attempt to catch my breath, I manically glance around, and my whole body melts when I notice Annabel standing beside Tom. Jesus. Thank God for that.

"What the hell is happening?" It's Jamie who asks this time, and he's not looking at Ava, he's looking at me.

I don't know what else to do, so I just shrug to show him I'm as clueless as he is, while Ava stays focused on whatever it is she's doing. Once the boxes have been moved, a wooden hatch is revealed in the ground. Ava pulls the handle sticking out of it, and it creaks open. She orders us to get in, and we do as we're told because none of us have a goddamn clue what else to do.

My head is aching less now, but my hands are shaking. Other than Ava, I'm the last to enter the small gap in the ground she's opened, and as I do, I realise it's leading to a basement. Usually, I'd rather amputate my own leg than jump into a dark pub cellar while being chased by something evil, but as well as the general panic induced situation, I feel drawn to it. I feel like it's going to save us. This is going to save us.

As I jog down the concrete steps, I feel a calmness begin to wash over me. There's a light at the bottom of the stairs, and I'm itching to get to it. Any pain in my head has vanished, and my lungs feel full of clean, fresh air. As I reach the bottom and join everyone else, I realise why this sudden outburst of positivity has overcome me. We're in the underground caves.

"Are you crazy?" Tom blurts as Ava appears behind me. "I'm not hiding out down here, it's creepy as shit!"

"We're safe in here, the caves are blessed," she snaps back. I think she's still pissed at Tom for, y'know, being half responsible for our near deaths. "Dark spirits can't access them, not easily anyway."

"What's the plan? Is there a plan?" Carmen questions hastily.

These caves are beautiful, mind you.

"We need to make it to the uni. That way, I can get my car and--"

"Uni's like a twenty-five minute walk away!" Tom whines, only pissing off Ava even more. I chortle.

"The route is, like whoa, totally faster, more direct. It'll be fifteen minutes at most."

Tom doesn't look convinced. I laugh at him again, and Ava shoots me a strange look. I don't know why people haven't relaxed more. We're safe now, and these caves are marvellous. The space we're in is narrow, so Ava nudges past us so she's at the front again. She has something in her hands, some kind of paper, but I can't make out what's on it.

As everyone moves forward, I follow with a slight skip in my step. I hum quietly. We're not running now, just walking at a fast pace, but I can tell Tom is resisting the urge to sprint. He's so silly. I fight back another laugh, but can't stop a smile from forming on my face.

"Right, wise up," Annabel hisses beside me. "Stop acting like you're high on something, okay? Now's not the time."

Rude. I ignore her. Jamie's barely said a word since we got down here, which is very unlike him because it's usually impossible to get him to shut up. It's great. It really is making this whole experience even more wonderful. I glance around the group, and everyone has a terrified expression on their face. How can no one else feel how amazing this place is?

"Felix, seriously, you need to be focused," Annabel nags in my ear again, and at first I go to laugh, but when I see the deadpan look on her face, I stop. "Ground yourself. We're still not safe. The second we leave here, they'll be back. Spirits can latch onto recognisable energy, just like I do with you, so we're not safe."

My logic knows she's right, and that these caves are just making me delusional again, but it feels so real, like this is reality, and everything outside it is pretend. And it feels so good. I want to just smile, and keep smiling because of how good it feels, but I push against every instinct and listen to Annabel. It's not over.

We've been walking for close to ten minutes now, and Ava has glanced down at the paper in her hands several times, so I've figured it's a map of some sort. We've taken numerous twists and turns, entered enormous rooms and tiny passageways, all the while making me realise how complex this whole underground system is.

The warm feeling still floods my body, but with the help of Annabel, I'm keeping myself grounded. Sort of. I mean, I did stroke a wall for a few seconds having gotten myself caught up in it. Everyone's a little calmer now too, other than Jamie who seems more on edge than ever.

"How long?" he asks, but it's mumbled so badly that I'm surprised Ava can understand him.

"Probably not even ten minutes now," she reassures him, but it doesn't seem to help much.

He's twitching slightly, and in my cave daze, I have to force myself not to laugh at him. Carmen has taken hold of my hand, and our fingers are linked together, and it feels nice. We should get married or something. Jamie's muttering something, but no one can make out what he's saying, so we ignore him. I do, anyway. He's lagging behind a little now too, which is inconvenient for everyone.

We enter a large room, which is empty except for a few boxes and some wooden chairs, and there's a small door at the end of it. Ava rushes over to it, so we follow suit, but as she goes to lower its handle her face drops. She tries again, but the door doesn't budge. She starts muttering something about it being locked, so I can't quite grasp why she doesn't just unlock it because there's an obvious unlocking mechanism on the thing.

"It's jammed, I don't..." she mutters. "It won't unlock."

"Let me try," Tom offers, and Ava steps aside.

Just like she did, Tom fiddles with the door, its handle, latch, lock, and everything else attached to it, but it remains stuck. I glance at Annabel because this kind of thing is perfect for her time to shine, but when I look at her, she's staring behind us with wide eyes.

I turn to face whatever it is she's looking at, and initially find myself confused because the only thing there is Jamie, and he's hardly fascinating. As Ava, Carmen, and Tom notice that I've spun around, I realise why Annabel is staring at him like she is. The usual grey colour of Jamie's eyes has vanished, and in its place is nothing but whiteness. He's twitching slightly.

"Nobody move." Ava.

She's frozen in place, her eyes locked on Jamie, and there's something in her voice I've never heard before. I think it's fear.

Chapter 29

Carmen goes to step forward, but Ava shoots her arm out to stop her. No one's speaking. Despite the fact both of Jamie's irises have pissed off to who the hell knows where, I can feel his gaze on us. Staring. From all my experience with the paranormal, I have never seen this before in my life.

"What's wrong with him?" someone asks, and it takes me a moment to realise it's me.

"He's--I think something has possessed him," Ava replies, her voice shaking. "I've heard of it, but I've--but I've never seen it happen."

"What?" Tom exclaims. "How has--You said we'd be safe here! How did something get in?"

"We are," Ava snaps back, "it must've gotten to him before we entered here, it--it takes a while."

While the two of them argue, I'm fixated on Jamie. His twitching has subsided, and he's standing perfectly still. Inhumanely still. Annabel has manifested beside me now, her body huddled up to mine, and I don't like that I can't reassure her. The cave daze is making me feel slightly sick now, and my mind is muddled with its calming effects and an unprecedented fear.

Tom and Ava have stopped sniping at each other, and all is silent again. I don't think anyone has any clue what the hell to do. We're just standing motionless, like sitting ducks waiting for whatever the hell is messing with Jamie to do something. I turn to Ava in hope of something--anything, to see her with her eyes shut. Her expression is calm and controlled, like she's focusing on something. I'm about to question her when for the first time, Jamie speaks.

"That's not going to work, quack, though the effort is rather charming." It's his voice, but it doesn't sound right. Like there's something off.

"What?" It's Tom who responds.

Jamie laughs. My eyes are still locked on Ava, and at Jamie's comment, she flinches slightly but quickly regains composure. What's she doing?

"Well, perhaps less charming, and more pathetic. In fact, didn't you call us pathetic a short while back? Rather hypocritical, don't you agree?" Jamie continues, and I'm trying to put my finger on what's different about his voice, but I'm struggling. "I've met worms who have possessed powers stronger than yours. I can barely feel a thing, bless your heart. A pathetic excuse for a quack, though you know that, don't you? You agree. You'll never be like your mother, Ava, try as you will."

Ava is visibly shaking. She's biting her lip, her eyes still shut, and she's muttering under her breath. What's he talking about? If this isn't really Jamie, how does he know Ava's name? Shit, shit, shit. What do we do? What does it even want?

"You three work on the door," Ava eventually says with strain in her voice, her eyes still closed and her mind still focused on whatever it is she's trying to do with Jamie's captor. "I've got its energy preoccupied, it'll be easier to open."

Jamie laughs. "You're going to require far more than whatever this is, quack."

Ignoring the comments, Ava snaps at us to go to the door again, and this time, we obey her. Tom's switching between yanking on the handle and desperately trying to turn the lock, but to no avail. I turn back around to face Ava and Jamie just as Jamie steps forward. The footstep is heavy, and he almost loses balance, but he's closer.

"Help her," a voice whispers, and it takes me by such surprise that I jump. Annabel stands beside me, her eyes boring into me. "Whatever she's doing, you can do it--You must be able to. Help her!"

I stammer. I can't. I don't know what to do. I don't know what she's doing. Tom is still bashing the door and trying everything imaginable to open it, but it's not working. Nothing's working. Jamie takes another shaky step forward. Shit, shit, shit.

"Ava, he's walking towards you, he's--What do we do?" Carmen yells.

Ava doesn't reply. I don't think she can. All her focus is on whatever it is she's doing. Annabel's voice is raised now, almost yelling at me to help Ava, but I don't know how. I'm too scared to try anything because if I do, everyone will catch on to me. They'll know. Every single person here will know.

Carmen's trying the door now, but her attempts are as useless as Tom's. I join her, but my hands are shaking so much that I'm only making it worse. Suddenly, something whizzes past me, almost knocking me over, and then there's yelling infused with laughter as that something--Tom--lunges for Jamie. He doesn't even get close. The second they collide, Tom is violently shoved against the cave wall. Jamie is laughing hysterically.

"You insipid fool!" He booms through laughter, as Tom scrambles up from the ground, dazed. "I apologise, I imagine that's far too complex of a word for you. To be frank, it's a miracle you obtain the mental capacity to count to ten."

As Jamie spits insults towards him, Tom backs away. He's limping slightly. Ava stays in the position she's been in for the past five minutes or so, but her face is pale. She's struggling. I have to be able to do something, I have to.

"No one likes you, Thomas," Jamie continues, his voice now steady and low. "You irritate them. You irritate everyone. Then again, you've never been one for friends, have you? Poor thing. It's only a matter of time until this piteous bunch cast you aside. You're nothing. No substance, nothing, just a brainless little virgin."

"Shut up!" Tom yells, but all it does is spur the creature inside Jamie on.

"Now, now, there's no need to shout. I'm sure you'll amend that small issue eventually, don't worry yourself. Well, it'll probably have to be with something deceased or another spastic like you, but then I suppose beggars can't be choosers."

"Oh, piss off, dickhead!" I snap, and what I've just done quickly dawns on me.

Jamie turns away from Tom in the corner of the room, and towards me. A wide grin spreads across his face, and now it's my turn. Whatever it wants to say, it can bloody well say it. I don't need anything to convince me I'm a useless piece of shit.

Out of nowhere, a sharp pain stabs itself into my skull. I clench my eyes shut, and lift my hand to my head. My ears are ringing. I try to push it out, and as immediately as it appeared, it's gone. What the hell? I reopen my eyes to see Jamie's blank irises digging into me, his lips curled.

The pain strikes me again. I push against it, squinting this time. The third time it returns, I'm prepared. This time, I don't let it go. I keep pushing. I force my eyes to remain open this time, and Jamie's entire face is twitching. His nostrils are flared, his lip is curled, and his teeth are grinding against each other.

Then I spot Ava in the corner of my eye.

Her arms dangle by her side, her hands clenched slightly as some colour returns to her face, and after having her eyes shut for over five minutes, they're finally open and are looking straight at me. She knows.

I briefly lose focus. Ava swears, I think directly at me, and quickly shuts her eyes to return to the focused demeanour she'd adopted before now. The stabbing pain returns, and I counteract it again. Jamie's face is twitching even more sporadically now, and he's grunting.

"Felix, get your spirit to work on the door," Ava demands, her eyes still shut.

"I don't have, I mean, I--"

"Get your spirit to work on the door!" she snaps, and I don't even have to say anything because Annabel obeys immediately. "Its energy is primarily focused on us, and there's only so far it can stretch." She takes a breath. "Carmen, Tom! Keep trying the door!"

I continue forcing all my energy against Jamie's captor, but it's straining every inch of my body. I'm winning; I can feel that I'm winning, that we're winning, but every part of me wants to let go. Suddenly, there's a clicking sound. It echoes throughout the cave. Then there's a long squeak. The door. They've gotten the door open. Holy--Thank fuck for that. My relief is short-lived because within seconds, the force pushing against me intensifies. I feel dizzied.

"Run through!" Ava calls to Carmen and Tom. "We're only five minutes or so away, so grab the map and go!"

"What about you?" Carmen questions hastily.

"I know the way, don't worry. Go!"

With that, Carmen and Tom make a break for it. Their footsteps echo behind them, but I can't concentrate on the sound for long. I continue forcing myself against the energy attacking us, but I'm turning weaker. I can feel it.

"Tell your spirit to push with us," Ava instructs. When I don't respond immediately, she swears and continues on. "Stop stalling! Do you even have any idea what you're doing? Your spirit can help us, tell it to help us. For the love of--What's their name?"

"Annabel," I answer quickly this time. No turning back now.

"Annabel, touch Felix, and focus on his energy. It will guide you to follow what we're doing." The calmness I'm used to hearing in Ava's voice has returned, and she speaks slowly. "It might feel strange, but it's normal, I promise."

Annabel, who's still standing at the doorway out of here, manifests herself beside me. She doesn't need to be told twice. She grabs my hand, but the moment she does, flinches and pulls away.

"It hurts," she stammers, looking up at me.

"Felix?" Ava questions.

"Yeah, hang on," I mutter back. God, my head is killing me. "I know," I whisper to Annnabel. "Just make yourself stay with it, okay?"

This time, I take Annabel's hand. She instinctively pulls away, but stops herself letting go completely. Jamie hasn't spoken since I started fighting him back, and I can only assume it to be a good thing. The weight of his energy lifts ever so slightly, but it's not because I'm letting go. It's because it's now three against one.

No one says a word, and it's so silent I swear I can hear Tom and Carmen in the far distance. Then without a slither of warning, the pressure disappears completely. Annabel's hand falls away from mine, and the intensity of all my focus being released almost trips me over. It feels like I've just emerged from being buried six foot underground.

Ava is running, but I'm not sure what towards because my eyesight is patchy, but I don't think it's out the room. She's bending down in the middle of it, and Annabel has joined her, but I don't know why. I stumble towards them as my senses begin to recover.

As I stop beside Ava, I realise she's crouched over Jamie. He's half sitting, half lying on the grey ground with a dazed look on his face, and I've never been more relieved to see his stupid grey eyes looking at me. His face is white, and he's blinking rapidly. Finally, I snap out of the stupefied state I was in, and make myself useful.

"I'll pull him up, and you just grab his arm and keep him balanced," I say to Ava, who clearly has no clue how to get him to stand.

She nods, and does as I instructed while I drape Jamie's arm over my shoulder and force him to stand, all the while not taking her eyes off me for a second. She looks pissed. Really, really pissed. Jamie is mumbling incoherently, but by the time we get him on his feet, he's able to stay half upright. Ava drapes his other arm around her shoulder, and we begin to awkwardly guide him towards the cave's exit.

"Will it come back?" I ask Ava as we approach the doorway.

"No," she answers simply.

"Why are--Where are Tom and Carmen? What happened?" Jamie says, finally regaining the ability to speak normally.

"Are you sure?" I question, ignoring him. "Can it not possess him again, or one of us?"

"It can't remain in here without a body to inhabit and protect it from the cave's blessing. We're fine. Whoa, how are you so clueless?"

Her question sounds more rhetoric than anything, so I don't answer it. It must only be five minutes or so until we finally reach our destination, but it feels like hours. Jamie can pretty much stand perfectly now, and he keeps asking us what happened, and we keep telling him we'll explain later. We've stopped outside a door at the end of a well-lit passageway, and as Ava goes to open it, I inhale a breath of air. Thankfully, this one opens perfectly.

"Carmen? Tom?" Ava calls up the stairs at the other end of it, and within seconds, there's a reply.

"Ava? We're here! Are you okay? Is everyone okay?" Carmen speaks at a hundred miles per hour.

After reassuring Carmen, Ava begins ascending the stairs while I follow behind with one of Jamie's arms still slung over me. At the top of these concrete stairs is a tiny room with a blue door at the other side of it. Other than Tom, Carmen and Ava standing in the middle of it, it's empty.

Wasting no time for explanation, Ava scurries towards the door, opens it, and hurries us all through it. Somewhat confusingly, as we step out of the compact room, we find ourselves standing in some girls' toilets. I'm surprised. I mean, they smell pretty good.

We leave the bathroom, Jamie now able to walk by himself, and I realise where we are within seconds. Ava was right. She really was leading us to uni. We're in The Cavern. We're on the basement level, so hurry upstairs to the ground floor. There's not a soul in sight. It's unnerving seeing the social hub of university so dark and deserted.

I don't know if it's because the numbing abilities of the caves have worn off or because in addition to the fact we're being hunted by something that wants to kill us, it's finally dawning on me that everyone here knows I'm not fully what I seem, but an intense sensation of panic is falling over me. I try ignoring it as we jog our way through the ground floor of the building, but it's dizzying me. Suddenly, there's a black shadow. No. Then another. It flies past my eyes. No, no, no.

We're getting close. As we pass a table loaded with stacked pamphlets, they're thrown into the air in a wild flurry. Something black whirs past us. We up our pace. Panic has flooded my whole head by now, and I can barely think straight, let alone walk straight. I don't know if it's because she notices this, or just because, but Carmen grabs my hand and steadies me. It helps. More black shadows. I try to reassure myself because there are no Trackers this time, but it doesn't help much.

Paper cups, napkins, coffee stirrers, and pretty much anything that isn't nailed to the ground are flung at us as we pass through the food court, but we can't stop. Finally, we reach The Cavern's main entrance. Carmen bashes the emergency door release, and just like that, we're free. As we step outside, it quickly dawns on me that this isn't just going to be a straight run to Ava's car because dotted around us like mould in a white room, are bursts of black energy.

Now, we run. Rubbish from the ground whirls in the air as we scramble down The Cavern's steps, and the trees that frame the adjacent road are swaying wildly. It's drizzling slightly, and the route we're taking is poorly lit. To make matters worse, as we run down the road, the streetlights' bulbs explode aggressively, making it near impossible for us to see where we're going.

Rubbish continues being thrown at us, and as we take the turning for our accommodation, I have to shove Tom out of the way of an incoming glass bottle. It scuffs me, but only on my hand.

"Where are you parked?" Jamie yells through the rain and rustling trees.

"Just outside!" Ava replies. "We're not far!"

We up our pace. Bursts of black explode around us, and despite the rain and crap being thrown at us every passing second, we eventually find ourselves in the car park we need. We're not even a hundred yards in when Ava falls, her car keys flinging out of her hands and crashing to the paved ground. Something throws them into a nearby bush.

Tom goes to lift her up, but she can't move. Something is weighing her down. There's a shadow figure above her, so to catch its attention, I bend down and somewhat stupidly throw some gravel at it. Stupid or not, it works. The bastard falls right into my trap. The second I feel a nudge, I force my energy against it. Ava is released. I turn my attention to the bushes where the keys were thrown to see Annabel floating them in front of her face. God, I love her sometimes. She throws them to me, and we're beside Ava's car within less than a minute.

I pile into the back with Tom and Carmen, while Jamie takes the passenger seat. Considering Tom is twice the size of anyone here, it's not an ideal set up, but now's not really the time to complain. Once inside, seatbelts aren't even a consideration. Ava starts the engine, and we're off before Jamie has even fully shut his door.

Now that my legs are no longer carrying the weight of my body, and the distraction of trying not to fall over has disappeared, I feel lost. Confused. My head is aching. My chest is tight. I can't keep still. It feels wrong to be sitting down, I need to be moving. We've left the uni's grounds now, but the black bursts continue to follow us. I furiously rub my hands together. Why can't I catch my breath? Shit, shit, shit. The panic is setting in again.

They know. Everyone knows. Not just Jamie anymore, everyone. Ava knows, Tom knows, Carmen knows. Every single person here knows. I'm trapped. I'm stuck in this car. I want to escape it, I want to run away. They can't know. No one can know. They think I'm crazy. They must do. I try to breathe in, but I can't, and I don't know why. Shit, shit, shit. My head hurts. I can't breathe. Why can't I breathe? I can't keep still, I can't think, I can't focus. Everyone knows. Everyone.

"What the hell, Felix?" Someone is calling my name, but I can't hear them properly over the throbbing in my head.

Are the bursts of darkness still outside? Are they still following us? Why can't I hear anything properly? I can't breathe. I still can't breathe.

"What the shit was that all about? Are you a messiah or something, what the actual shit?" I think it's Tom.

"He can interact with them, it's complicated," someone replies.

I think it's Jamie. Yeah, it must be.

"Wait, you knew about all this?" Tom's eyes are on me. My vision is turning more and more blotchy so I can't see him, but I can feel them piercing into me. "Bloody hell, thanks for telling that loser and not me, mate."

I didn't want to tell anyone. I don't want to tell anyone. I just want to be normal, that's all I want. I don't want to see these things. I don't want this. I don't want any of this.

"Felix! Felix, calm down!" Ava.

Does she know I can't breathe? Do they all know? Can they tell? Black spots flood my vision, and I don't know if it's the dark spirits or if there's something wrong with me. Voices are shouting, but I don't know what they're saying.

"They're latched onto his energy, they're following him, and his energy is like a flashing light to them right now! It's too manic!"

"He can't help it, I think he's having a panic attack!" Carmen?

It doesn't feel like I'm here anymore. Maybe I'm not. Maybe this is all in my head. Maybe I'm in the middle of a hospital suffering from a psychotic episode. Maybe Annabel isn't real. Maybe my parents aren't real. Maybe there never was an accident. Maybe none of this is real. I feel sick.

"Don't! It could go badly, I--If he is having one, it might be dangerous!" I think it's Carmen again.

"It won't be any more dangerous than this!" Ava snaps back. "Tom, just do it!"

I use the little energy I have to turn my head slightly to look at Tom, and that's when I see him with his eyes squinted shut and his fist raised, moments before it hits me square across the face.

Chapter 30

"**U**gh, move, you're barely touching him."

"Yeah, maybe because I don't wanna kill the guy? Pretty sure I almost have already."

"Shut up, you're exaggerating!"

"Um, no I'm not, did you miss what happened back there?"

Voices continue to argue, and as I slide back into reality, I begin to realise that holy shit, my head hurts. I try to raise my hand to it, but my body is limp. I can't move anything. I take a deep breath, only for it to intensify the pain. My face feels like it's on fire.

"Just move! Let me attempt it."

I open my eyes, but my vision is blurred. Something harshly shakes me, making me feel even more off balance than I already am.

"Bloody hell, calm it!" the other voice snaps. Tom?

"For Pete's sake, move! The both of you!" a girl's voice intervenes, and I can't remember whose it is, but it's nice.

I try to take another deep breath, but it's still painful. Less so than before, but not enough to make me want to try again. I can make out shapes now--figures, but it's dark and it's making me slightly disoriented. I must still be in Ava's car. I feel someone shift their weight on the seat beside me.

"Felix? Felix, can you hear me?" Finally, I recognise the voice as Carmen's.

I try to respond, but my mouth is dry. God, I'm tired. A hand brushes across my cheek, and it's cold. I blink in an attempt to focus on Carmen's face, but it just makes me feel dizzier.

"Hey? Felix? Say something."

I don't know if it's because I'm regaining my strength, or because it's Carmen who asked, but I do as I'm told. What I say is a nonsensical splurge of unidentifiable sounds, but I mean, hey, technically I'm saying something. Carmen responds with a soft laugh, and as my vision straightens out, the first thing I see are her yellow-brown eyes and soft, tanned face.

"You okay? Here," she says as she turns around to grab something from behind her. She brings out a bottle of water, and hands it to me.

I mumble what I hope sounds like a thank you, then grab the bottle from Carmen's hand like my life depends on it. God, I'm thirsty. As I sip from the bottle, I realise I'm slouched over, so shuffle about a bit to sit upright. I'm still sitting in the middle of Ava's car, while Carmen leans in from the door with her knee balanced on the seat next to mine, and just outside it are Jamie and Tom. Then everything hits me like a kick in the groin. The séance, the caves, the possession, The Cavern, the car. Everyone knows.

It takes me about ten minutes to properly regain myself and leave the car. It turns out Tom punched me in the face to knock me out and omit my energy earlier, which wasn't the kindest gesture, but it seemed to work so that's that. There sure aren't any crazed dashes of blackness around anymore, anyway. My eye is bloody killing me though.

Ava drove us to a remote B&B just over an hour out of the city, and she's in the lobby booking us rooms to sleep in for the night. It's almost midnight, though, so we might struggle a bit. She kind of looked like she wanted to rip my head off last time I was conscious, so part of me wants to avoid Ava at all costs. I'm currently outside with everyone else and they're looking at me like I'm a literal alien though, so I decide to go on in and join her before they grow the balls to start asking questions.

The lobby is small and narrow, and as I reach the end of it, I spot Ava speaking to a middle-aged balding guy sat behind a wooden desk. I think the carpet is meant to be red, but it's faded to a dull pink with some questionable stains dotted around it. It smells kind of damp in here too. Carmen, Tom and Jamie have followed me in, and Jamie is whispering something to Tom. Probably something about me. As if on cue, when we stop beside Ava, she spins around.

"Groovy, okay, so we've got a double, and a family room, so you guys can have the family room while Carmen and I share the double," she announces, and before anyone can respond, she's charging up the stairway behind the reception counter.

We have to half-jog to keep up with her, and honestly, I was hoping we'd all just retire into our assigned rooms, and spend the night in a deep, peaceful sleep. Naturally, that's not the case. Ava leads us to hers and Carmen's room, and when I ask where ours is to make my escape, she just spins around, stares at me in silence for at least ten seconds, then smiles.

"No."

Um, okay then. She grabs my arm and violently pulls me into her room, while everyone else follows. Here we go.

"Sit," Ava orders as she points at the large double bed in the centre of the room.

She still has her eyes locked on me. Carmen takes the bright blue armchair beside the bed, while us guys hop onto the large mattress. It kind of smells like something died in here, and I'd usually comment on it, but I don't think now's the best time. Annabel has joined us by this point, and she sits cross legged on the floor beside Ava, who stands over the bed with her arms crossed.

"So?" Ava asks with raised eyebrows.

I don't look around the room, but I know everyone's eyes are on me. I can feel it; it's crawling through my skin. There must be something I can say--an excuse. Anything. I glance at Annabel in hope of some support, but she just shrugs with a slightly down-turned mouth. Even if I did try to bullshit my way out of this, Jamie knows. As if I could anyway; they literally saw me performing some ghostbuster shit out there. I take a deep breath, and do what I always do. I shrug.

Ava rolls her eyes. She's tapping her foot methodically, and every time she does so, a tiny cloud of dust bursts from the carpet. It's hypnotising to watch.

"For the love of--Are you even listening?"

I snap my attention back to Ava, who's chewing her lip, and apologise. "No, uh, yeah--I mean, yeah, sorry." I dart my eyes around the room, and every person is focused on me. "Look, can we--can we do this tomorrow? I promise I'll explain, I just... I need some time."

Ava mumbles something under her breath before saying, "we don't have time, we don't know if we're safe, or if--"

"Yeah," Carmen interrupts her, and turns her eyes from my face to Ava's for a few seconds. "We can deal with it tomorrow."

"Whoa, Carmen, it's not that easy. No one can see them, okay, no one. He's either lying--Well, Jamie is, or this is even more serious than I--"

"Ava, we're all shattered, scared out of our brains, and Felix was just knocked straight out for almost an hour, probably mid panic attack, okay? I don't think any of us are in the right state of mind for this right now, let alone him."

Everyone is silent after that. My eyelids are heavy, and if we sit around saying nothing for any longer, I'm probably going to pass out right here on the girls' bed. Eventually, Ava nods, then walks out of the room. Carmen goes after her. With a sigh, I lie back on the bed. For a skanky hotel, this thing is comfy as shit. Well, either that or I'm too exhausted to notice any springs digging into my back.

Jamie awkwardly moves out of the way to avoid me. I don't know why he's acting so weird; he knew all of this already. Tom's staring silently at the beige wall opposite us. There's a ringing sound in my ear, and as I shut my eyes, I focus on it until I'm so used to it that I don't notice it anymore. Instead, I listen to the blood pumping in my head. It's like my ears are pulsing, and I count each one. One, two, three.

I think Jamie and Tom are speaking, but I can't make out what they're saying over the sound inside my skull. Four, five, six. I keep counting until I forget to, so start again. It's quieter now. I think Jamie and Tom have gone. One, two, three. I wonder if Annabel is still here. Four, five six. Something soft brushes against my bare arms, and it's warm. Seven, eight, nine.

My breath is out of sync with the blood pulsing in my head. It's slower. Ten, eleven, twelve. The mattress I'm lying on lowers a little. Thirteen, fourteen, fifteen. Wait, isn't this Ava and Carmen's bed? I should get up. Sixteen, seventeen, eighteen. The only lamp that was lighting the room must turn off because everything turns to total blackness. Wait, what number am I on?

I'm awoken by a pillow being thrown at my face. I jump up, and for a moment, I forget where I am and wonder why I'm lying--well, now half-sitting, in a random bed in a run-down B&B in the middle of nowhere. It doesn't take me long to remember. Carmen sits at the end of the bed, her hand delved into a tiny box of supermarket branded cereal. She's grinning.

"Y'know, a hey Felix, it's time to get up would've done the job," I mumble.

Carmen shoots me a wink. "Please, I'm not that nice." She grins as she throws me a small box of cereal, and I'm practically ravenous, so I'm soon throwing said cereal by the bucket load into my mouth. "Well, saying that, Ava wanted to wake you up an hour ago, but I convinced her to let you sleep in some more, so really, I'm the hero here."

I respond by throwing the limp pillow she threw at me right back at her, but she's been awake long enough to have her wits about her, so dodges it.

"Thanks for saving my arse last night," I say, rubbing my eye, only to flinch at the pain from where Tom whacked me in the face. "Can't say I was feeling the third degree by Ava at the time. Did she--Did you guys sleep here last night? Sorry, I didn't mean to fall asleep."

Carmen waves her hand in the air. "It's all right, although if you don't explain what the hell is going on within the hour, I might have to throw you off the roof of this place."

She laughs, but I'm not entirely convinced she's kidding.

"And yeah--Well, I did, but Ava slept on the single in the guys' room, which I'm sure you can imagine Jamie loved when that meant sharing a double bed with Tom." She laughs. "I kept my hands to myself, don't worry. I mean, to start with, I'm pretty sure it would've been sexual assault considering your state, and the whole, y'know, being unconscious thing." She throws a handful of cereal into her mouth. "Can't afford that sort of lawsuit."

I'm a little thrown by how cheery, and generally talkative, Carmen is this morning. If roles were reversed, after seeing the things I was doing last night, I would be staying at least five feet away at all times. Then again, maybe that's why she's acting overly chatty. Maybe she's trying to hide the fact she's scared of me.

As Carmen and I make our way downstairs, and I make my way to my second breakfast, my legs feel like they could cave in on me any second. I thought I'd slept okay, but I still feel shattered. Worse, if anything. It doesn't help that I'm terrified of seeing Ava. If she's even half as pissed as she was last night, this is going to be horrific.

Surprisingly, no one is in the compact dining room when we step into it. No one appears throughout the meal either, and so as time goes on, I begin feeling less like I'm on the verge of a severe panic attack.

"They're in the beer garden out back," Carmen says, and it takes me a moment to realise what she's talking about.

"Oh, cool, makes sense," I reply with a mouthful of bread.

"Jamie was going to wake you and do the whole breakfast thing because he--Y'know, he knows about stuff, but we thought it'd be better if I did."

"Yeah, good shout, he's annoying," I mutter, which Carmen responds to by slapping my arm across the table, and telling me not to be mean. Her eyes tell me she one-hundred percent agrees with me, though. "I'm not gonna, like, summon a demon to shit on your breakfast, by the way. You don't need to be afraid," I joke, but the last sentence comes out a little too seriously.

Once we've finished in the dining room, I finally grace Ava, Tom, and Jamie with my presence in the beer garden. It's probably the nicest part of this hotel, and a lot bigger than I figured it'd be. Despite it being a warm, bright day, the garden is pretty empty. The group are sitting around a picnic bench, and while Ava and Jamie look like they're drinking some kind of fruit juice, Tom has a bottle of beer. I kind of want to join him.

Annabel is already sitting with everyone, which throws me slightly, but hey, it's a free country. Ava spots me the moment Carmen and I step outside, and she's opened her mouth before I've even fully sat down on the bench beside Jamie.

Surprisingly, "I'm sorry," is the first thing she says to me. "Carmen told me about your family's accident, and I just--Whoa, I'm stupid sometimes. I just assumed you'd grown up around spirit talkers. I shouldn't have, sorry."

I shrug it off with a mumbled it's fine. I should probably be annoyed at Carmen for telling Ava about my family, but I'm not, and it's hardly a feeling I want to force. It's inevitable that it was going to come out sooner or later anyway. Everyone's eyes are on me again, and I just can't be bothered to avoid it anymore. So I explain everything.

I skim over the basics; the accident, the dead parents, the general I see dead people thing, but explaining the weird shit that's been happening recently is more complicated. Anything I forget is either filled in by Jamie, or I'm reminded to mention it by Annabel. No one else speaks throughout, and Ava's dark eyes don't leave my face for a second. Once I've said all I have to say, still no one speaks, but Ava starts to nod slowly.

"The Trackers," she eventually says. "What's the closest one came to you?"

"Uh..." I stammer a little, not quite sure why this of all things is the first question she has for me. "What d'you mean? Physically?" I ask, to which Ava nods. "Um, I mean, one grabbed my shoulder, I guess, in The Cavern's--"

Ava gawks at me, her mouth literally hanging open. "Oh, whoa. Whoa. You let one touch you?"

I don't think I've ever heard anyone say whoa so aggressively.

"Well, yeah, the dickhead wouldn't tell me anything, so it got to that level. Bit of a personal space issue, sure, but--"

"No wonder they latched onto you! Your energy would've stood out like a sore thumb to them after one of their Trackers had made a physical connection to you."

Ah. Well shit. My bad.

"Sorry, you don't--You wouldn't have known that. I just, whoa, okay." She groans, and begins rubbing her head. "This is bad. I don't know what this is, but it's really bad."

Well that fills me with confidence. If Ava doesn't even know what the hell is going on, there's no way anyone else here will. Tom is about to speak when Ava calls out to someone behind me.

She jumps up from the table quicker than I've seen anyone ever move, and as I turn to look at what's distracted her, I see her hurrying towards the patio doors her parents have just stepped out of. They seem to have brought a guest too; their dead bartender. Hey, good shout. Maybe they'll be able to tell me whether or not I'm about to be slaughtered by a mass of demonic dead people.

Chapter 31

Our table is too small for another two additions, so we move from it to plant ourselves onto a larger, round one. During the moving process, I attempt to go grab a drink, but get roared at by Ava, so don't dare move. Tom offers me some of his slightly warm beer, and the fact I accept the offer says everything about my current state of mind.

I'm not sure how to react to Kato and Mosi's bartender friend, who's standing over Kato's shoulder opposite me, so I just play it safe and ignore him as I always do. I'm soon forced to endure another round of the explanation process, this time to Kato and Mosi. I can't quite decide if I'm more or less afraid of these two than I am of Ava. Once finished, it's quiet again. This silence lasts longer than the one that followed my first explanation.

When Kato eventually breaks that silence, she leans forward slightly and looks at me with an expression that's impossible to read. "Prove it."

"Uh, what do you--I mean, how?" I ask, tripping over my words.

"If your claim is true, you'll know how."

What? My heart suddenly feels like it's bouncing around my body, and everyone is eyeballing me. What does she want me to--Oh, shit, that's why they brought the old stiff, isn't it? They want me to acknowledge him. Eyes continue boring into me from all angles, and I know I should just look up at the guy and say something, but I'm frozen.

I can barely bring myself to speak to Annabel in front of Jamie half the time because it feels so strange, let alone acknowledge a random spirit in front of everyone in the middle of a run down B&B's beer garden. I've started tapping my feet. What's wrong with me? Just look up, you idiot. Everyone knows everything anyway, it doesn't matter. It doesn't matter.

"Okay." I sound about as confident as a puppy on its way to having its balls cut off. I clear my throat, take a breath, then look directly at Mosi's deceased bartender. "I'm guessing that's what you're referring to."

I make an awkward waving motion towards the spirit, and while everyone else's response is to look for something they can't see, Kato keeps her gaze on me and tilts her head slightly. She nods. I think she wants me to expand.

"The, uh, guy who hangs out at your pub a lot," I continue. "He fixes up badly poured pints. Kinda old. A lot of tweed."

I have such a way with words, don't I?

Kato and Mosi look at one another, while Ava gazes wide eyed at them to gauge their response. The curious, and probably somewhat concerned, glances of strangers are beginning to be shot in our direction, and it's making me want to crawl under the table and hide for the rest of eternity. The bartender has disappeared now that his job is done, and after some more silence, Kato nods her head slowly. She pulls her wild hair back, and pins it up off her face.

"Right," she says, clapping her hands together. "Family name? Is Reynolds part of a double barrel? Or did you change it?"

Straight into the family questions. Fantastic. Love it. I kind of want everyone to piss off. There's no use in Tom or Jamie being here--the only one who really needs to be here is Kato. I hardly want to make any more of a scene than I'm already making though, so I bite my tongue and say nothing.

"Nah, that's it," I reply to Kato.

"No, it can't be. It's not one of the twelve families."

Nope, that's definitely it. She can consult my birth certificate if she doesn't believe me. I want to roll my eyes, but fight it. What is it with Ava and her family's determination not to stray from their ghostie literature for five minutes? I mean, c'mon, I think I know my own surname.

Kato's eyebrows furrow. "It must be your mother's side. What's her maiden name?"

"Uh, Reynolds," I answer, which makes Kato look ten times more confused than before. "My folks never married. I took my mum's name--no clue why."

"Right, so what's your father's surname?"

"Brennan. Not sure how you say it, but I always say it like it rhymes with--" I stop in my tracks when I notice a look on Kato's face that resembles that of someone who's just witnessed a coyote bite a small child's head off. "What? What is it?"

Kato, Mosi, and Ava are darting their eyes at one another like they have some genetic twitching condition, leaving me no closer to understanding what the heck is going on.

"Ava, dear," Kato finally says, "you and your friends go and start getting all your stuff together. Your father and I will finish sorting this out here."

Sorting this out? Why does it sound like they're about to beat me up? Ava opens her mouth to speak, but says nothing when Mosi raises his eyebrows in response. She nods quickly, then stands from the table. She grabs Jamie's arm, who was sitting beside her, and pulls him up as they move around the table.

Carmen does as she's told when Ava asks her to head back inside, but Tom whines about wanting to hear all the 'cool ghost shit'. That gets him a sharp jab in his side from Ava, so he eventually does as he's told through complaints. I almost stand myself, but am getting the vibe that's not really the idea. The only people still here with me are Kato, Mosi, and Annabel. She sits beside me, mimicking the leaned in position Kato has adopted.

"What do you know about your father's family?" Kato asks, to which I shrug. "Did you know them? Did your parents ever speak about them?"

"Well, I mean, I can't remember," I reply with an awkward laugh that comes out sounding more pathetic than humorous.

"Yes, of course, sorry," Kato apologises.

"They couldn't be traced or anything, I don't think--I mean, after I was in hospital, there was no sign of anyone on my dad's side, which I guess is why I ended up in care or whatever," I expand. "I didn't have much family on my mum's side, so yeah, that's that." I pause. "I'm gonna guess you know more about that?"

"Yes. It's quite... It's difficult to explain."

Okay? Kato and Mosi glance at each other for the umpteenth time. I'm not completely sure why Mosi stayed; I don't think he's said anything this whole time. Annabel is looking up at me now, most likely waiting for a response to Kato's ambiguity, but I've got nothing.

"The Brennan's were always very... quiet, I suppose the word is--Well, perhaps private is a better word. We didn't know them personally, and I believe only one or two other families did, but we heard some wonderful things--an Irish family, in case you weren't aware. They were very close, extremely in touch with spirits, and were said to be some of the best spirit talkers."

As Kato continues raving about how fantastic my father's family were, it gradually dawns on me that I've heard all this before. Approximately eleven years ago. I know what's coming. I know this buttering up is leading to a shitstorm, so I just say it. No point dancing around the subject.

"They're all dead, aren't they?"

It's the only thing I've said with any shred of confidence all day, and it's oozing with the stuff. I don't make any emotion out of it, I just say it. Nice and plain. Annabel's eyes are boring into me, her mouth agape, which I don't fully understand because she must've figured it out.

"Oh, I didn't realise--Well, oh, were you told in hospital?" Kato says with surprise in her voice.

"Nah, I just guessed," I mumble in response. In an attempt to make light of the situation, I then continue on to say the weirdest thing I possibly could say. "Dead family is kind of my aesthetic."

Kato stammers slightly at first, then releases an awkward chuckle before going on to explain why every member of my family is dead. It took people a while to notice, apparently, with them being so private. So I guess they might've been rotting a while. It's generally accepted they were killed by dark spirits, which my cheery family road trip story reaffirms, but nobody knows why or how.

My folks' accident is the first actual revelation of how it happened, least with how they were killed. It could've been different for the others. The only reason anyone found out about the whole family being wiped out is from a séance, which resulted in the death of a member from a different family. All sunshine and rainbows then.

At least it now makes sense why Kato ordered everyone else to leave; breaking the news to someone that not only their direct family, but their entire ancestral line was violently slaughtered by angry spirits isn't best done in front of an audience of teenagers.

Kato and Mosi watch me with careful gazes, and everything about this situation is reminding me of when I was stuck in a hospital as an eight-year-old, surrounded by grown-ups watching my every move with downturned mouths and eyes brimming with pity. Annabel is sitting beside me with a face like a slapped arse, but I just shrug. I'm used to strangers I'm supposed to know dying.

Chapter 32

"What does it all mean?" I ask in attempt to steer things away from the subject. "In the grand scheme of things. I mean, what do we do now?"

Kato sighs. "We... We don't know. I'll try and figure it out--look into the literature to discover any clues in history, trace any spirits who may be able to help. In the meantime, all of you need to keep moving. Don't stay in one place too long. Those evil spirits are sensitive to your energies now, and the longer you stay in one place, the more concentrated your energies become."

"Aren't the others safe?" I question. "Someone clearly wants my neck in a noose, sure, but they've got no reason to go after the others."

Kato shakes her head. "They're not safe. Whatever it is that's after you will use the others to locate you, and if you're not there when they track them... Well, dark spirits aren't particularly known for their patience and understanding."

To cut away all the frills, I've basically screwed everyone over, and they could quite literally all die because of me. Isn't that just the best thing ever? Everyone should be my mate. If I wasn't in a public space with the spirit talking parents of my flatmate, I'd probably be hitting something by now. What do these things even want from me? What would they gain from murdering me? What did they gain from killing an entire bloodline?

"I'm gonna guess going back to uni is out of the question, right?" I ask, refusing to dwell on questions that can't be answered.

Kato responds with a soft smile and a shake of her head, and finally, Mosi speaks. "We've brought the jeep with all your stuff," he explains. "Ava's insured to drive it as of today, and you should be able to get any assignments done on the road. It's not ideal, but there's not much else you can do."

I nod. Annabel, who's been sitting quietly this whole time, looks like she's about to speak but I cut her off before she can. She probably has a million and one questions, all of which I'm not in the mood to address right now. I need a break from all this crap.

"I better go get my stuff together," I say, standing up from the table.

"Do you not have any more questions?" Kato asks, forcing me to stay put.

"Ask her why I couldn't speak to Ava when I tried," Annabel butts in, finally getting her say.

"Not really, I guess it's just a lot to take in," I half lie. I probably will think of a million things later, but I need a break from all this for five minutes.

"Felix!" Annabel snaps at me from my side. "Ask!"

"Of course, yes," Kato says softly. "When you do think of any, Ava will be able to answer most, and we can answer those she can't. Don't hesitate to ask, dear."

I respond to Kato with a thumbs up, which naturally makes me look like an imbecile. I've just been told I'm the sole remaining member of my family after the rest were brutally murdered, and whatever did that has now made it its mission to slaughter me and all my friends, and the way I choose to end that conversation is with a thumbs up. If that doesn't symbolise how screwed we are, I don't know what does.

Annabel yells at me to ask her question again. Before I'm able to scurry away in a flurry of awkwardness and sheer embarrassment, Kato stops me.

"You need to remember," she says, her voice quiet. "I realise it's not quite that simple, but it's just that--Well, you see--"

"To put it bluntly," Mosi interrupts, "we can't help you. Not enough. The only people who can really know what these spirits want, why they did what they did, why they're doing what they're doing now, are the ones who experienced what started all of this, and you're the only one left who did." He lifts his eyes slightly, and locks them into mine. "And you're running out of time."

Annabel starts whining at me the second I'm back inside the B&B. I was right; she does have too many questions to count, and I assure her they'll be answered, but that doesn't satisfy her. While everyone loads their stuff into Mosi's jeep, I take the opportunity for five minutes alone in my hotel room. I collapse onto the bed, the mattress' springs digging into my back, and stare at the white ceiling.

"Shit," I say at nothing. "Shit. Shit. Shit."

"Just ask them one before they leave, please!" Annabel.

I sigh, then shut my eyes. My head feels like it's spinning, and it could be as a result of anything ranging from the punch in the face

Tom gave me, to the news of my entire family being dead and buried. No wonder the authorities couldn't track them after the accident. I open my eyes, then sit up on the bed to see Annabel's glare digging into me from the other end. Her arms are crossed, her lips pursed, and her eyebrows narrowed. Then it hits me.

"You can remember," I mutter.

"Huh?" she questions, her face softening.

"I'm not the only one left, I mean, not technically. You can remember too." I straighten up, and begin to speak more quickly. "My memory loss was from a physical injury, and I might never get it back, but yours wasn't. Yours is like the memory loss of any spirit; it'll come back if you try hard enough."

Annabel shakes her head. "I'm slow though, Felix. I can still barely even remember fragments of when I was alive, and it's already been eleven years. We don't have another eleven to fix this."

I shake my head. There must be a way to speed up the process. The memories are there, she just needs to unclog them. We can ask Kato. She'll know if there's a way. This is it, this is the answer. It has to be. Annabel can remember. She has to.

As I hurry out of my room and jog down to the small hotel lobby, I scout out Tom, who's trying to carry way more bags than physically possible. I hurry over to him, and grab two from over his shoulder.

"Hey, have Kato and Mosi left yet?"

"Don't think so," he replies slowly.

As we walk outside to the car park, he scans my face in a way that suggests I'm about to summon Satan himself. I hope this walking on eggshells thing doesn't last too long. It's a pain in the arse. Mosi's jeep is about the size of a house, so it's hardly difficult to spot among the modest cars dotted around the cobbled car park.

As I notice Kato helping Ava with a bag, I go to call after her, but find the words stuck in my throat when I realise that standing among the frail trees that line the car park, barely visible among the straggly branches, is a Tracker.

"We need to leave," I say blankly as I throw the bags I'm carrying into the jeep's boot.

"What?" It's Carmen who asks. She's sitting in one of the back-seats, and turns around to look at me.

"We need to leave," I repeat. "Just trust me."

"Whoa, no!" Ava snaps, suddenly appearing beside me. "No more of this ambiguity. What is it?"

By this point, Mosi has joined his daughter, and is looking at me inquisitively. Kato seems distracted with Tom and his hundred bags, but Jamie has picked up on what's going on from the vehicle's passenger seat. I can feel his bug eyes on me.

"Tracker," I mutter.

"Everyone in!" Mosi yells before I've even finished saying the word.

Without question, everyone does as they're told, other than Tom, who unsurprisingly has no idea what's going. I keep my eyes on the Tracker as I sit beside Carmen in the jeep, and I'm unsure of whether to be pleased or unnerved at the fact that I'm in next to no physical pain. A visit from one of these clowns usually gives me a splitting headache, but I just feel a tad bit numb at most.

Mosi is shouting orders at us, and everyone is in a mad fluster, but I just close my eyes. I keep the image of the Tracker in my head, its gangly limbs dangling like the branches of the trees it's hidden in, and the frown on its face as big as ever. There's still a ruckus going on in the jeep. I'm not sure if I'm imagining it, but there's a force pushing against me. I push back. Slowly, I open my eyes. It's still there. I keep pushing, and then within a few seconds, it's gone, and I'm left feeling dazed. Kind of dizzy. Huh. I think that worked.

Suddenly, something nudges me hard in my side, and I whip my head around to see Carmen's light eyes. Tom, who's sat on her other side, is peeking round her to stare at me in a slightly less subtle way.

"Sorry, what is it?" I question.

"For the love of--" Jamie groans from the passenger seat. "We're all going to be dead within a day relying on this idiot. It was nice knowing you people."

"Has anything else appeared?" Kato asks me, ignoring Jamie's comment. "We can't sense anything, but want to be sure."

The jeep's windows are rolled down, and Mosi is leaning in on Ava's side while Kato stands beside him outside. Per usual, all eyes are on me.

"Oh, nah," I reply. "I got rid of it."

Kato raises her eyebrows in what I can only guess is surprise, but seems content with the answer. I'm ninety percent sure Ava's parents think I'm useless, and am probably about to lead their daughter to her death, not that I can blame them. The banishing of a Tracker is probably a much needed boost to my reputability.

Once Kato and Mosi have said their goodbyes, adorning Ava with too many kisses to count in the process, we head out of the car park and onto the road. We don't have much of a plan of where we're going, just that it needs to be far away.

Chapter 33

Our plan to drive as far away as possible lasts about fifteen minutes. There's logic behind it, and it's strongly based on Ava's newfound trust in me, which while I am appreciative of, may be a critical mistake on her behalf. I'd started rambling about getting Annabel to remember the whole dead family scenario instead of me, which Ava perceived as a good idea, but it turns out there's a severe lack of understanding about the way a spirit's memory works.

Spirits themselves often have a far better grasp of that sort of thing, to which I mentioned the one I encountered at the haunted manor house. When I revealed said spirit must've been from at least two centuries ago, Ava nearly had heart palpitations.

Despite the fact almost every ghost story ever involves dead folk from centuries past, it turns out a spirit that old is actually extremely rare, and often extremely knowledgeable. So that's where we're headed. It could be an entirely fruitless mission that'll get us all brutally murdered, but I'm remaining optimistic. That's worked so far. Sort of.

Between the time we set off and the time we pull up to the manor house, we encounter no murderous ghosts, so I'd like to think the journey is a success on the whole. The ticket queue isn't too long, but five minutes after joining it, Jamie is already whining.

"Must we pay for our tickets? Frankly, ten pounds each is extortionate for such a poorly orchestrated tour, and even if it was of decent quality, I image it's exactly the same as last time."

He keeps talking, but I'm too mentally drained to tell him to stop, while Tom and Carmen are too focused on me to even really notice him droning on.

"... Just wait around the outskirts of the building in hopes of what we're searching for will come to us. Is that not feasible? I'm still reeling over the horrid conditions at that bed and breakfast. I mean, honestly, how can they expect anyone to sleep when the bar remains open until ridiculously late? The last thing I wish to be doing right now is queuing for an unreasonable length of time to spend money on something so--"

"Shut up," Ava finally interjects. She shoots Jamie the warmest smile I've ever seen, then turns back to face the front of the queue. She really is a beacon of light in an otherwise hellish world, sometimes. Jamie stammers, but shuts up, to which Ava responds to with a "thank you."

Around ten minutes later, we're inside. It smells older than I remember. Like burning wood. We just bought regular entry tickets instead of a guided tour, so much to Jamie's relief, they were seven pounds instead of ten. We immediately begin scouring the building for an empty room, which ends up proving tricky due to the fact barely twenty percent of the house is open to the public, and so most areas are filled with tourists.

At the realisation that finding an empty room will be impossible, I take the next logical step. We're in one of the long hallways, and towards the end of it is some rope with a 'no entry' sign placed in front of it. After checking there's no one else around, I duck under the rope, and wave my hand for the rest of the group to follow.

"You can't go in there!" Jamie whispers in a way that makes it sound like he's shouting. It's actually quite impressive.

"Call me an anarchist," I reply sarcastically. "C'mon, before anyone else shows up."

My friends glance at each other, but soon follow my lead as I turn down a hidden part of the house. Jamie complains the whole time, naturally. I'm not sure what I was expecting, but this hallway looks no different to any of the areas open to the public.

"How do you summon these things?" Tom asks, and what I can only perceive as an attempt to answer his own question, he begins bobbing his head around while whistling and clicking his fingers.

"We're not looking for a dog, you imbecile," Jamie snaps.

"I'm hoping she'll recognise him," Ava replies somewhat absent-mindedly as she scours the hallway. By 'him', I'm assuming she's referring to me. Bit rude.

All the hallway doors are shut, so we risk it, and Carmen subtly pokes her head into one of the rooms. She turns back to us, nods, and steps inside. I'm assuming that means the coast is clear. We follow Carmen into the room, and it's nothing special. Well, as non-special as a room in a fancy manor house can be, anyway. It's a bedroom; not an especially bland one, but nothing outstanding either. Carmen inspects the door as everyone sits down and makes themselves comfortable, then turns back to us. She's chewing her lip.

"Can you get your, uh, thingy--I mean, your--Annabel. Could you get Annabel to keep watch or something? There's no lock." Carmen asks me, followed by an awkward laugh.

I'm silently pleading this tip-toeing around me shit doesn't last much longer because it's excruciating. I nod, and before Annabel has the chance to whine about it, cast my eyes over to the bed where she's landed herself. She mutters something inaudible, then disappears. I'll just assume she's guarding the door outside. Tom, Carmen and Jamie are sitting on the bed, while Ava sits on the floor. I'm too fidgety to sit, so stand above Ava.

"Do we need to get the Ouija board or some--"

"No," Ava replies before I can even process Tom's query. "Please no. Really no. Indisputably no."

I think that's a no.

"Right, go ahead," Ava says, looking up at me.

I glance around the group, but they look as confused as I do. "I might need a clue," is all I say.

"What? How can you not--" Ava stops herself, then closes her eyes for a second. "Sorry, sorry, I--Whoa, I just, I'm still in the process of figuring out the depth of your understanding."

"It's about as shallow as Tom's understanding of nuclear physics, as I think is well established by this point," Jamie mutters.

Is this pick on Felix day or something? Screw these guys, I'm feeding them to the demons next time.

"Hey, what's that supposed to mean?" Tom retaliates. "I was only a few marks off a C in my Physics--"

"Can we do this later, please?" Carmen interjects. "Kinda have other priorities right now."

Tom clamps his mouth shut, but the silence doesn't last long as Ava starts questioning how I know if there's a spirit around, how far my ability to sense stretches, and all kinds of spiritual crap like that, and I don't know how to tell her I can't sense shit. The only reason I ever know there's some poor dead bastard around is because I physically see one. When I inform her of this, her eyes widen.

"Whoa, so you've literally never been able to sense a spirit without seeing one?" she questions, to which I shrug and shake my head. "Hm, that's not ideal," she mutters, then suddenly perks up before I have the chance to be offended. "No worries, I'll focus on that. I imagine the spirit has picked up on your energy by now anyway, so just keep an eye out."

All eyes are on me as Ava shuts hers, and I'm not too sure what I'm waiting for. Is the dead lady just going to poof into the room out of nowhere? I mean, that's literally what ghosts do, I guess, but I don't see how whatever the hell Ava's doing can aid that. Just as I'm about to question the whole thing, the small boy I met last time I was here appears about a centimetre away from my face, and I absolutely shit myself.

I trip backwards, almost falling, and for a moment consider the possibility that I might have to add a heart attack to my medical records. The boy is laughing his guts out, while everyone gapes at me, perplexed. It's a perfectly reasonable response on their part because to them, I literally just jumped about a foot backwards, almost collapsing right into the enormous wardrobe behind me.

As I regain myself, I realise that whatever the hell Ava was doing worked. Tugging at the boy's arm to pull him back is the female spirit we trekked here for.

"Robert!" she says, smacking his arm. "What did I say?"

Ava is asking me what's going on, while the wary faces of Carmen, Jamie and Tom grow more concerned by the second. I turn back to the spirits to see the boy still receiving a telling off, and Ava's asking me more questions. Multitasking is hard, man.

"They're here," I say to Ava before grabbing the spirits' attention. "Hey, uh, hi. Yeah, sorry to show up unannounced. You good?"

You good? Am I all right? Jesus, I'm severely unqualified for this.

"Apologies, he's been awfully bored of recent," the female spirit responds, finally addressing me. She raises her eyebrows at the boy, then nods to me. "Robert?"

Robert stares at the floor, shuffles his feet, then mutters what sounds like a "sorry" in my direction.

In fairness to the kid, if I was dead, I'd literally do the exact same thing.

Chapter 34

"I was hoping you'd return," the spirit continues with a soft voice. "Our run in with that horrid creature intrigued me deeply, and I must say I have been concerned for you."

"Felix? What's going on? What is she saying?" Ava unknowingly interrupts.

The female spirit smiles again, then nods at me as if to give me permission to return to earth and interact with the flesh and blood in the room.

"Oh, hey!" Annabel suddenly appears beside the woman. "We've got heaps of questions."

"Annie, you're meant to be keeping watch!" I snap before turning to Ava. "Sorry, one second."

"The kid's guarding, it's fine," Annabel reassures me with a wave of her hand, and I quickly scan the room to notice Robert's gone. Annabel turns back to the female spirit. "Long story short, I need to remember my life, especially the leading up to death part of it. Thing is, it needs to be fast. We're dealing with pretty tight time limit."

"You're in danger?" the spirit asks it as a question, but it sounds more like a statement.

"I'm bored, can I have a look outside?" Tom interjects from the bed.

As Annabel relays the Oujia board catastrophe to the spirit, she wanders over to Ava and places a hand on her shoulder. Ava's eyes are shut, and hers and the spirit's thin lips are curved upwards slightly, and it's all just looking a tad bit too cult-like for my liking.

Annabel's still telling the story, despite the fact the spirit's clearly occupied with something else right now, and Tom's still asking for permission to move. With Ava sitting crossed legged on the carpet looking somewhat possessed, and me just generally flapping around the place, I don't think Carmen and Jamie know where to look.

"Do you know spirit talkers who may have known, or had contact with... Sorry dear, I can't recall your name," the female spirit says, suddenly removing her hand from Ava's shoulder. Her eyes land on me.

"Felix," I fill in.

The spirit tilts her head slight. "Your parents named you that?" she asks, to which I nod. "Strange. My name's Clara Arlington. My husband and I once owned this house, hence my being here. Anyhow, yes, do you have any contact with, or know of any spirit talkers who would've known your family before they passed?"

I guess she was listening to Annabel, after all. I go to open my mouth, but Ava beats me to it. "I know others, I--Well, one family who did. They're a little... tricky to deal with, though."

Oh, sweet, Ava's joined the party. That must've been what the satanic ritual was for.

"She can hear you now?" Annabel butts in, going completely off topic. "How do I do that? I want to speak to other people." I don't think she means for it to, but it comes off as desperate.

Clara chuckles slightly, then shakes her head. "Guides can't generally communicate with the living beyond their human, least not unless in the direst of situations."

"What do you--Oh, no. No, I'm not his--I'm his sister, sorry, I thought I mentioned that."

"I am aware. You're also his guide."

I laugh. I actually laugh out loud. Piss off is Annabel my spirit guide. I might as well strap a neon sign to my chest that reads Hi, my name is Felix Reynolds, and you want to kill me if she's the one in charge of ensuring I don't kick the bucket.

"Sorry," I quickly apologise as I notice the perplexed look on Clara's face. Well, everyone's, for that matter. "I just--I don't think she is. I mean, Annabel's not really the spirit guide type... She was still alive when I was born, so it's not even possible, right?"

"I am so the type!" Annabel argues in response before anyone can say a word. "You've made it through the first nineteen years, have you not?"

"Barely," I mutter.

"Would it be an accurate assumption to say her life ended as a direct result of prolonging yours?" Clara asks, ignoring mine and Annabel's bickering.

Right in with the heavy questions, Jesus.

"Yeah," I reply as it dawns on me that's exactly the case. "Yeah, she saved me."

"Guides can alternate throughout a lifetime. Self-sacrifice is the most common cause for losing one, and self-sacrifice on a living's part is often what assigns each new one," Clara says matter-of-factly, then softens her voice as she turns back to Annabel. "The only time you're likely to possess an ability to communicate with anyone else from the living is if your brother were in a life-threatening situation, to seek help or draw attention to whatever the danger may be."

I glance at Carmen, who's in the process of telling Tom to shut up. She saw Annabel the night I decided to take a nap on the side of the road in sub-zero temperatures. I can't argue against the fact that all of this makes perfect sense. Shit. I guess Annabel really is my spirit guide.

"Ha! See! You'd be dead without me, you arsehole," Annabel snaps, a hint of playfulness in her voice.

In all fairness, I can't deny that.

"The family who knew Felix's," Ava says, bringing the conversation back to the matter at hand. She briefly turns her attention to me. "Sorry, I know you and your sister probably have, whoa, heaps of questions, but we don't have much time." She shoots an apologetic smile, then turns back to Clara. "The family, how can they help?"

"Well, as you've already established, Felix or Annabel must re-member what they're currently unable to," Clara explains. "Unfor-tunately, there's no guaranteed way to trigger Annabel's memory, but interaction with people from her past should accelerate the process." She looks at Annabel. "The main issue, dear, is that you're preventing yourself from remembering. Whatever it is you can't recall is painful, and so you've closed yourself off to any memory of your life in fear of it leading to the surfacing of traumatic experi-ences."

Oh, great, so I'm finally getting a grain of insight into my mysteri-ous childhood, only for it to be the fact it was so awful my sister has repressed any memory of it. I glance at Annabel, and based on her face resembling a smacked arse, she's on my wavelength with this one.

"That isn't to say your life was ghastly, but there was darkness in it. I would imagine the period leading up to your death can't have been too pleasant," Clara continues in response to Annabel's frown.

Oh, there we go. It wasn't all bad. Just a bit traumatic. Silver linings and all.

"Hopefully communicating with the family who knew yours will stir something within you, and what you absolutely cannot do is resist it. Your instinct will be to, so much so that you may not even realise it, and so a conscious effort must be made to welcome any slither of--" Clara stops dead in her tracks. "You must leave."

"What is it?" Ava questions.

Her voice is measured, but her eyes have narrowed. Not sure what they're freaking out over, everything seems fine to me. In fact, I'm about to say how fine everything seems when in the corner of my eye, I spot a dark figure. Oh, piss right off.

"Don't look at it," Clara says in a voice so controlled, it's soothing. "Don't look at me, or Annabel." She can only logically be referring to me, but she's looking directly at Annabel. "It can only sense your presence. There's no way for it determine who you are unless you make it obvious. Don't look."

I don't know if it's because I know I can't, but my eyes strain as I force them to look anywhere other than at one of the three things I can't look at. How can it not know who I am? Every other Tracker has.

"What's happening? What is it?" Jamie asks from the bed.

Surely it knows it's me, even just from our conversation. Unless it can't hear us. Are Trackers deaf? I'm about to question Clara's logic when it occurs to me that my first response to every Tracker ever has been look straight at it. Shit. I actually hate myself.

"Guys?" It's Carmen this time.

"Leave. Behave as if you've simply finished in this room, and are leaving. Behave as normally as you can," Clara says, still focusing on Annabel.

That's kind of a big ask, but figure it best not to voice my opinion right now.

"There's a Tracker here," Ava says with chirp in her voice, which I can only guess is her playing the role Clara's assigned us.

I'm going to assume I was right and Trackers can't hear for shit. Either that, or Ava's just royally screwed us all over. At the mention of the 'T' word, Jamie, Carmen and Tom's faces drop. God help them if they ever saw what the things looked like. Ava tells everyone to remain calm and act normal, then stands up. I'm still forcing myself not to look at Annabel, Clara, or the Tracker.

"Where is it?" Tom asks, bobbing his head around like a chicken as he stands, having clearly ignored every single thing Ava has said. "Oh, shit, sorry. Just wondering if there'd be a cold spot or something where it was, y'know, like in the films. Is that true?"

Ava looks like she wants to punch him, but resists. Instead, she just hushes him as everyone leaves the bed and follows her to the door. Annabel has left the room, but I can't be sure about Clara. I've not looked at where she was standing since she told me not to. The Tracker manifests itself beside the doorway, and I barely manage to stop myself from flinching. My head's beginning to ache. Holy shit, this is hard.

Tom's still blabbering about something, which in fairness, actually helps in the sense that it's keeping me distracted from the mangled demonic thing standing a few feet away from me. Then, as Jamie is walking through the doorway, Carmen's eyes move to directly face the creature. It shifts its body towards her as if locking its gaze onto her, moves an inch closer, and I panic.

"Carmen!" I blurt, pulling her back from the creature.

Carmen spins around, confusion plastered onto her face as Ava turns to me, her eyes the widest I've ever seen them, and it's only then that the degree of my monumental fuck up hits me. Oh, crap. Before I can do anything else, the Tracker is right in front of my face, its hanging arms more limp than I remember.

Clara shouts something from somewhere, but before I can make sense of what she's saying, a shooting pain races down the left side of my body. I vaguely make out the shape of a claw-like hand on my shoulder before I black out completely.

Chapter 35

Once the ringing in my ears has ceased and the blackness has disappeared, the scene I expect isn't the one I find myself in. I don't see my parents, I don't see Annabel. There's no car, no road, nothing. It's all new. I'm in a forest, least I think it is. I see a lot of trees, anyway.

Everything looks big and I'm peering over someone's shoulder as they hold me, so I know this isn't happening in real-time. I know it's another vision. We're being chased. The dark bursts are chasing us. My present self knows I shouldn't be, but my past self is staring at them as they follow us. I want to look at who's carrying me, but my younger self can't take his eyes off the dark energies.

"No! No, no, don't look! Don't look!"

The voice is too muffled for me to figure out its gender. I'm cursing my younger self for not understanding why it's so important not to stare at the dark shapes. We keep running. I don't know if we're running anywhere, or just running away from what's chasing us. Whoever's holding me keeps telling me not to look, and I keep not listening. They push my face into their neck, blocking my view completely. It smells of sweat and aftershave.

I think I'm crying. We keep running, and it feels like we're never going to stop. As I begin to give up hope and question if this entire thing is my mind playing tricks on me, the person holding me removes their hand from my head, and we come to a halt. They swoop me down, and plod me onto the muddy ground.

I'm surrounded by branches. They're scratching my bare skin, and it's making me cry even more, and the person keeps saying sorry and telling me to try and be quiet. I think we're in a bush. Or a low hanging tree. I don't know, it's dark. It's really dark. I'm beginning to sweat as panic eclipses my thoughts, and I don't think it's my younger self suffering. What the hell is happening?

Finally, my apparent saviour crawls into the branches I'm tangled among and crouches down in front of me. I can barely make out any features through the shrubbery and darkness, but his eyes are big and his shaggy hair is sticking up in all directions. He keeps glancing behind him.

"Okay, buddy?" he says shakily, and now that we're deadly still, I desperately try to take in all his features despite the darkness making it near impossible. "Just try to be quiet. It'll stop, I promise. Close your eyes, okay? Just close your eyes."

His face is old, but his voice doesn't sound as jagged as I'd have expected. I want to ask him who he is, and where we are, and what's happened to my family, but I have no power over my younger self. My younger self just keeps crying.

"I won't let anything hurt you, Felix. Okay? Hey, listen, you're safe. I promise." The man pulls me into him, and I smell his aftershave again. "I promise."

I don't know how long we sit there, or how long it takes for me to stop crying, but it all comes to an end eventually. The man pulls himself away from me, puts his finger to his mouth in a hushing motion, then quietly crawls back out of the branches. He returns soon after, with relief plastered on his face. He pulls me out of the shrubbery, picks me up, and we make our way through the forest again. This time, though, we don't run.

As we emerge from out of the trees, I see an all too familiar scene, except now there are no bursts of black or white. My parents car stands motionless, the bumper hanging off the twisted metal of its front. My dad sits in the driver's seat, dead. Annabel lies on the bonnet, dead, and my mother lies on the road, dead.

The man holding me shoves my face into his neck again. I don't think he realises I've already seen it all. We're heading towards the car, and my present self can't understand why. When the man opens one of the back doors, I'm even more confused. He sits me down in one of the seats. I'm staring at my dad in the front. I think I'm starting to cry again.

"Felix? Felix, listen to me, don't look there, okay? Look at me," the man orders, but younger me doesn't listen. He takes my chin and forces me to face him as he crouches down outside the car. "Don't take your eyes off me, okay?"

It's lighter here than in the forest. There are no street lights, but there are no more trees to block the moonlight. The man runs his hands through his hair to move it off his face. Now that there's more light, I can see he has a wound on his forehead. Dried blood is splotched all over his face, and his lip is swollen. I can't tell if he's my dad's age or older.

"I have to keep you safe, okay? I'm sorry. I'm so sorry, I don't want to do this." The man's voice cracks as he speaks, and behind him emerges the brightest white light I've ever seen. "I have to keep you safe, I don't know what else to do. I'm sorry, it's too dangerous for you to remember. I love you, okay? I love you."

The light grows bigger, and I'm engrossed. It's blinding me, but I can't turn away. It gets brighter and brighter until all I see is white, and with the snap of a finger, darkness. Cold, unadulterated darkness.

I wake to a warm feeling in my hand, and the smell of wood. It's comforting, so much so that I briefly consider keeping my eyes shut and staying here forever. Then I remember what I just saw, and where I was before it happened.

"Oh, shit, sorry," I mutter, trying to lift myself up from the lying position I'm in. "My bad."

"Oh no you don't!" Carmen almost screams at me as a hand shoves me back down.

It's probably a good thing. I feel kind of sick. And I can't really see. Everything's blurry. I can make out the vague image of Carmen's face above mine, and within seconds, another few appear in the form of Tom, Annabel and Robert.

"Hey, he's alive!" Tom calls out, but is immediately hushed by several people.

The warm feeling is still in my hand, and as I lift myself up more slowly this time, more faces appear until everyone and their dog is staring at me. It's then I realise the warm feeling in my hand is Carmen holding it.

"Are you okay, son?" Clara questions as I manoeuvre myself into a sitting position. Carmen goes to release my hand, but I stop her. "I tried to banish it before it could touch you, I'm deeply sorry, I--"

"It's cool," I reply, to which Clara shoots me a perplexed expression. "I mean, it's fine--I'm fine, it's my fault."

Everyone is sitting around or near me, but Clara stands beside the large window with downturned lips. I scan the room for any danger as I bring myself wholly back to reality, and find no sign of a Tracker anywhere. As orderly as ever, it takes seconds for Ava to start questioning me about what I saw. Once I've explained the whole thing, everyone other than Clara looks like they're finally confused to the point of being entirely done with my bullshit. Hell, I'm done with my bullshit.

"Though it's of course impossible for me to understand if the forest has any deeper relevance, who the man was, what any of it means in the grand scheme of things, or anything of that sort, I believe that answers the question of your memory loss," Clara begins, shedding some light on a dire situation. I stare back, not quite grasping what she's trying to get at, and so she continues. "A spirit wiped it. One with good intentions, it seems, though the reason why remains unclear, least to me."

"Spirits can do that?" Ava questions, her eyebrows raised.

"Rarely. It's rather complex and requires a great deal of energy, so usually only the most powerful are able to, though Felix being a child would have made it easier. It would've meant less memories to erase, a less complex mind."

I go to make a joke about how my mind hasn't developed anymore complexity since then, but stop myself when I see the serious expressions on everyone's faces.

"What? So it's not a physical injury? Can I get it back?" The questions leave my mouth so fast, I can barely understand them myself.

"What's being said?" Jamie questions. "What physical injury?"

I'm quickly discovering that having a conversation with a group of people when the majority can't see or hear several of its members is a bit of a pain. I brush Jamie off.

"Technically, yes." Clara's words sound promising, but any trace of optimism is quickly crushed. "However, it can only be reversed by the spirit who did it. Either that, or one that is extremely powerful, and finding another capable of such a thing will be tremendously difficult. I've been here for nearly two hundred years now, and have never met a spirit powerful enough."

Well, that sounds promising. Jamie butts in again to ask for an explanation, and this time, Ava panders to him and explains the whole scenario. The room explodes with conversation in an attempt to decode the entirety of my life, and I know this is the last thing I should be feeling now, but I'm done with it. I'm just so done with it all.

I excuse myself, saying something about needing the toilet, and leave the room. I'll call one of them if something else tries to kill me. Either that or just let whatever it is put me out of my misery. The latter is growing increasingly tempting.

I manage to leave the building without being caught by staff in any off-limit area, and find myself a quiet patch of grass within the manor house's needlessly large garden. It's gotten cooler since this morning, but it's still dry and sunny, so there are a few people around. Mainly families. Picnics, I figure. I don't really think, I just stare at the families. My phone rings, but I ignore it.

"You should tell them whenever this stuff starts getting too much for you." Annabel. "They'll understand. Well, maybe not Tom, but the rest will."

I don't look at her because I have this sickly feeling that if I do, all I'll see is her body strewn over my parents' car.

"I'm fine," I lie, not even trying to hide it anymore.

Annabel sighs beside me, but I still refuse to look at her. I wait in anticipation of a sarcastic comment or insult, but instead, feel a warm sensation. I look down to see my sister's arms wrapped around me, then turn my head to see hers on my shoulder, and I don't know why but I really want to fucking cry.

Chapter 36

We stay like that in silence for a few minutes until my phone starts ringing again. I intend on ignoring it, but that gets me a telling off from Annabel. As I reach into my pocket to answer though, the ringing stops, and something ruffles my hair, making it fall messily onto my face.

"What was that for?" I whine as I fix it, and Carmen plops herself onto the grass in front of me.

"For disappearing and making Ava panic that you've been murdered or demon-napped, or both. The demon-napping would come before the murdering, I'd assume," she replies as she picks a daisy from the ground and throws it at me. "And for ignoring my phone call. Rude."

"How'd you know I was here?"

"Dunno, think I'm just good at figuring out where your preferred place of moping will be wherever we go."

She grins at me, so I throw a chunk of grass at her. Carmen giggles, but her smile quickly fades.

"Listen, I'm sorry about how I've been over the past day or so" she begins, all hints of playfulness disappearing from her voice. "All this crap must be literally driving you crazy, and me acting weird around you can't exactly help. It's just--I'm getting used to it, and I'm really trying to work on it. I mean, two days ago my only concern was whether or not you fancied me, and now it's whether or not I'm going to be possessed by a literal demon and whether or not you fancy me."

I laugh genuinely for the first time since we set off on this bizarre road trip. "Being possessed by a demon is probably the better outcome of the two, honestly."

Carmen nods in agreement with a wicked smile, and despite the shadows under her eyes and undone hair suggesting she's struggling with all this, she's rapidly making me feel like everything isn't, indeed, going to shit. I must be zoning out because Carmen taps my leg. She leaves her hand there as I return to the present.

"You're exhausted, Felix. Mentally." The joking tone has disappeared from her voice again. She shifts a little awkwardly. "And I know you've convinced yourself that you can't possibly be traumatised by your past because you can't remember it, but--"

I go to argue, but Carmen hushes me.

"Look, I know nothing about this ghost stuff, but based on what I have learned and whatever intuition I have, I know there's no way for us to get through this if you keep shutting yourself off and pretending you're not fazed by any of it. You've had a shit time of it, Felix, a really shit time of it. You've grown up without any family, and now you're literally stuck inside your own head watching them die without having any clue why, or what it all means. I don't care what you say; that's horrific."

Carmen finally takes a breath, and it's followed by a stammer that drifts off into nothing. My heart is beating so crazily that I have to resist looking down at my chest to see if it's obvious, and I'm angry. I'm really goddamn angry, and for a moment I think I'm angry at Carmen, but I know that's just a ruse. I'm not angry at her, I'm angry at everything else.

I'm angry that even after all my visions I still can't remember the people who saved my life, I'm angry I've gotten everyone else involved in my bullshit, I'm angry I grew up without an opportunity to stay in one place for longer than a few years, I'm angry I spent Christmas Day alone, and I'm angry I'm cursed with this stupid ability.

"I know," I say, and try to laugh, but my brain doesn't compute, so I don't even smile.

"Felix! Oi, Felix!" a familiar voice yells from behind me.

Carmen rolls her eyes. "Here come the rest of the budget ghost-buster gang."

I snicker and turn my head to see Tom calling me, with Robert skipping beside him and Ava. Jamie and Clara follow a few steps behind. Ava's got her parasol again, which momentarily confuses me because I'd not noticed it with her at all today, but then I remember nothing about Ava makes sense, so don't delve any deeper into it. I'm soon internally questioning her again as she starts reaching down and picking flowers from the ground. Hardly seems like the time. Tom and Robert reach us first.

"Mate, you need to stop doing runners," Tom whines at me. "We need to piss off out of here in case one of your creeper friends fancies paying us another visit."

"Felix," Ava says matter-of-factly as she and Clara stop beside me, a bunch of flowers in her hands. "You can't keep disappearing without telling us, it's--"

"Yeah, yeah, I know," I mutter as I stand up. "Sorry."

"You must leave." Clara speaks before Ava can say anything else. "Every second you spend here puts you in grave danger."

No pun intended, I hope. I nod while flashing my most convincing optimistic smile, but can't imagine it's any good. Carmen jumps to her feet, and we begin heading back towards the house. Everyone's rushing, but I'm just trying to resist running back into the garden to hide in a bush for the next few centuries.

"Your additional abilities, what are they besides psychokinesis?" Clara asks, suddenly appearing beside me and scaring the shit out of me.

"Huh?"

"Moving stuff!" Robert chirps, who also scares the crap out of me with his sudden appearance, but less so than last time.

Clara hushes him. "Moving objects without touch. Energy manipulation, if you will," she elaborates. "What can you do beyond that?"

We move into the main hall where we're surrounded by people, so I keep my head down as a means to make it seem like I'm not talking into thin air. Everyone's still moving fast to reach the car.

"Uh, nothing?" I say slowly, not sure if that's the right answer.

Clara nods. "One's control over energy manipulation is primarily dependant on personality. It comes far more naturally to those with a focused, stable disposition. Erratic personalities always have a poor grasp on their abilities, unfortunately. " I think that's an insult. It feels like one. "Practice, however, will improve it. It's unfortunate the ability has intensified so late into your life."

"What, can most people start being able to do this stuff earlier?" I question as we exit the building.

"Yes. Your attempts to suppress your abilities, alongside your severely deficient knowledge of the spirit world will have delayed the process."

I nod. Every word Clara speaks beats even more confidence out of me, and I kind of really don't need this now. As we head towards the car park, I notice Ava is still picking flowers. Hell, she's picked so many that Tom and Carmen now have a pile each. I don't even bother questioning it.

"Are you coming with us?" I enquire, the scale of how useful Clara is only now hitting me.

"I can't. Whatever is chasing you may visit here, and I must be present to protect the younger spirits that reside here." She glances at Robert, who's now laughing at Jamie arguing with Ava over something. Probably flowers. "Even if so, there isn't much more I can help you with."

We finally reach the car, and Clara and I come to a halt.

"The person you met before, the other one who could see spirits," I say, suddenly recalling something Clara said last time I was at the manor house. "Can they help? Where are they now?"

Clara shakes her head. "It was years ago, not long after I passed myself. She..." She hesitates, clearly unsure of whether she should say what she says next. "She chose not to be a good person, and that choice caught up to her."

As I go to question what that means, Clara changes the subject.

"Your girlfriend spoke truth," she begins as she nods at Carmen, and I go to correct her, but figure it's not important. "Your aura is dark, not through any form of evil, but through a heavy sadness. A little anger, but largely sadness. Your mind is muddied and unwell, and that must be your priority. If you cannot banish the demons inhabiting your head, then you've no chance of defeating those outside it."

"Ready?" Ava interrupts.

I spin around to look at her, having been so engrossed in what Clara was saying that I forgot where we were and what we were doing for a moment. I nod. I'm not ready. I've never been more unprepared for anything in my life. We say goodbye to Clara and Robert, who wish us well, which is old time ghost talk for good luck trying not to die, and huddle into the car.

I sit in the front seat this time. Ava has filled the thing to the brim with flowers, and finally, I question what the hell is going on.

"Is anyone gonna explain why I've got flowers poking into every orifice of my body?"

"Ew," Jamie mutters, explaining nothing.

Ava giggles, then rolls her eyes. Then she begins loudly humming some melodic tune. At this point, I'm honestly starting to question if I have any trace of sanity remaining, and if none of this is actually happening and I'm going to wake up on a psychiatric ward.

"Flowers warn off negative spirits, remember?" she says, and then what she was singing immediately hits me. That bloody nursery rhyme.

I shrug. Whatever helps her sleep at night.

"I'm fairly sure picking them was illegal," Jamie intervenes. "Considering we stole them from a privately owned tourist attraction. I can't believe I let you all drag me into it."

"Put some in your pockets," Ava murmurs, ignoring Jamie completely. "It helps."

I nod, but don't even touch a flower. Well, if you don't count the ones that are under my arse and nudging me in the face. Ava starts the engine and pulls off, and within a few seconds of realising I've not filled my pockets with daisies, she scowls at me. Being slightly terrified of the girl, I do as she says and grab a pile, shoving them into my jeans and jacket pockets. She nods, then smiles.

"So what's the plan?" Carmen asks from the backseat. "Head to visit this weird family who knew Felix's and go from there?"

"Yes," Ava says plainly.

"What's difficult about them, anyway? They're not gonna sell me out to the arseholes trying to murder me, are they?"

We're stopped at a red light, and so Ava turns to face me. "They don't traditionally interact with other spirit talkers, and no." She pauses. "Felix, whoever it is that's chasing you, whatever it is, it could've easily harmed you by now. It doesn't want to kill you." She releases the clutch as the light turns green, then turns back to look at the road. "It wants something from you."

Chapter 37

I can always tell when Mum is thinking. Her eyebrows crease ever so slightly, and she runs her tongue along the back of her bottom teeth as her dark eyes stare directly at whoever it is she's speaking with. To the untrained eye, her expression doesn't flinch, but having known her for nearly nineteen years, it's a look I can identify instantaneously. Why on earth she doesn't just ask him is totally frustrating.

When I query exactly this, Mum raises her eyebrows with a sigh. "If he has any knowledge about the spirit world, Ava, we need to let him come to us."

Ugh, I don't have the patience to wait an entire lifetime.

"Some spirit talking families are extremely private, you know that, and it's not our--"

"But he's so weird, and not just like, whoa, nineteen-year-old white boy weird. Whenever I ask him about spirits, he shrugs. Who shrugs at a question like that? Well, he shrugs a lot, but that's the kind of thing people don't just shrug at. There's someth--"

"Ava," Mum says slowly, forcing me to stop talking. "I've already told you not to try and coax something out of him."

"It's groovy, I've asked him about spirits, like, once," I lie. I click my tongue as I lean my head back against the sofa's armrest. "You and Dad both agree there's something he's not telling us, we know he's got a spirit attachment, and whoa, what about his aura? You've never not been able to read someone's aura bef--"

"Ava," Mum interrupts. "End of discussion. The important thing is that he knows we're here to talk to whenever--if ever he feels ready to."

I sit back up and go to open my mouth again, but Mum digs her eyes into my own before I'm able to get anything out. Despite her putting a hard stop to our conversation, her expression returns to the contemplative one decorating her face a few minutes prior. She's obviously just as intrigued by Felix as I am.

With a long sigh, I jump up from the living room sofa, and an-nounce my plan to head back to the uni apartment. As I'm leaving the room, Mum reminds me to stop bugging Felix about spirits, which I pretend not to hear.

A short while later, I'm letting myself into the apartment, and both Jamie and Felix are occupying the living area. Perfect. Jamie's talking loudly about something, and it sounds like he's complaining, although I'm not sure who to because Felix is hunched over a thick textbook as he scribbles something into it.

"Ah, Ava!" Jamie calls over to me from one of the sofas near the window. "Do you harbour crockery in your room?"

"Yes," I reply as I stop beside Felix, who's sitting on one of the kitchen stools.

He hasn't removed the nail polish Carmen decorated his nails with a few days back, so they're still a bright maroon colour. It's quite cute.

"Hey, Felix, what's the youngest person you've known who's died?"

"What? No, it's--I mean, dirty crockery," Jamie elaborates. "I'm trying to prove a point that it's disgusting and barbaric to leave used plates around the apartment, which Felix seems utterly oblivious of."

"I don't--What do you mean?" Felix replies as he shifts his attention towards me.

I roll my eyes, then peer at the open book in front of him. He's drawn faces over a bunch of mathematical diagrams, and drawn a fire-breathing dragon attacking a sketch of a bridge. A bunch of cars and stick figures are diving off the bridge with speech bubbles screaming help!, and there's a giant butterfly overseeing the scene.

I feel rather sorry for Carmen, but I suppose you can't help who you're attracted to.

"Butterfly wings are more rounded than that," I tell him as I point at his drawing.

"Oh, nah, that's Mothman," he says as though it means anything. 'Y'known, urban legend? All round legend, if you ask--"

"What's the youngest person you know who's died?"

Felix stammers, and Jamie calls my name, but I ignore him. Felix still doesn't answer my question, and I swear talking to this boy is like trying to draw blood from stone. His green eyes are wide, and he looks even more so like a deer caught in headlights than usual.

"Your spirit attachment is definitely young," I explain as I sit down onto the stool beside Felix, and continue speaking as I lock my eyes onto his increasingly blank face. "I'm not great with ages, but I'd not say, like whoa, crazy young or anything. Maybe a teenager, but probably younger than us."

"You sure you're not mistaking this whole spirit attachment thing for Jamie? The guy stalks me like a fly, and not sure if you've noticed, but he produces this continuous whining sound that--"

"Shut up!" Jamie interjects.

While I'm entirely aware this is one of Felix's many, many blatant attempts to evade spirit-related conversation, I have to admire his ability to enrage Jamie within the matter of seconds. He starts laughing at Jamie's outburst, and the dimples in his cheeks grow deeper as I cross my arms. I hum to myself while I wait until he's finished.

"What's the youngest person you know who's died?" I repeat for, I'm fairly certain, the third time.

"It's--You must have something mixed up," Felix replies, then shrugs. Of course he shrugs. He mutters as he moves his eyes from my face, and starts doodling again. "I don't know anyone young who's died, or anyone who's died generally,"

Bullshit. Everyone knows somebody who's died.

I follow Felix's movement with my eyes as he continues drawing in his textbook, and the energy surrounding us--the energy filling this room is undeniable, is so blatant that surely even a non-spirit talker could feel the electricity of it. There's someone else here.

We're all heading to The Cavern's bar tonight before we return home for Christmas, and I'm desperately hoping Felix gets extreme-ly drunk because while, yes, this may be totally immoral, I want to take advantage of any opportunity I have where he's likely to be more honest. It's groovy because it's not like I'm forcing him to get drunk, right? If something happens to be revealed off the back of his intoxication, Mum can't scold me, right?

A lot of students have already left campus for the holiday, so as Carmen, Felix, Jamie, Tom and I wander into the bar, there are plenty of tables to choose from. With a grin, I skip towards a booth in the centre of the room, and spin around mid-skip to check the others are following me, which they are.

Carmen's laughing as she skips a few feet behind me, her curled hair dancing in-synch with her body, but the boys are walking behind with hands in their pockets as if they're cool or something; it's totally embarrassing. In fairness to Felix, he's not included in that because he's instead completely engrossed in everything Carmen is doing in a not at all subtle way.

"Whoa, so when are you going to ask Carmen out on a date?" is the first thing I say to Felix as he joins Carmen and I in the booth.

"Ava!" Carmen hisses in a whisper.

Felix starts stammering, and if it wasn't for the dark stubble covering them, I'm fairly certain his cheeks would be red. These two make me want to bang my head against a wall sometimes. I don't know why they won't just admit they fancy each other because it's even more obvious than Felix's blatant familiarity with the spirit world.

"How often do you shave?" I ask Felix as Tom and Jamie join us at the table.

"Are we talking about shaving? Shaving what?" Tom interjects. "I used to shave my ba--"

Jamie loudly, and rather aggressively, hushes Tom before he can finish his sentence. Before I can interrogate Felix any further, he stands--well it's more of a stumble, really--from his seat and announces he's going to fetch us some drinks. As he walks towards the bar, I'm fairly sure he's scowling at something. He does that a lot: pulls faces at nothing. I did contemplate the possibility of this being some evidence towards him being a spirit talker, but upon further contemplation, I think he might just be weird.

I excuse myself from our table to use the bathroom, and upon my return, Tom pounces at me with a rather stupid question. He's questioning me on whether I'd rather eat nothing but cucumber for the rest of my life, or only ingest liquids. I tell him it's a stupid question because cucumber contains over ninety percent water.

"No, but if you had to, like, say your life depended--Oh, if the ghosts' lives depended on it! Think of your favourite ghost that you've met, and--"

"The ghosts' lives? Ghosts are already dead, you idiot," Jamie says with a sigh.

"Did you just admit to the possibility of ghosts being real, Jamie?" Carmen chimes in.

"What? Ugh, no, I just meant--"

"Too late, you've already stepped in it," Felix interrupts. "Sorry, mate, you're now officially number one ghostie connoisseur." Felix bops his head around Carmen to look at me. "Sorry, Ava, you're out."

Tom and Felix both start laughing, although Tom's laugh is more of a guffaw, and he gives Felix a high-five as Jamie starts muttering under his breath. Carmen leans back in her seat and rolls her eyes, but she's biting her cheeks in a totally obvious attempt at disallowing herself to smile. I watch Felix's animated face in silence as I sip at my glass of Coke. While he acts like a clown far too often for it to be healthy, he's the only one who remembers I like lime in my cola, not lemon.

Given we don't arrive back at the apartment especially late, Felix and Tom are both rather impressively inebriated. Most of us have early starts tomorrow morning, so nobody stays in the living area for very long, but I make a base on the floor at the end of the room. I rest my back against the wall so I can peep through the long window overlooking the narrow lake below our apartment building to watch the ducks.

I'm fairly certain Felix's spirit is here. I can feel its energy in the air, and although Felix's bedroom is situated the other side of the living area wall, the niggling sensation underneath my skin is too strong for there to be any bricks separating us.

"Hello?" I call out.

Within seconds, the energy scatters. Damn it.

I don't have the opportunity to dwell on the spirit's disappearance for too long because far sooner than anticipated, the blue door at the other end of the room swings open, and Felix barges in. He always makes food when he's drunk; even if we grab a takeaway on the way home from a night out, he will undoubtedly make something in the kitchen within an hour of us returning home.

Felix takes a few moments to spot me sitting in the corner, and he's already in the kitchen area by the time he does.

"Shitting hell, what--Hey, Ava, what are you--Why are you sitting on the floor?"

"Ducks," I explain.

Felix blinks at me as though I just said something ridiculous. He looks a little like a duckling right now, his wavy hair sticking up in all kinds of directions.

The energy has returned to the room, so I assume Felix's spirit has followed him in, and the spirit seems... I'm not entirely sure; it's

difficult to tell without it making a connection with me, but
impatient, or annoyed.

"Your spirit is agitated," I try as Felix bends down to o
cupboard near the floor.

He chortles, then mumbles something under his breath, but
nothing to me. He stands back up with a can of baked beans in ha
which he throws onto the counter with a questionable amount
force, followed by a loud bang.

"Oops, sorry," he mumbles. "I swear the counter was closer.
Does--Hey, do you want some beans?"

"No, thank you, I'm groovy."

Felix shrugs, then spins on the spot to grab something from the
cutlery drawer. He's still wearing his oversized brown jacket, but
when I ask him if he's cold, he furrows his eyebrows as if confused. I
watch as he pulls a huge kitchen knife from the cutlery drawer, and
I widen my eyes as he wedges the blade into the edge of the can.

"Whoa, Felix, what are you doing?" Despite my questioning, Felix
continues to stab the tin can. "Wait, I've got a can opener, you
don't--"

He stops ramming the knife into the can, and lifts it to his eyeline
to, I assume, read the label.

"It's cool, it's vegetarian," he says with a shrug, and one final stab
which bursts the can open as an orange liquid seeps from inside it.

He drops the knife onto the counter with as much force as he did
with the tin earlier, only it lands far more quietly. Huh, that's rather
stra--

"Did you say you wanted some? Can't remember," Felix queries,
shifting my attention back to his face as he gestures the can of beans
towards me.

...re, and he shrugs once more as he tears ...the can further open. He then retrieves a ...drawer, and somewhat stumbles over to plop ...d floor opposite me. I stare at his hands as Felix ...fork into the can, and he begins eating the cold ...from it.

...e if we can feed the ducks from up here?" he questions ...th full of beans, then nods at the window beside me. "Can ...t beans? I think bread makes them explode or some shit."

...re's defintiely something wrong with him.

...n dying to know what his parents are like. Perhaps that's it; ...rhaps his parents aren't spirit talkers, at least not knowingly. It's impossible for someone from a non-spirit talking family to have abilities, but he could have a distant relative who's part of one of the twelve families. It's uncommon for abilities to manifest in distant relatives, but it's not entirely unheard of. Maybe he has abilities, but simply doesn't realise it.

I'm about to offer a spirit-related helping hand for the umpteenth time, but hold my tongue as Mum's words echo around my head, followed by the promise I made to her. Ugh, fine, I'll let him eat his beans in peace. For now. Besides, if anything strange happens to him, he wouldn't let it get so far that it becomes dangerous, right?

"Nah, on second thought," Felix says, and I return my focus back to the drunk teenager sitting opposite me. "I'm too hungry to share. Fuck the ducks."

"Fuck the ducks," I repeat.

Epilogue

"It's not cheating if I can't help it. I mean, it's--Hey, would you accuse a deaf person of cheating in a sign language contest?" I pause for dramatic effect. "No, you wouldn't. Same energy."

"Right... I'm not even going to bother explaining the sheer lack of logic behind that statement," Jamie replies slowly like the sarcastic swine he is. "And besides, you can tell Annabel not to help."

"You realise there's fifty grand at the end of this, right, Jamie?" Carmen chimes in with raised eyebrows.

I grin at her from across the table because yes, thank you! Jamie responds with a huff and an eye roll, but zero comeback. He never tries to argue with Carmen or Ava, and I've got no clue if that's a reflection on them, or on Tom and me. Probably the latter. We're idiots.

The upcoming challenge revolves around breaking into a house, then stealing something from it as evidence. It's practically made for me--well, made for anyone with a ghostie friend or sibling--because Annabel will be able to sniff out any obstacles before I can even risk crashing headfirst into them. The challenge commences this ourselves to a late breakfast in one of

ᴄuss what to expect later. If the Texans can

breakfast, that's for sure.

ment with a shrug as I finish chewing on my

tell Annabel what she can and can't do. Female

and all that."

see you struggle,' is Annabel's cheery response from

wsill at the end of the table. "Would be funny watching

something stupid that gets you killed, and hey, a bit of death

hurt anyone; I can vouch for that."

ѕh!" I hiss as if anyone else can hear her not backing my corner,

ᴎe snake.

"What?" Jamie questions.

"She said stop being mean to me."

"As if."

This time, I'm not a total idiot, and shoot Annabel a glare instead of telling her to shut up. Master of deception, that's me.

Jamie's just bitter he's not playing the game himself. Carmen, Tom, and I are all competing while Ava babysits Jamie, which she assured us was entirely voluntary but bloody questionable. Tom would have one-hundred percent been eliminated by now if it wasn't for Annabel. The last challenge was walking a plank between two decaying water towers, and the sole reason he didn't plummet to his gory death was thanks to Annie using her energy to keep him upright. The guy can barely walk straight at the best of times.

Whatever happens, we've agreed to split the prize money five ways, which was dumb as hell because Jamie's loaded. It's just that I felt kind of guilty about dragging him and the others out here